Wha

MW01671419

Just finished this intrigu... ...... about time travel; I love the fact that it 'flip-flopped' so each chapter lapsed in time... WELL DONE. GREAT first novel and it looks like the end is a new beginning…sequel? Would make a good TV series or movie!

Adele Steinberg

TIME TRESPASSER ROCKS!!! The premise is unique. Not just the usual time travel tale, but one with meaning. A slave master goes forward in time and learns that everything he has based his life on is bull. (Or does he?) The book is very well researched and not only did I gain insights into slavery's foundations, I got a real sense of what it was like to be a slave. The multi-layered story takes the reader back and forth in time as we get to know multiple characters that are directly and indirectly involved in the many ramifications of slavery. My favorite parts are when the slave owner comes face to face with the very people he and his kind have oppressed for so long. His reactions ring true and give us a satisfying sense of justice so long denied. Read this book, not only for the history, but also for the suspense and intrigue.

Howard Marshall

Just finished Elaine's excellent tale, Time Trespasser. WOW. Could not put it down. So well written. What a premise. She really pulled it off. Left me wanting a follow up. Read this book!!!

Malcolm Campbell

Finished the book tonight. Loved it. Amazing how you intertwined stories. The time transitions were easy to negotiate and the characters so interesting. Loved the ending.

Cathy Bedal Chase

This book is amazing and needs to be made into a movie!!! I read Time Trespasser during my beach holiday last week and couldn't put it down! I followed this read by another book called "Wild", which HAS been made into a movie. Wild WAS good, however, it paled in comparison to Time Trespasser. This is a MUST READ and needs to make it to Oprah's book club!

Patricia Grom

Time Trespasser

Time travel is real...
isn't it?
Enjoy!
[illegible]

Also by Elaine Weeks

The Best of the Times Magazine

Postcards from the Past

500 Ways You Know You're From Windsor

Windsor Then

A Forgotten City

Walkerville - Whisky Town Extraordinaire

Time Trespasser

A master.

His slaves.

A crack in time.

Elaine Weeks

WalkervillePublishing

2017

Time Trespasser
A Master. His Slaves. A Crack in Time.
Weeks, Elaine, b. 1956

ISBN: 978-1-927591-03-1

cover design Chris Edwards
cover photo Jon Estwards
author photo Howard Weeks

published by Walkerville Publishing Inc.

716 Windermere Rd.
Windsor, ON N8Y 3E1
519-255-9527
walkerville.com

this edition
printed in the United States of America

In Memory of

Bonnie Bridge Sartor

For Chris, Jon and Rosalie,

and anyone who has ever wondered,

"what if?"

I had crossed the line. I was free;
but there was no one there to welcome me
to the land of freedom.
I was a stranger in a strange land.

Harriet Tubman

In Einstein's equation, time is a river. It speeds up,
meanders, and slows down. The new wrinkle is that it
can have whirlpools and fork into two rivers. So, if the river
of time can be bent into a pretzel, create whirlpools
and fork into two rivers, then time travel cannot be ruled out.

Michio Kaku

"We hold these truths to be self-evident,
that all men are created equal..."

The Declaration of Independence
of the United States of America

Author's Note

I was watching a few minutes of an NBA game about three years ago when something occurred to me: I could remember when almost every player was Caucasian and there were only one or two African American players on the floor, but now it's the complete opposite. I was taken aback by this realization, especially as this had happened during my life time.

I wondered what would someone from long ago think if they were watching this game? And then I thought, what if that someone was a plantation owner who owned hundreds of slaves?

Wouldn't that be an interesting book?

And so it began.

1837

A Little Black Magic

THE GIRL PLUCKED TWO EGGS OUT OF THE BASKET, hid them in her skirt and limped over to the slave quarters. She forced herself to move without haste so as not to draw undue attention.

Ole Mary was shelling peas on her stoop. She could tell who was coming without even looking up. The girl slipped the eggs into her hand before anyone could see. She had managed to bring the old woman some rum a few days before.

The girl's face was tight with worry. She whispered, "He'll be gone by mornin'?"

Ole Mary nodded. "Spirits see to that."

"Where he gonna go?"

"Away. Far away. Don't know where."

"He gonna come back?"

"Far as I know it, they never come back."

The girl glanced back at the Big House. Soon it would be night. The hint of a smile softened her drawn features for a moment.

She nodded her head. "Good."

Then she limped away.

1

October 10, 2011

Wherein a journalist has an awakening.

HE NUZZLED THE SPOT JUST BELOW HER EARLOBE with his lips. She pressed into him for a second, and then pulled away. He backed off, but saw that she was smiling. He smiled back, waited a few moments, and then tilted her chin up to give her the look. He felt her body give a slight tremble.

B z z z z z z ...

She stared past him, made a little sound and stood up to go. He caught her hand and pulled her back down beside him.

"Where you going?" he asked.

B z z z z z z ...

"What the hell is that?" she said pointing at something near his head.

"What?" He turned to look.

She gave a little scream and he glanced back just as her face split into two pieces.

"Christ!"

His eyes flew open. His phone.

He grabbed it off the bed side table. An all too familiar face on the call display stared at him.

"Fuck."

He waited a couple of more buzzes to calm down, sighed, and against his better judgment, swiped 'answer'.

"This had better be good, Jake."

"Rise and shine, Martin."

He instantly felt his blood pressure go up a notch. He counted to three and said, "Jake. It's the crack of dawn. And you're interrupting one of the best dreams I've had in a very long time."

"Yeah? Well, you can tell me about it at Starbucks. I need to see you, pronto."

"Now? You're kidding, right? It's not even 7!" Then a nugget of worry crept into his brain. "Hey, did something happen? Is there an emergency?"

"You could say that," Jake chuckled. "I'll tell you at Starbucks on 3rd. 8 a.m."

Martin jammed the heels of his palms into his eyes. "Jake, it's my day off. And it's supposed to make up for the overtime from that last story. Remember? C'mon, tell me what's up. Or, FaceTime me. Later. Much later."

"Nope. I really wanna tell you in person. I'll make it worth your while. Trust me. And it can't wait 'til Monday. Honest. See you at 8."

"Jake—"

Click.

"What the fuck?" He threw his phone on the bed. Every now and then, his boss insisted on an early morning meeting even though he knew Martin wasn't a morning person. It was like Jake took some kind of perverse joy in torturing him like this.

He switched on the TV and flipped through the channels. There was nothing of any import on the news networks. Then he quickly checked his Facebook and Twitter feed on his phone. Nothing.

He pulled the covers over his head.

Do NOT want to get up. I need sleep, dammit.

A minute later, he yanked down the covers and glanced at the clock. He made a face.

"Why me, Lord?"

Untangling his long legs from the sheets, he slouched over to the john. Switching on the light hurt. He peered into the mirror and morosely rubbed the stubble on his chin.

"Ugh. Shouldn't have had that last beer," he muttered at his reflection. Then he shook his head. "Nope, not gonna shave."

He flicked off the light and looked at his bed. The dream had long slipped away.

"You're late."

"By five minutes, Jake." Martin choked back what he really felt like saying.

Jake pointed at the empty seat in front of him.

Instead of sleeping in to start off a nice long weekend, why am I about to sit across from someone I'm starting to loathe? Martin asked himself. What is wrong with me?

He set his coffee cup down and dropped into the chair opposite his boss. At least Jake had picked a table by the window. Placing his laptop bag on the empty seat, Martin hoped he wouldn't need to crack it open. He took a fortifying gulp of espresso.

"Ok. I'm here. So, why all the mystery, Jake?"

His boss swiveled his head to scan the coffee shop. It was surprisingly quiet. They were alone except for an older guy way on the other side of the room reading his paper and a fine looking redhead at the counter shaking cinnamon into her latte.

Martin smiled to himself. Who's he worried about? The FBI?

Apparently satisfied they wouldn't be overheard, Jake leaned in close, and, boring his squinty blue eyes into Martin's, drawled, "This is gonna be big."

The blast of his foul morning breath forced Martin backwards out of sniffing range. "Yeah? How so?"

To his dismay, Jake leaned in even closer and whispered, "I just got privy to some inside info. And I want you to promise me you won't tell a soul. I know I can trust you, right?"

Martin nodded warily.

"Listen. Do you remember when we ran that piece on Ira Walker?"

"Um, not really, but I know who you're talking about. Up and coming actress known for offbeat roles. In fact I just saw her latest movie. It was good. Seems like she's going places."

"Oh yeah, she's going places, all right," Jake smirked. "High places and low places too."

Martin opened his mouth for a second and then clamped it shut.

"Jake, what are you asking me to do?" he said tightly.

"I want you to do a story, obviously."

"Me?"

Clearly he'd been tricked into this meeting. Resentment began to boil inside him.

"Look, shouldn't you be waking someone else at the crack of dawn to meet with you about this? Someone like, uh—Dee Dee?"

"Dee Dee? No, Martin. I want you on this. It will give the story more cred if it comes from you, 'cause I gotta say, the stuff I heard is pretty unbelievable." He snickered and took a gulp of his coffee. "You do this story and your bonus will be almost as insane."

Martin stared at the dribble of java glistening on Jake's pockmarked chin and realized he felt like puking.

"Hold that thought, Jake. Need to use the rest room. Not feeling so hot."

His boss gave a little snort. "Feeling a little rough there, buddy boy?"

Martin stood up without bothering to respond. In the Men's Room he slapped his face with a couple of blasts of cold water and then took a few shaky breaths, trying to calm himself down.

What was this meeting really about anyway? he asked himself as he ran his hands through his curly hair, flicking drops of water onto the mirror. He held onto the edges of the sink and watched the water running into the drain for a few moments before turning off the tap. No doubt it was about money, he guessed. The Net's been doing a number on print ad revenues, so I bet Jake's gotten orders from up high to pull out all the stops.

Mechanically wiping his hands and face on a paper towel, he looked hard at himself in the mirror. His light brown skin was dull and pasty, and the bloodshot green eyes staring back—courtesy of last night's beer binge, coupled with lack of sleep—were flat and glassy.

He suddenly felt an overpowering desire to talk to his older brother. With a lurch, he realized he hadn't thought of him in a while.

Guess I've finally gotten used to Solomon not being around. Well, it's been ten years so I guess that was bound to happen.

He dropped his head.

What I'd give to hear his voice again. Shit. No doubt he'd give me an earful. Can almost hear him. Probably say, 'Hey bro, did you happen to forget you graduated top of your class from one of the best schools in the country? Aren't you supposed to be a respected journalist for a national newspaper?'

He fired the crumpled towel into the garbage can, and then stifled a burp.

Ugh. Coffee's definitely not mixing too well with the beer.

"You're drinking too much, Martin," a voice whispered.

He gave a little jump. The hairs on the back of his neck lifted up.

Did I just hear that? Could have sworn I heard my name.

He checked for feet under the stalls. He was definitely alone.

A few seconds later he heard the voice murmur again.

"You're better than this, right?"

What the fuck? That sounds like my brother! "Sol?" he said and then gave a quick laugh. What am I doing? No one hears their dead brother talking to them.

The voice again. A little louder this time. "Man, you a slave now to the almighty dollar AND to a boss who obviously has zero respect for you?"

Holy shit. It *was* his brother!

"Sol! How....where are ..."

He heard the bathroom door opening. He spun around. The guy who'd been reading the paper came in. Martin managed a nod. Then he closed his eyes and took a long, shaky breath to calm himself down.

Sol, if that's you, he thought, I don't know how in the hell you're talking to me right now. Jesus. This is insane.

He opened his eyes and looked at himself in the mirror again. He looked a little crazed. He slowly shook his head, then took another deep breath.

My brother's right. But do I have the stones for this?

He moved to the door and pushed it open. There was Jake, sprawled in his chair, phone stuck to his head, eyeballing the redhead with the latte.

He stood in the doorway, willing himself to move. Was he becoming someone's *boy*?

His brother's voice whispered in his ear again.

"You ain't nobody's 'boy', Martin."

Martin whispered back, "No... no man, I'm not."

"Do this, bro. You got better things coming."

"Ok. I'm going." Martin squared his shoulders and strode over to the table. Grabbing his laptop bag he stared down at his boss.

Jake gaped at him in irritation. "What took you so … Hey, what are you doing? We're not done here yet."

Martin stared down at him. "Yes, we are, Jake. "

"Martin, we aren't done until I say we're done!"

"Jake. We're done. I quit!"

Martin turned on his heel and marched out of the coffee shop. As he passed by the window, he could see Jake glaring at him. He gave him a little wave.

Heading back to his car, a huge smile lit up Martin's face. He hadn't felt this proud of himself in a very long time.

"Did I really do that?" he asked himself, shaking his head.

"Yeah, Martin, you did," he heard his brother say. "I'm proud of you, too."

"Thanks, bro," he whispered.

2

May 4, 1837

Wherein Jacob Williams makes a delectable discovery.

HE'D INSTRUCTED HIS OVERSEER TO WHIP ANY SLAVE guilty of damaging his cotton crop whilst picking it. Whether new or old hands, or done by accident, they would all get the same punishment—10 lashes on their naked backs, and, at his discretion, salt rubbed in for good measure. With nearly 300 slaves, it was essential they all knew their place.

A few were on the receiving end of the whip more than what was good for them. One—a big strong buck and the tallest slave Jacob had ever seen—could be a hard worker, but only when he chose to be, it seemed. Jacob got the distinct impression Jeremiah was born that way. Even when he was still a pup, he was a handful—talking back and trying to escape whenever he could. Of course, he would never get far. The first time he'd disappeared, the hounds sniffed out his hiding spot in the woods the very next day. When he was carried back to the plantation, Jacob's father ordered a lashing, but since Jeremiah was just a child, only seven strokes—one for each year of his life—instead of the usual 70. But within a couple of years, didn't that boy run again? He'd avoided capture for a few days. When the men caught him, Jacob's father ordered one of his toes severed as a lesson.

After Jacob's father died, Jeremiah had become Jacob's concern. More than once he'd considered selling the slave, but he always reconsidered. While his size and strength virtually guaranteed a good sale, Jeremiah's reputation as an uppity slave would knock the profit down to make any deal worthwhile. And, since he'd gained some excellent new stock from him, Jeremiah was in fact more valuable to Jacob as his property, no matter how high falutin' he got.

Now that Jeremiah had so many offspring, Jacob hoped his running off days were over. Nevertheless, he'd instructed his overseer to keep a sharp eye on him, especially as Jacob sensed that Jeremiah was aware of his 'special' status. Slaves needed to be in fear to stay under control.

Jacob's overseer had just alerted him that morning that the slave was acting up again He'd decided to ride out to the field to check on his prized buck before deciding what his punishment should be. Though he was working in one of the far fields, Jeremiah was easy to find; he stood a full head taller than any other slave. Jacob walked his horse closer to watch him work. Though it wasn't even mid-morning, the day was muggy and promised to be much hotter by afternoon.

Jacob toyed with his whip as he observed him work. Jeremiah didn't let on he saw him, but Jacob knew he was aware of his presence and was more than likely putting on a show for him. Nevertheless, he was mollified to see the nigger pulling the fuzzy white blossoms quickly yet delicately from the prickly pods. For such a large man, he had a deft touch.

The sun was becoming intolerable. Jacob nudged his horse over into the shade of a nearby grove. He'd been talking with a fellow plantation owner a few days earlier who'd explained that occasionally, the mere threat of punishment was all he needed to keep a slave under control. Jacob decided, after a few more minutes of scrutiny, he would try that tactic and spare Jeremiah—but just this once.

He was about to turn his horse around toward the Big House when he got a glimpse of the girl. She was picking a row over from Jeremiah. Jacob would have missed her if Jeremiah hadn't squatted down for a few moments. Jacob urged his reluctant horse back out into the sun a ways down from where Jeremiah was working so he could get a better look at her. Bewitched, he observed the girl's elegant small hands fly as she effortlessly plucked the blossoms. She'd been taught well.

Jacob felt himself growing hard as he contemplated the delights concealed under her graceless garb. Despite her shabby coarse cotton skirt and blouse, her beauty was unmistakable—skin the color of rich, brewed coffee, a slender petite body, but most assuredly all woman. A cool, calculating smile hovered on his thin lips as he watched her. He was amused how she coyly kept her eyes lowered to her work.

Yes, she would do, he decided. Most assuredly, she would do.

Out of the corner of his eye, he saw Jeremiah had lifted his head.

"What you looking at, boy? Get back to work!"

Jeremiah ducked his head and did as he was told.

Near day's end, Jacob summoned his overseer. The man rode up holding his hat and his whip in one hand and mopping the sweat off his brow with the other.

"Hot one today, Master Williams."

Jacob nodded and stared off into the distance.

The overseer jammed his hat back on his head and waited for his boss to speak. He noted how Jacob's large green eyes glittered in the bright afternoon light. He was reminded of the wolf he'd seen when he was just a boy. He'd been scared near to death.

"I saw a girl working in the south cotton field today," Jacob said finally.

"Yeah, boss."

"Never saw her before."

The overseer cocked an eyebrow as he waited for him to continue.

"She was just a little bitty thing, but a good worker. And a beauty. If I'm not mistaken it seemed Jeremiah was trying to hide her."

"Uh, that would be Sadie," the overseer replied after thinking a moment. "One of his pups. Hm. She usually works in a different field. Not sure why she was over there today."

"Sadie? The last time I saw her she was just a child," replied Jacob as he stroked the cleft in his chin. "My, oh my."

Suppressing a smile, the overseer waited. He'd served Jacob Williams for many years and could readily predict what he would say next.

At last, Jacob cleared his throat and announced, "I do believe Miss Sheila needs a new house servant. That other one has run off, as you well know."

"I'm sure they'll catch her soon, suh," the overseer said quickly.

"Of course. Stupid wench. And she'll pay for it. I'll make sure of that."

"Yes, boss. I know you will."

"Well, then. I'd like Sadie to take her place. Have her start working in the Big House day after tomorrow."

The overseer nodded again. "An excellent choice, suh."

Jacob dismissed the man and headed toward his house. Lost in thought, he took his sweet time climbing up the wide front steps. Pausing on the stoop, he lifted his hat to mop the sweat from his face with a large scented handkerchief. He turned back towards his land and saw that the setting sun had turned his pure white cotton fields the enticing color of ripe peaches.

He sighed. It was always a bit of a dilemma for him to decide whether sunset or sunrise was his favorite time of day. While dawn suggested the potential of new profit, dusk allowed him to contemplate his magnificent kingdom in all its glory as money continued to be made by his slaves. They would continue to pick until it was too dark to see.

A self-satisfied grin slid across his face as the sun gradually slipped below the soft white blossoms. He had much to be thankful for. Though, of course, he, of all people, deserved it all, didn't he?

He took in a deep breath. The lush scent of oleander blossoms commingled with the tantalizing aroma of roasting meat emanating from the kitchen of Big House. He turned the gleaming brass doorknob of the heavy oak door and stepped across the threshold. The smell of the roast grew so intense he immediately began to salivate. He almost shivered at the thought of the succulent meat tonight and of a more delicate offering in the very near future.

Oh yes, how he looked forward to feasting upon this latest girl's delights.

3

May 5, 1837

Wherein a young slave questions her existence.

BARKING DOGS. THE CRACK OF A WHIP. A SCREAM.

Sadie's eyes snapped open.

Suzanne. They found her?

No light through the chinks in the cabin walls yet. Her younger sisters and brothers whimpered. Ma whispered, "Hush, now."

Sadie yanked the rough blanket over her head.

"Oh pray! Oh pray!" cried the girl. "Have mercy!"

Sadie clamped her hands over her mouth, to keep from yellin': It is Suzanne!

The rasp of male voices. "You can pray all ya want, bitch, but Master Williams said 70 lashes and that's what you gonna git!"

Oh, why can't Sadie still find some comfort in prayer?

He never answers. Me, I'm just one more slave girl askin' for His mercy. Too many of us for Him to pay attention to one more slave.

She winced as the lash continued to find its mark not so far from where she lay.

The ugly voices again. "The master say to tan your hide, but your hide already tan, ain't it, girly?"

Suzanne's howls grew louder and ever more pitiful.

Sadie added her own silent scream: That girl ain't no animal!

She shut her eyes tight trying to squeeze back tears. But that's just what they think we are, ain't we? Just beasts ... beasts that walk on two legs and can talk, that is.

Her mind flashed back to the morning Massa sent her baby brother on an errand to the plantation t'other side of the hill. He came back cryin' and hardly able to talk. When Mama finally calmed him down, she got it out of him what happened. A slave man was gettin' rolled all over the yard inside a barrel that had shingle nails driven into it. Sittin' on a block was his Massa, laughin' at his cries. The slave doin' the rollin' wanted to stop, but Massa told him if he did he'd get himself a long lashin'.

Not so long ago, Massa Williams punished a slave man by gettin' him shoved into a box just big enough for him to squeeze into. Overseer nailed down the top leavin' only a little bitty hole for him to get some air. That was a coffin with a livin' man inside. Left him there for two days in the hot sun. By the time they let him out he was nearly dead. And why did he get such punishment? 'Cause he didn't take his hat off when Massa passed by.

The whipping finally stopped. Suzanne's cries had died off long before. A voice grunted, "Ya'll think twice now before you decide to run off again, won't cha, you dirty wench!" The other man laughed and they rode off with the hounds yelping in their dust.

Oh, them dogs, thought Sadie. Massa called 'em *nigger hounds*. When she was a little bitty girl, she was made to run off a good ways, and then overseer sent the hound pups on her tracks. Silly she thought it was fine sport at the time. Then she realized them pups were being trained to hunt colored people. Sometimes the hands were called in from the fields and made to run around and climb up trees with them hot on their heels. And every single day a pot of good hominy got cooked up for them hounds. They always got the victuals leftover from Massa's table, too. Whenever she saw them gnawing on a good piece of meat, she wished she were a dog.

The night was quiet now except for the moans and whimpers of poor Suzanne.

How'd that girl find herself enough courage to slip away? Poor chile. Didn't get far enough.

The cabin door next to Sadie's creaked open. Someone slipped out to ease Suzanne up and carry her inside. Her moans turned into screams again as her wounds were bathed and covered in salve.

Why some people born slaves, Sadie asked herself once again. Why others born masters? She gave a little moan. And how come I was born a slave?

The horn would be blowing soon. She must sleep. Pressing her ears hard to block the sounds drifting over from the next cabin, she conjured up the letters stored for safekeeping inside her head—the letters Ole Tom's been teaching her, whenever he dared.

Then she shivered.

If Massa or overseer ever found out, it'll be me in that box.

4

August 9, 2012
Wherein Jacob has a rude awakening.

He felt absolutely wretched, but he'd expected that. The spinning sensation was something new, however. He felt weak and so terribly dizzy. On his fourth attempt to get out of bed, he nearly spit up onto his covers.

He closed his eyes and while he waited till the room righted itself, he took stock. At least he was in a bed, which he assumed was his, although he very well could be mistaken. He'd had some brandy—a great deal of it, he had to admit—at the dinner table the night before. His wife had left him there after a particularly bitter argument. What happened next was a bit of a mystery. He wasn't even certain if he'd made it to his room. Perhaps he'd blacked out—again.

Once he had his coffee, he would feel better. Snaking an arm out from under the sheet, he groped about until he felt the fringe of a tassel. He gave it a tug and then opened an eye. To his relief, the spinning had stopped. He saw that he was most assuredly ensconced in his own chambers.

Did someone carry me in here last night? I can't seem to remember a thing.

He almost felt disgusted with himself. He needed to be sharp as he had a long, busy day ahead, but in his present state he wasn't quite sure if he would be up to it. The sooner Samuel arrived with his coffee the better. That, and some dry toast, would help set things straight.

The room seemed brighter than usual. The morning was wearing on. Damn. He must have slept in. Glancing at the windows he saw that someone had pulled the drapes wide open.

He frowned. Was Samuel already in here? If so, why didn't the imbecile bring me my coffee?

He sat up, clutched his head and fell back onto his pillow moaning in agony. Mother of God! Why do I drink so?

After lying still for several more minutes, the throbbing in his head lessened. He willed his mind to return to the day's matters. He had an important afternoon meeting with the overseer; amongst other things they were discussing what to do about this year's crop. The wet spring had held planting back and every grower in the region was worried. And with cotton prices seemingly on the decline, this was very concerning indeed. He might have no choice but to auction off a couple of slaves to make up for the impending losses.

He gave a little snort. Indeed, there were one or two who had been quite troublesome of late that he might be better off without. And Samuel might soon be added to the list.

"Damnation!" he growled. "I can't wait here forever. I have to get on with my day!"

Maneuvering himself out of bed he stumbled over to the air closet to piss. As he stepped back into the room he detected faint voices. At long last. "Samuel! Coffee! This instant!"

Several minutes passed, but still no Samuel.

"By God," he muttered, "if that bugger doesn't get in here soon I'll sell him by sundown!"

He fumbled into his robe and poked his head into the hall.

"Samuel!"

He cocked an ear to listen; it seemed the voices were drifting up from the Great Hall. He started toward the landing to investigate, but had to stop short as his surroundings began to spin again. Falling back hard against the wall he closed his eyes until things settled down. Several moments passed before he felt steady enough to move to the railing and peer down into the Hall.

His mouth fell open. "Good Lord!"

Three strangers—two men and a woman—stood in the foyer, talking.

Who invited a harlot into my house? Look at her! Her frock is exposing her legs!

He stared hard at the trio, trying to make sense of what he was seeing. And who are those men! They're dressed like paupers! Where are their vests and cravats?

His knuckles whitened as he gripped the railing hard to keep himself from falling over it. After a few more moments of scrutiny, he revised his opinion as to the gender of the two men.

My God. That one there's a woman! In trousers!

Then, to make matters even worse, a big Negro stud—black as soot—strode in through the front door. The three strangers turned to greet the buck.

"Welcome to the Williams Plantation, Mr. Monroe," the trousered woman said and extended her hand.

"What?" Jacob sputtered.

"My name is Louise, and this is Cathy and Stuart."

"A pleasure to meet you, Mr. Monroe," said the white man giving the darkie's big black hand a firm shake. "As restoration work has just been completed on the Big House your class is the first to take a tour."

"You there! What are you doing in my house?" Jacob croaked pressing a hand to his chest. His heart was pounding so hard he felt it might burst.

To his consternation he received no response. Instead, the group ignored him and continued their conversation.

"Please, call me Patrick," the big nigger said looking quickly around.

The bitter liquid filled Jacob's mouth again. He spit it over the rail in the nigger's direction, then watched in disbelief as the long, shiny strings of saliva disappeared before reaching their target.

"What? That's impossible!" he cried, leaning over the railing to see whether his spit might have landed on the floor.

"The kids are very excited," the nigger said. "I'll tell the driver to let them off the bus." He added with a toothy grin, "Get ready! They'll have lots of questions!"

"As do I!" shouted Jacob before a coughing fit overcame him.

Again there was no response from the intruders.

Jacob scowled at the scene below. This must be some kind of sorcery. How can I be invisible to this vile lot?

He felt so wretched, he decided to go back to his chambers and lie down. Touching the wall to keep from falling he wobbled down the corridor to his room and collapsed onto his bed. As he stared out the window, he tried calming himself, but his brain was bursting with questions.

How did those three get into my house? Where are my servants? Why would they allow a nigga in my front door? Why were those people treating him as if he were their equal? And why can no one see or hear me?

Then something terrible occurred to him. Forcing himself to rise once again, he made his way over to his chamber's fireplace where a large mirror hung above the mantelpiece. He stood swaying in front of it, feeling relieved but foolish by his notion that he had somehow become invisible. He wasn't all that pleased by what he saw in the mirror, however: messy gray curly hair, flushed freckled face dripping with sweat, green eyes—not surprisingly red and tired looking—and wide, thin lips that were pulled down into a grimace.

"God in heaven. I look a sight," he groaned as he wiped his face with the sleeve of his night robe. "Samuel! Where are you?"

Then he sucked in his breath.

That big darkie had said: 'touring the plantation'! I will NOT have trespassers snooping about my house. Christ, those bastards are behaving as if this is their property. And what sort of nonsense was that about 'kids'? Is that black barbarian about to bring goats into my house?

He sniffed in indignation. And then he felt a glimmer of hope.

Sheila. I must talk to Sheila. Perhaps she can explain all this.

Taking care not to fall, he staggered out his door and then covered the short distance to her chambers. About to knock on her door, he remembered: she'd found out about Sadie. Most likely she was avoiding him. Well, he would have to make it up to her, somehow. He rapped on the wood. Hearing no response, he knocked harder, then tried the knob.

The room was empty; her bed made up.

"Darling?" he called through dry cracked lips. "Are you there, Sheila?"

He waited a few moments in case she was indisposed, but was not rewarded with a reply. He lurched across her room and stepped out onto her balcony in the hopes he would see his wife outside with the children.

What he saw horrified him.

What's happened to the garden? And my crops! What in Christ's name has happened to my crops?

He peered up and down the length of the house and scanned the pathetic garden. His wife and children were nowhere in sight and his scant fields were devoid of workers. His eyes strained to pick out a sign of life—anywhere.

A distant whine, which appeared to be coming from the adjacent side of the house, caught his attention. He craned his neck toward the sound.

"Mother of God!"

An enormous black and yellow spider was inching its way along several rows of cotton. He watched dumbfounded as bare stalks appeared in its wake.

Retreating to his chambers Jacob fell onto his hands and knees. Then he began to shake. Never had he felt this cold before—not even on the bitterest winter day. Hot tears started burning down his icy face, but he found himself powerless to hold them back. He looked at his bed, which stood like an oasis in the desert, only a few yards away. Could he drag himself there?

Inch by painful inch, he crawled his way over, paused for a few moments to get his breath and then heaved himself onto the bed. He clawed at the covers with stiff fingers and pulled them over his body.

He stared at the ceiling, trying to calm his shattered nerves. Gradually, he started to feel warmer. If only the answers to the extraordinary morning would reveal themselves in the plasterwork.

He felt he should try to recall as much as possible from the previous day, which now seemed so long ago. He forced himself to think back. Bit-by-bit, memories began to solidify.

As far as he could remember, the day before had passed without incident. That all had changed at dinnertime. There had been no company, for once. The children had said their goodnights and were taken off to bed. Sheila had been largely silent during dinner, but soon after his first brandy was placed in front of him, her accusations about the house girls buzzed like angry wasps around his head.

It wasn't the first time he'd endured a tirade from her, but he had never seen her quite so furious. She wouldn't hear his excuses. "You said there would be no more!" she had screamed before storming out of the room.

He scowled.

Whoever the scoundrel was who had told her about Sadie would soon regret it.

His mind then entertained a horrifying possibility.

The brandy. Could Sheila have slipped something into it? She'd been angry enough to harm him.

He gave his head a slight shake.

No, no, I'm much more valuable to her alive. Who, then?

His green eyes narrowed.

A slave. But, which of them would dare?

The face of Jeremiah seemed to float before him. He considered the apparition for a moment, and then shook his head.

No, that nigga wouldn't risk it. His family and every other slave would suffer the consequences.

Rubbing his whiskery face Jacob was reminded of the day's mysterious disappearance of his servants. Where was Samuel? And Winston? The two of them should have shaved and dressed him by now. But they, along with everyone else that should be bustling about were missing.

He closed his eyes and cursed.

How is it that I am lying here like a helpless invalid? Is there not a soul on my property that I know, or who knows me? Have I been abandoned?

His brain ached for any sort of explanation, no matter how far-fetched. Suddenly, his eyes flew open.

Might those invaders downstairs be play actors? But, why? Who would bother staging a play such as this? It all seems more like a sort of dreamland—.

He groaned with relief. Of course. It was all a terrible nightmare.

Grasping the skin on his left arm with his thumb and middle finger he gave it a fierce tug.

"Ouch! Dammit!"

He rubbed the sore pinched spot as the grandfather clock in the parlor downstairs struck once.

"One o'clock? How is it possible?"

His eyes slid back toward the windows. A slight breeze stirred the lace edges of the drapes, as brilliant afternoon sunshine flooded into the room. On a normal day, he tried to wake just after dawn. He realized he had woken late, but could it possibly be one o'clock already? Where had the time gone?

Shrill voices emanated from the first floor; his attention returned to the problem of the trespassers.

What now? Christ, I can't just lie here. I am the Master of this plantation. I MUST take control!

With strength emanating from some unknown reserve, he abandoned his bed yet again and snatched up the fireplace poker.

"I will take control!" he said aloud.

He tottered down the hall to the landing and peered over the railing into the Great Hall.

"My God!"

A seething mass of piccaninnies had pushed their way into his house. It looked like they were about to steal everything they could lay their hands on. He watched in horrified fascination as they pointed small boxes about while speaking a sort of gibberish. He could make out an English word here and there such as 'awesome' and 'cool', but there was no making any sense of it.

The big nigger shushed the mob and began introducing them to the trio who proclaimed to be in charge of his property. Jacob could not watch another moment. Waving the poker over his head he screeched, "You there! Get out of my house!"

Once again, there was no response.

Desperate to get their attention, he smashed the poker on the handrail. "GET OUT! I WANT YOU OUT! ALL OF YOU!"

A few faces turned to peer up at him.

Though sweat was pouring down his body, Jacob barely noticed. He was so very relieved they had finally noticed him.

"Oh!" said the harlot. "You're early!" Turning to the trousered woman, she said in a low voice, "My goodness. He seems a little angry. I wonder what's wrong—"

"Of course I'm angry, woman!"

The white man looked up at him with a stupefied expression. "Ok, sorry! We didn't know you were ready to go on." He cleared his throat and turned back to the other invaders, who were staring up at Jacob as if observing an apparition.

"Everyone. I'd like you to meet Mr. Jacob Williams, 'Master' of this plantation."

"Correct!" Jacob bellowed. "Now leave my house at once or I'll have y'all arrested for trespassing!"

5

October 11, 2011
Wherein Martin explains himself.

"YOU QUIT?"

"Yes, I did."

"Oh, my goodness. But, why?"

"Short answer: I just couldn't take it anymore. And I am sick of Jake."

"I see. At least, I think I see. You're not worried about giving up that kind of income?"

"No. Well, I have to admit, that's kind of why it took me so long to do this. But when he began having me poke around in people's private lives, the money seemed tainted somehow."

"Hm."

"Yeah. I'm not proud of that. I've been pretending what I was doing was ok. But it wasn't."

A pause at the other end of the line.

"Mom? You still there?"

"Yes, I am, Martin."

"You know I didn't go to journalism school to end up becoming a high-paid Peeping Tom. And my boss, who I finally realized is evil incarnate, just wants dirtier and dirtier stuff. I don't want to be part of that anymore."

Another pause. "Well, you know what?"

"What?"

"I'm proud of you, Martin. I do believe you did the right thing."

He sighed with relief. "Thanks, Mom. You don't know how good it is to hear you say that."

"But, what are you going to do next?"

He gave a dry chuckle. "I hate to admit it, but I don't know—yet."

"Oh."

"I know. I know. Listen, I didn't even realize I was going to quit until—" he hesitated before going on. Should he tell his mother that her long dead son had given him advice from the grave? It might upset her and she would probably think he was crazy. In fact, he was half convinced he'd been hallucinating.

"Until, what?"

"Well, until my boss dragged me out of bed to a meeting this morning—on my day off. I guess you could say I had, um, a revelation. I could see what a bastard he was ... that he was just using me. Seems like all he cares about are ad revenues and sales—doesn't give a crap about good journalism at all."

"So you quit right then and there?"

"Yup. Just wished I'd had the nerve to do it sooner. Well, anyway. I did it today and now all I have to do next is figure out what I really want to do with the rest of my life."

There was a pause on the other end of the line and then he heard a small sigh. Martin wondered if he was about to get a lecture.

"Now, look," she said at last. "Take your time, all right, Sugar? It's important that you make sure that whatever you do next, it's the right thing—something that will make you happy."

"Hm, something that will make me happy. Wow. There's a novel idea," he said, his voice gloomy.

"What do you mean, sweetheart? How could you not be happy? Ok, I understand the job has gotten to you, but otherwise, I thought you were very content, although of course, you haven't found a nice girl yet."

He gave a weak laugh. "Ok, Mom. I'll level with you."

"Yes?"

"Sometimes I feel guilty."

"Guilty? What for? The stories you wrote? You didn't really have a choice, did you?"

"Well, yes, I do feel guilty about some of them, but there were a lot I was damn proud of. And I guess I was trying to suppress the guilty feeling for a long time."

"Oh, Martin."

"What I mean is, things have always come too easy for me, Mom. School. Friends. Jobs. Money. And then I got this job and I thought, all right! You're on your way, man, but I started second guessing myself within a year or two. Wondered if maybe I was being touted as the 'token black wunderkind'. But yeah, the money was good, and started getting even better, and it somehow made it all ok."

"Don't feel guilty, Martin. You're so smart and talented! You earned those scholarships and you deserve to have a good life.

Sometimes things just work out better for some people."

He sighed. "Well, I know, Mom, but look, it's like this: when I see someone who's homeless begging on the street, especially if they're black, I get this feeling that could be me. I could be sitting there on the sidewalk, or huddled in a doorway, or whatever. But, I've been lucky."

"And smart, Martin. Very smart."

He gave a little laugh. "Yeah, well, I think success has a lot to do with luck, too. So, I usually give them some money, even if I suspect they will spend it on booze or crack. But hey, they're human beings. I can't just walk by."

"You always were the soft one, Martin," she said with a slight catch in her throat.

He figured she was looking at the family portrait on the mantle. The one taken just a few months before the accident. She'd lost her first-born son and he'd lost his only sibling.

He thought again of the otherworldly conversation he'd had that morning. Perhaps Solomon had been with him all these years, after all.

"I guess so, Mom," he said, hoping she wouldn't cry. "So, anyway, I saw a guy downtown a few months ago, sitting on a dirty, old comforter by the curb. Probably about my age. Staring straight ahead and holding a little sign that said he couldn't find a job and his wife was pregnant."

"Oh, goodness. That's so sad."

"He seemed so depressed and lost. Even when I put twenty bucks in his cup, he barely looked at me. I thought, wow. What would it be like to have no hope?"

"That was nice of you to help him out a little bit, Martin."

"It was nothing, Mom. I mean it. I felt like the money was just so I would feel better, not him. But I think something clicked inside me that day."

"How so?"

"I think my gut was telling me I had to change my life, Mom. It just took me a while to listen to it."

Or, was that my brother trying to get through to me? he wondered.

"That man certainly could have been giving you a message, Martin," she said. "Why don't you think about helping people like him? Maybe that's your destiny. If you're determined you can make it happen. And, who knows? Perhaps you'll find a nice girl along the way." She gave a little laugh.

"Hope springs eternal, huh Mom?" he said, thinking, she never gives up, does she?

"Well, I'm not getting any younger, Martin."

"Don't worry, Mom. My life is changing so it's possible things might change in that department too."

"That would be nice. Very nice."

"Look, I've gotta run."

"Ok. Bye, Sugar. Love you."

"Love you forever, Mom."

Clicking off his phone he said to himself, ok man, you'd better do something proper with your life now. 'Cause If you don't, how are you ever gonna face Mom again?

6

August 9, 2012

Wherein Jacob wakes up to his worst nightmare, then is snatched from his home.

"SOMEBODY!" CRIED LOUISE. "CALL 911!"

Stuart quickly punched the numbers into his phone while his colleagues knelt beside 'Mr. Williams.' Moments earlier, the staff, class, and teachers had watched in disbelief as the man had lurched down the stairs into the Great Hall. Swinging a fireplace poker, his face beet red, eyes bulging out of his head, 'Mr. Williams' had clutched his chest and collapsed onto the floor, the poker falling at his side on the rug.

"Wow!" said a student as the class crowded in, peering at the man lying on the floor. "It looked like he was about to kill somebody!"

Patrick raised his arms. "Ok! Calm down, class! This gentleman needs air… please move back."

The parent volunteers stepped up, nudged the class back a few feet and got them settled down.

The emergency operator came on the line and Stuart gave her a quick run down of the situation.

"I think he's stopped breathing!" Louise cried, "Oh my God, the defibrillator's still on order! Does anyone know CPR?"

"I do," replied Patrick kneeling down beside 'Mr. Williams', who appeared to be turning blue. "Someone get a pillow for his head please!"

Cathy slipped away and returned with a cushion from the settee in the parlor, which she slid under the man's head. She'd also grabbed a throw, which she laid over the lower half of his body to prevent him from going into shock. Patrick began compressing his chest with large capable hands and then pinched his nose shut to force air into his lungs.

"That was a close call, guys,' Cathy said in a low voice to her co-workers. "I wonder what could have gotten into him?" "

"Geez, I haven't got a clue," responded Louise, gulping in some deep breaths as she tried to pull herself together. "God, I'm shaking like a leaf. Hope he's ok!"

"What incredibly bad timing," said Stuart under his breath. The two women shot him a stern look, and then turned back toward Patrick who had resumed compressions.

Jacob's eyes fluttered open, then widened in horror to see a black face hovering just above his own.

He fainted before he could order the darkie to remove his filthy hands from his person.

7

May 8, 1837

Wherein Sadie has a close call.

RUNNING, RUNNING, RUNNING, RUNNING FASTER than ever before. Sides aching–can't hardly breathe...

The howls gettin' closer...

Don't look back!

River shining through the trees...

C'mon... keep running... water will throw them off. Praise God I learned to swim! Almost there... just a little bit more now...

Tripping, falling, falling face down in dirt and leaves.

Hand grabs the back of my neck.

"Sadie! Wake up! You're going to catch it if you don't get a move on, girl!"

She turned her head to see Ma looking down at her in the gloom of early morn. She blinked her eyes. How did she fall back asleep with Suzanne carrying on so?

She wiped away tears bent on sliding down her cheeks.

Freedom seemed so close.

"Hurry, Sadie! Hurry, girl!"said Ma giving her a pinch.

She leapt out of her cot.

"Here, quick now, eat some pone."

She did as she was told, though she could barely get the food down.

"Now move it, girl," said Ma. "Don't want to give Missus no good reason to whip your hide, too!"

8

August 9, 2012
Wherein Patrick and his class
have a thought provoking experience.

After the drama in the Great Hall and subsequent departure of the 'plantation owner' who was taken away by ambulance, the rattled staff of The Williams Plantation Historic Site worried that opening day would be a flop. It was therefore a huge relief when the other re-enactors, including the house servants and field hands, took their places after the ambulance left and went on with the show as if nothing had happened.

The Antebellum Big House, filled with flowers and furnished with carefully restored period pieces, looked magnificent. When Patrick and his student group reached the second floor to explore the family quarters, there was some excitement about the bed in the plantation owner's suite; it looked like it had been slept in.

"Evidently that re-enactor took his role very seriously," commented a parent.

"Or maybe he came in early and took a nap?" suggested a girl.

Patrick stared at the rumpled bed, wondering if he was the only one who felt the discovery unnerving.

For the remainder of the Big House tour he found it hard to concentrate. He couldn't seem to stop thinking about the incident in the Great Hall. He felt better when they began the second part of the tour: the growing operation. Urban development had eaten up hundreds of acres of the original plantation, but with the fifteen or so acres remaining, the estate had been revived as a working plantation with cotton, corn and other vegetables, and included some fruit crops like blueberries, strawberries, raspberries and peaches. The students were fascinated by a huge, yellow spider-like machine that crawled down the cotton rows picking the bolls.

Then it was time to visit the slave quarters. Unlike most of the nation's preserved plantations that tended to "whitewash" their unpleasant past, management of the Williams Plantation had chosen not to shy away from this unsavory historical aspect, which was why

Patrick had been so eager to visit. In fact, he had started organizing the field trip as soon as he'd heard it would be open to the public. He felt it t would be the perfect supplement to his African-American History curriculum.

Patrick's class paused on the rock hard earth in front of a row of three small log cabins to hear some words from a middle-aged slave re-enactor. She was dressed in a simple homespun long cotton skirt and loose fitting cotton blouse, her hair twisted into tight cornrows.

She smiled and bobbed a little curtsy. "Hello, y'all. My name is Ole Jen. A long, long time ago, I lived in one of these here cabins. Once there were dozens just like it, but since they were all made of wood, most didn't survive the years after full Emancipation in 1865. These here ones are just 12 feet by 18 feet each. Believe it or not, up to 10 to 12 of us slaves would live in a cabin and each only had one or two rooms."

As Ole Jen paused to let this sink in Patrick noticed several of his students looking askance. Despite his state of mind, he had to smile. He had grown up in a large family. Not only did he share his bedroom with two brothers, there had been just one bathroom for five kids, including two sisters—plus his parents and Auntie. It was a crowded existence and he often longed for privacy, let alone peace and quiet, but compared to this tiny dwelling, it was like living in a resort. He assumed many of his students' houses were much roomier than his childhood home had been so the thought of living cheek by jowl in a place like this was probably incomprehensible to them.

The group followed Ole Jen to the second cabin, which looked exactly like the first. "Some cabins were bigger and built in different spots depending on the rank of the slave. Even though us field slaves did such hard, valuable work, we were stuck in shacks. Artisans and the black overseers or slave drivers had the best houses. Next came the domestic servants. Even worse off than us field hand slaves were the children's gangs and the sick or elderly who couldn't work no more."

One of the students stuck a hand in the air. Ole Jen nodded at her. "So what happened if a woman was like, pregnant or just had a baby?"

Ole Jen gave her a rueful smile. "Well, she would have to keep on working right on up to the day she delivered and right after that too.

She would take that baby with her out to the field strapped onto her back. Or she would have to leave it under a tree near the field for hours at a time. Once in a while a dog or a hawk would take one.

"What? Oh my God!" the girl said. The girl next to her piped up. "That's so sad!"

Ole Jen looked down for a couple of moments. "That's right, those were real sad days. In fact, at least 20 percent of the slave children died before the age of five. Most of us slaves were unhealthy 'cause of all the hard work, whippings, and our starchy diet lacking in protein and vitamins."

A boy raised his hand. "But, wouldn't plantation owners want to keep their slaves healthy so they could work harder?"

Ole Jen gave a little grunt. "You would think so, but most of them didn't and there usually weren't no proper medical care neither. Luckily, we had some knowledge of the herbs and roots could help cure us. Passed down from the old ones that came from Africa. And thank goodness we had song and prayer to sustain us."

She gestured toward the cabins. "It's time. Go right on in."

Patrick and the parent volunteers had split the group up between the three cabins. He followed seven students and a parent up the two wooden steps and over the threshold of the first structure. As the cabin lacked windows it took a few seconds for his eyes to adjust to the dim interior. There was little to see. A stone fireplace with a large blackened hearth crouched in the middle of one wall. Six simple wooden chairs surrounded a roughly hewn table topped by a carved bowl and pitcher. Pegs poked out of a couple of walls, some with a few items of clothing hanging on them. And there were half a dozen narrow wooden beds, just a few inches above the dirt floor, with only coarse thin blankets for bedding.

There was a profound silence.

One of the mother volunteers murmured, "To think this was where enslaved people had actually lived. My, oh my."

From the corner of his eye, Patrick saw one of his students lie down on a bed. "Man, this is hard as a rock!" the boy pronounced. "I wouldn't be able to sleep for even one second."

There was some nervous laughter, but then everyone remembered where they were and it sputtered out.

"I think after a long day in the fields, you would sleep, Lawrence," said Patrick. "Just think, only six beds in here so some slaves would have to share or else sleep on the hard dirt floor, which would be muddy if it rained. And that was after a long, long day of hard labor in the boiling sun or in a hot kitchen."

"And maybe after having their bare backs whipped," whispered a girl. They had stopped at the whipping post just a few yards away from the cabins.

In spite of the dim light, Patrick noticed tears glistening on several faces.

Ole Jen appeared in the doorway. "Y'all have any questions?"

The same parent asked in a hushed voice, "Do they know the different families who lived in these cabins over the years?"

Ole Jen nodded. "We have a few names, but nobody could find all the records. The Masters sometimes broke families up. They would sell parents or children to other plantation owners as punishment and sometimes that meant they were sent to other States. And they would split up the husbands and wives too."

"Slaves were basically livestock," muttered Lawrence.

"Animals. That's all we were in those days," agreed another boy.

Patrick listened quietly. At the start of the school term he had asked his students to share any passed down family stories about the days when their ancestors had been slaves. He was not surprised that many didn't know much about those days. When slaves were sold, they were often never seen or heard from again. Runaways that had not been caught often disappeared without a trace. Some of the escapees may have purposely avoided being traced to prevent capture and could have died years later without anyone knowing their story.

And some families just didn't want to talk about those times. It was too painful to remember. Trying to find out his own history had been tough for that reason, but Patrick had managed to pry some information from his granma before she died.

When he was organizing the field trip, he'd worried about some students who might come away from it feeling a bit shell-shocked. He'd warned his class that it wouldn't be like a trip to the zoo or the art gallery. Fortunately, he'd prepared a debriefing for the bus ride back to the school and for the following week.

"Whew!" said a girl, wiping her forehead. "It's so hot in here!"

"Yes, let's get back outside everyone," said Patrick checking his watch. "It's about time to head back to school."

As the group straggled toward the bus, the scene in the Great Hall replayed in Patrick's mind. The look on that man's red, sweaty face had completely unnerved him. He gave a little shudder. What he had seen in the man's glittering green eyes had been pure, unadulterated hatred.

9

August 10, 2012

Wherein Jacob receives two unthinkable surprises.

This is the day of Jubilee,
God's going to build up Zion's walls!
The Lord has set His people free.
God's going to build up Zion's wall!
We want no cowards in our band,
God's going to build up Zion's walls!
We call for valiant-hearted men.
God's going to build up Zion's walls!
Gonna take my breast-plate, sword and shield,
God's going to build up Zion's walls!

MOUNTED ON HIS FAVORITE HORSE, Jacob tilted his hat further down to shade his eyes from the late afternoon sun. The crushing heat of the previous week had lifted and now the weather was glorious. He gazed at the hunched over field hands who dotted the endless rows of cotton before him. Was there another sight more pleasing to the eye than an expansive cotton field in bloom full of pickers? They were proof positive that his fortune was growing larger every day. Their rhythmic, beautiful voices singing the old bible song complemented the idyllic scene.

He allowed himself a small sigh of contentment. How pure it

looked. Like drifts of new-fallen snow.

A slave straightened up. Rubbing his lower back, he turned to face Jacob.

What's he doing? thought Jacob, his reverie broken.

After regarding him for a few moments, the slave began to walk in his direction.

Jacob frowned. "What do you think you're doing there, nigga? Get back to work, boy!" he barked.

But the slave continued to approach. He was big and at first Jacob assumed it was Jeremiah. But, instead of a rough cotton shirt and loose breeches, this darkie's garb was strange: tight blue trousers and a yellow shirt with short sleeves that ended at his elbows. A straw broad brimmed hat was squashed onto his large head. On his feet he wore shoes as white as freshly picked cotton.

The singing had stopped. The only sound Jacob could hear was a rhythmic, pulsing noise that seemed to come from nowhere. His eyes darted over the fields hunting for his overseer.

More and more slaves were straightening up to watch the nigga walk toward him.

"Dammit! Where is that overseer?" Jacob said. He could feel his chest starting to pound. The slave was now only a few yards away.

And that's when Jacob's horse vanished from beneath him.

"What the?"he gasped, turning this way and that. He looked up into the slave's dark, intense eyes, then quickly dropped his gaze to see *his* bull whip dangling from the darkie's big paw. He fell on the ground and tried scrabbling away from the big buck, but couldn't budge an inch—his legs were buried up to his shins in hard dirt.

Then there was an ear-splitting crack. Rawhide whistled past Jacob's face, nearly taking off the end of his nose. He cowered in front of the darkie, trying to yank his legs out of the ground, while keeping a close eye on the whip. But it was no use. No matter how he struggled, he was stuck as firmly as a fence post. Where was his overseer?! He saw that the other slaves had begun moving towards him.

"Get back!" he cried.

The nigga towering above him chuckled to see Jacob's predicament. He crossed his arms across his broad chest, the whip draped over a powerful bicep. He tipped his hat at Jacob.

"How do you do, Mr. Williams?"

Jacob's mouth worked, but words would not come.

"Allow me to introduce myself. My name is Patrick."

Jacob continued to gape at him in silence, though his mind churned with countless questions.

"I have come to take you on a journey," the slave continued.

"What's that?" whispered Jacob. "A journey? Where?"

The slave inspected his whip and then gave him a long look. "I'm sure you'd much rather go with me than feel the bite of this rawhide."

Jacob flinched. But then, from somewhere deep inside him, a surge of anger replaced his fear. "You wouldn't dare!" he growled, hoping he sounded braver than he felt. "You're not going to take me anywhere, nigger!"

The slave frowned. "Very well then. I'm sorry you feel that way, Mr. Williams. I guess you'd rather have a whipping, then?" He raised his arm in preparation to strike.

"No!" Jacob screamed as he tried yet again to pull his legs out of the ground, but they remained rooted in place. "You can't—you have no right," he screamed again.

"Mr. Williams?"

"Get away from me, you beast!!"

"Wake up, Mr. Williams!"

He opened his eyes. A petite young woman wearing small round spectacles was leaning over him. She had a thin black snake draped around her neck.

He gave a little shriek and pulled away from her.

"It's all right, Mr. Williams," she said patting his hand. "I think you may have been having a bad dream. You need to stay still or your intravenous will come out."

His eyes swiveled around wildly as he took in his surroundings.

Large, white room. Other people in beds. A strange yet familiar sound pulsing close to his head.

He turned back to the woman.

"Who are you?" he croaked.

The woman removed her spectacles and smiled, "I'm Doctor Shields."

"Doctor? How...?"

"You're in good hands here, Mr. Williams. You're in a hospital. You had a heart attack, but your condition is improving."

"What's that? My heart was attacked?"

She smiled again. "You were lucky. Not a severe one, but you will have to stay here for a few days."

He was finding it difficult to focus. He closed his eyes.

"A woman doctor?"

She pursed her lips. "Well, Mr. Williams, it is the 21st century, so yes, one or two women doctors are practicing."

He opened his eyes and frowned at her. "What did you say? The 21st century? What do you mean, woman? I don't understand."

Perhaps he's foreign, she wondered. "Well, as in, after the year 2000."

"2000? What is 2000?"

This time when she smiled he noticed the dimples in her cheeks.

"Uh, 2000 and 12," she said and tilted her head to gaze at him steadily.

Despite his confusion, Jacob couldn't help but notice how attractive she was. Then his eyes narrowed.

She is trying to bewitch me!

He forced himself to look away.

"I insist on seeing a real doctor."

The dimples vanished.

"I am a real doctor, Mr. Williams."

She started to say something else, but then crossed her arms and stared at him, apparently lost in thought. Then she nodded her head. "Well, if you insist."

He nodded. "I do insist."

She headed for the door, but stopped short a couple of feet away. She looked over her shoulder at Jacob. "I'll have another doctor come to ask several questions, since we don't know all that much about you. You arrived without identification."

Bristling, he said, "I'll have you know that I am none other than Master Jacob Williams, and I want to be returned to my plantation at once!"

He saw her stifle a chuckle before she pushed through the door.

He scowled.

"Of all the nerve!" he muttered under his breath. "Witch!"

10

January 14, 2012
Wherein Martin discovers he's been an ostrich.

HE WAS LEAVING A RESTAURANT WITH SOME FRIENDS when Martin saw him again. The young guy who'd been begging for money to support himself and his pregnant wife was being herded into a police van, along with several other vagrants. Just before the officers slammed the van door shut, the man lifted his head and stared right at Martin. Martin met his gaze and then gave him a slow nod. He got the uncanny feeling the guy was sending him a message: *Do* something.

When Martin got home he went straight to his desk, Googled homelessness in Memphis, and then immediately got slapped upside the head. He was stunned to read that in 2011, his city was designated the poorest in the entire nation. The economic meltdown of 2008, which led to the worst recession since the 1930s' Great Depression, had done a real number on Memphis. According to Partners for the Homeless, there were at least 1,800 people living on the city's streets or in shelters. And those were the ones they knew about. The agency just couldn't find the rest; they were tucked away in alleys, parks and "cat holes"—the street name for abandoned buildings. Added to the mix: the mentally ill. Once affordable mental health care had been snatched away by the federal government, some had little choice left but to roam the streets.

Martin had some knowledge of the problems facing this fringe of society, but clearly, he'd been keeping his head in the sand, just like the vast majority of Memphians, he figured. It was a hell of a lot easier for those who weren't homeless to assume homelessness wasn't their problem—that people chose to live on the streets. Martin chided himself for unconsciously accepting that way of thinking for so long, especially as he'd been a journalist and was trained to look at both sides of a story. He just hadn't bothered before.

Wondering what efforts were being made to combat homelessness, Martin did a bit more Googling and stumbled upon *Opening Doors*, President Obama's comprehensive strategy to help prevent and end homelessness. When Barack Obama got into the White

House based on his platform of "Change" back in '08, Martin had been ecstatic. Unfortunately, Obama had inherited a mess. Not only did he take his oath of office right as the global recession was bearing down, he'd gotten stuck with a U.S. housing disaster that had caused millions to lose their homes, and he'd been saddled with a nearly $500 billion deficit.

Now Martin understood just why change was so crucial. In spite of Obama's Congress, which was composed of many anti-Obama Republicans and Tea Party members with their right wing agendas, Opening Doors had managed to pass. It was going to ramp up that summer.

The image of the panhandler's face popped into Martin's head again. And then he knew. This was how he could answer the guy's silent plea; he would apply for an *Opening Doors'* grant and establish a day shelter. But Martin's shelter would be different. The few shelters that existed in Memphis did not accept families and only the ones for women allowed children, which meant that families were being broken up. Martin's day shelter would fill that void.

11

August 10, 2012

Wherein Abby requests a second opinion.

HER FINGERS QUICKLY PUNCHED AN EXTENSION on her office phone.

"Roger Eaton."

"Hi Roger! It's Abby. Miss me?"

"Abby. Who wouldn't?" he chuckled, pleased to hear her voice again. "How was your trip?"

"Amazing. And God knows, I needed it."

"Good. I hear ya. Three more weeks and then Vegas, here I come. Can't wait."

"I bet."

"Are you trying to be cute?"

It was her turn to chuckle. "Um. Not really. Listen, Roger, I could really use a shrink."

"You? Thought you just said your vacation was amazing."

"Not for me, wise guy. Patient: middle-aged male, mild-to-moderate heart attack. I have a feeling you'd like to see him."

"Because…?"

"Because he was very disoriented—emphasis on the 'very'. He didn't seem to know what year it was—he didn't seem to get what 2000 was even—and he said some other strange things too."

"What kind of other 'things'?"

"Well, for example, he said women couldn't be doctors."

"Hmm. He may have a point there."

"Ha, ha, very funny," she said. "But seriously, at first the man kind of ticked me off, but then I wondered if maybe his attack had triggered amnesia. Or maybe it's causing hallucinations. I recall studying that phenomenon, but I've never had a patient with this condition. You?"

"Yes! I had a case like that a number of years ago. A woman. Didn't recognize her husband or kids. Even called herself by a different name. Thought she was from France." Roger grinned at the memory. "And I remember she even spoke with a French accent. It was quite amazing."

"Interesting. So, you might be the perfect person to check this guy out for me. He came in without I.D. And, oh, I almost forgot. The man says he owns a plantation."

"Well, that's plausible."

"Maybe. But, listen Roger, you know that old cotton plantation just out of town?"

"Yeah. Creepy place. Isn't it being fixed up?"

"Yeah. It's a historic site now. Apparently, it just opened. And that's where the ambulance picked this guy up. Staff said he was working there as a re-enactor. A class of students had just come into the Great Hall of the house when there was a commotion on the landing. Apparently, the patient was standing up there screaming like a mad man and then he charged down the stairs swinging a fireplace poker around. That's when he collapsed."

Roger gave a low whistle. "Is that right? I have to admit, I'm intrigued. Well, you're in luck, doctor. It seems my next patient had a bit of a meltdown and needed tranquilizing. So, your timing is quite excellent."

"Great! Room 350D. I'll see you there in five?"

"Sure thing."

"You're the best. Thanks!"

"My pleasure."

After hanging up, Roger ran his fingers through his mop of curly hair and thought back to his "French" patient and how rare a case it was. His curiosity about the so-called "plantation owner" was definitely piqued. He took a couple of more bites of the tuna sandwich he'd been eating when Abby called, grabbed his lab coat, and headed down the corridor.

12

May 1837

Wherein Sadie runs—again.

AFTER THE CANDLES AND LANTERNS WERE SNUFFED OUT in the Big House and all was quiet in the slave quarters, Sadie's fingers closed around the small bundle tucked under her head. Without jostling her little sister who snored gently beside her, she eased out of her cot and slipped through the door of the cabin. She stopped for a moment to listen, praying that she hadn't woken anybody up. If asked what she was about, she would say she needed to use the necessary.

When she didn't hear anybody call her name, she started moving, tilting her head up to scan the sky. It was a cool, clear, blue-black night. So many pinpoints of light crowded together it took a few moments before she found it: the North Star. Ole Tom had told her to follow it—said it would lead the way. Along with all the other stars—there weren't no moon that night—it was the only light she would have.

She began to creep toward the woods.

"No!"

Sadie froze, then crouched down onto all fours to peer into the velvety, thick darkness. She couldn't see a thing.

"Have mercy. Please, have mercy!"

Sadie released the air she didn't even know she was holding in her chest.

It was Suzanne.

Poor thing's cryin' out in her sleep again.

She blew a little kiss towards the slave cabins. "Goodbye, girl", she mouthed. "Hope I got better luck than you."

Then she felt a quick pang of shame. She sent a quick silent prayer to Suzanne: I hope you try running again one day, girl, and make it!

Sadie took off toward the woods. Staying low, she sped past the rest of the cabins. Her first goal was to reach the cover of the trees. She couldn't let the memory of Suzanne's screams the night the men caught her and whipped her outside the cabins worry her none. Sadie had scars on her own back to prove you didn't have to try runnin' away to get beaten bloody. The lash had gotten her when she hadn't picked enough cotton and another time when she was too slow gettin' to the field.

Right now the only thing she should think of was getting as far away from the plantation as she could before it grew light. She wouldn't let herself think about Mama, Papa, her sisters or brothers either. Didn't want to think about what they would feel or think the next morning when the horn blew and they saw just her sister in her cot. There had been no chance to say goodbye. She hadn't dared say a peep to even her Ma about her plan. They would have all told her she was crazy—that she wasn't strong enough to survive—that she would get lost and eaten up by wolves.

But, she knew in her heart she could do it. She had to. And right now she was almost at the trees.

Ole Tom told her there were folks above the Ohio River who would help anyone who made it to its banks. He explained how the river was the line between the slave States and the free States.

No use frettin' over how far that might be.

She was sure scared, but if she didn't run, matters would be a whole lot worse. When Massa's daughter told Missus what her poppa was doing to Sadie in the parlor, Missus would sure enough see to it that she got punished something terrible.

It wasn't until the sky began to blush pink before Sadie's steps slowed. Geese honked high above the trees. She turned her face up and was gladdened to see them form an arrow as they flew north after the winter. They would show her the way, too. She allowed herself a tiny smile. Then she heard dogs howling in the distance. Her smile vanished as the hairs on her arms and the back of her neck lifted up.

"Sweet Jesus! They know I'm missin' already?" she whispered.

Her tired eyes tried to pierce the shadowy woods. She wondered if it was an early hunter? She shuddered. No matter. Anyone spotting a Negro girl out on her own would know she was a runaway.

A glint of something in the distance caught her eye. She stared at it hard.

Water. Like in my dream. I just knows it.

Dashing through the trees, she found a narrow stream. Plunging in she splashed along for a ways to cover up her scent. Once or twice she nearly fell into the deeper part near the middle, but caught herself in time. She kept going until finally she figured it safe enough to get out. Sloshing back out onto the forest floor on the other side of the stream, she knelt down to gulp down some of the cold water, and then ran off a good ways until she found a place to hide herself during the light of day.

She kept pushing north night after night. After her rations petered out, she ate whatever she could scrounge up—berries, leaves, sometimes a bit of cooked meat if she came across a cabin and dared herself to steal it. Some days she went to sleep with nothin' in her belly to keep it from growlin' like a bear and she worried someone or something might hear it! And then there were those nights on the move when she was so weak from hunger she thought she was going in the wrong direction. She would panic until she could prove to herself that she was heading north.

Every dog that barked in the distance and each twig that cracked because of some varmint in the woods spooked her bad. Sometimes she didn't know how she kept herself going. It was keep moving, or die. And she didn't want to die. She wanted to be free. She wanted to live where no one forced her to do their biddin', where she could learn anything her heart desired, where no one could lash her, and where she didn't have to worry about Massa pushin' his cock inside her.

At long last, a great river lay before her.

"Please Lord, oh, good dear sweet Lord," she prayed, her lips moving to murmur the words just loud enough that maybe He would hear her this time, "Please, let this be Ohio at last! Please! Please, Lord."

The river was too big to swim and she was too tired and too weak to keep on going. She buried herself in some leaves on the bank, said one more prayer, and then everything went dark.

She wasn't certain how long she slept, but when she began to slowly crawl out of her nest, the sun had just about set. Blinking her eyes, she took a good look around.

A big, black man was standing twenty paces away. And he was staring right at her.

She screamed.

"Shhhh," he said, putting a finger against his lips. He walked toward her slow and reached out his hand. "It's all right now, chile. Y'all come with me."

13

August 10, 2012

Wherein Jacob receives a quick psychoanalysis.

After the witch left the room, Jacob closed his eyes. He was in pain, but had chosen not to let her know. If he were to leave this wretched, alien place and return to his plantation as soon as possible, he would pretend he was well.

Despite his bravado, it was difficult to move without wincing. The strange pulsing sound assaulting his ears didn't help matters, nor did the disembodied voices requesting a nurse or a doctor to report to such and such a room. It was all making him feel quite woozy.

Taking care not to be observed, he studied the three people lying in the other beds in his room. He grimaced; it appeared at least one was a darkie. Fortunately, they all appeared to be asleep.

The nightmare that woman had woken him from was still fresh in his mind. He thought about the mysterious slave in the cotton field. Why was he dressed that way? Then he gave a small gasp. It wasn't a slave. It was that big nigger he'd seen in his Great Hall!

He heard a whooshing sound. In walked the witch with a tall white man at her side. He didn't have a snake around his neck like she did.

This must be the doctor at last, thought Jacob.

The pair approached his bed. The man was smiling. The witch was not.

"How do you do, Mr. Williams? My name is Dr. Eaton," said the man.

"I am happy to see you Doctor Eaton," Jacob said. He frowned at the witch who gazed at him with her dark, penetrating eyes. He quickly averted his face to look back at the doctor.

"Can you please see to it that I am released as soon as possible? I feel quite well, doctor."

"Mr. Williams, you've had a heart attack. I think it would be wise if you remained here a bit longer," Dr. Eaton said. "Now, I'd like to ask you a few questions, if you don't mind."

"What is it you wish to know?" Jacob sighed and fell back against his pillow.

"My colleague here tells me you own a plantation. Can you tell me a little about that?"

"I suppose," he said, shooting the witch a suspicious look. "My plantation is the largest in the county."

"Is that so?" the doctor responded with interest. "What's your crop?"

"Well, cotton is my big money maker," his brow furrowed as he remembered how the rain had delayed planting, and at the memory of the monstrous spider eating what was left of his cotton, "but I also grow corn and some lesser crops as well."

"I see. And who works for you on the plantation?"

"I have an overseer, five drivers, the house staff and the field hands of course."

"How many altogether then?"

"At the moment, I have 272 head, although I may have to sell one or two if the cotton yield is down to make up for the loss."

The doctor looked taken aback. He exchanged glances with his colleague and then said in measured tones, "Excuse me, but did you say, 'Head' and 'sell'?"

Jacob opened his mouth to speak, and then abruptly closed it. He wasn't quite sure he liked these questions.

The doctor looked at him closely and continued. "Can you please tell me exactly what you mean by those words, Jacob?"

The door whooshed open again. Jacob saw a short stocky Negress clad in pink trousers and a baggy pink blouse step in to the room. Jacob ignored the doctor and watched with suspicion as she did something to the patients opposite him. Then she turned and approached him. He wasn't fooled by the smile on her face.

"What do you want?" Jacob demanded.

"Hello, Mr. Williams. It's time for your pain medication," she said.

He shrieked, "Oh, no you don't! You're fixing to poison me!" and knocked the pills out of her hand. "

14

February 1838

Wherein Sadie sees how she will always be tied to the Master.

"PUSH GIRL, PUSH!"

"I can't... I can't... it hurts! I want my Mama! I want my Mamaaaaa!"

"I know... I know it hurts, girl ... y'all be all right ... soon, soon now ... Unh huh, I see it. I see the head! Baby's coming! Give me a big push now, ya hear?"

Sadie pushed as hard as she could, screaming even louder than when she was getting a lashing. She just couldn't seem to help herself.

"I'm sorry! I'm sorry... don't mean to yell," she panted when the pain eased up a bit.

"I know, I know it, girl," assured Ole Maggie. "All right, easy now... no more pushing for a little bit. Just rest up now. You're almost there—"

A cool wet cloth was placed on Sadie's forehead and a soft voice whispered, "Look at me, Sadie. Look at me. You're in good hands, sweet girl."

Turning her head she stared into the kind blue eyes of the old white lady who had taken her in. Sadie managed a weak smile.

"Ok, that's better now, dear. You're a strong girl, Sadie. Have faith. It will be all over before you know it."

Sadie nodded. This white lady wouldn't lie to her. She was a good woman. She'd allowed her into her home and nursed her back to health. The man named Joe brought Sadie there after he found her in the leaves that day she woke up by the river. She was hungry and so scared, but Joe found her like he knew she'd be there. He'd gently taken her hand and helped her to her feet, then picked her up like she was a little child when he saw she was too weak to walk even one step.

Sadie hadn't spoken to a soul in so long and was so weak she hardly had any voice, but she'd whispered to him, "Oh, I was so scared. Now I'm found. Thank you, mister."

He'd smiled and said, "Yes, you've been found, girl. Now hush, chile. You save your breath. We're gonna take good care of you."

Then he took her to the house where this white lady lived. It was as if he had taken her to an angel. A few mornings later, when Sadie had felt a little stronger and could sit up, the lady came into her room holding a small tray. On it was a spoon, a white cloth napkin, a glass of water and a steamin' bowl of what looked like mush. The old lady had cocked her head and studied Sadie. "Ah, I see you're feeling better."

Sadie had nodded and then answered in a low, shy voice. "Yes, I am, missus. Thank you, missus."

"Very good. Now, please, call me Margaret, dear," the lady said.

Sadie had given her a nod.

The lady placed the tray on the side table and then sat down next to her. "All right then. I've got some of my special gruel here. It will make you feel stronger. Shall I feed you?"

"Oh, no, no. You don't have to do that, missus."

"I do. And it's Margaret, dear."

"Yes, Missus Margaret."

Then the old woman laughed. "Oh, dear sweet girl. You are precious."

Sadie blinked. No one had ever called her 'precious' before.

Then Missus Margaret had looked at her real close. "All right then, I'm sure you have many, many questions. I will try to explain a few things while you eat."

And then she'd told Sadie how Joe had once been a slave too and how he'd started helping her find runaways before the white wolves could catch them. She'd explained how they found many lost souls, and had nursed pretty near all of them back to health, then helped them get set up in her little community. Missus Margaret called it *Harmony*.

Another pain began building inside Sadie's body, wrenching her back to the present. But this time her cry was not so gut twisting. After the pain subsided, she took a quick look down and saw the top of the ole midwife's nappy head between her two skinny nut-brown legs. Sadie watched, catching her breath, as Ole Maggie took some clean white rags from the table beside her. The cloths glowed in the black, black skin of her hands. The midwife lifted her head a bit and Sadie saw her eyes grow round. Then a big smile lit up her face.

"Almost there, girl!"

And then, another long moaning scream escaped Sadie's lips.

Ole Maggie said, "You can do it, chile. That's the way..."

And a few moments later, Sadie heard, "You did it girl. Unh huh. You sure did. I caught him!"

"Oh, Sadie! You are so brave," cried Missus Margaret.

But all Sadie could think, as she lay on the bed gasping for air, was that she didn't care one little bit about what she'd just done. All she cared about was that she'd gotten it over with.

"Oh my, my, my. You got yourself a nice baby boy," cooed Ole Maggie. She cut the cord, cleared out his nostrils, and then gave him a couple of quick pats.

A son! Oh Lord. I have a son, thought Sadie.

And then she heard him. She heard his cry. It was loud and clear.

"Oh, he's a little bitty one, but he'll grow big and strong," assured the midwife "Come on now, girl, take a look."

But Sadie didn't want to see. She only wanted to sleep. She just wanted to sleep and sleep and sleep. She didn't want to see what Massa had done to her. No. She didn't ever want to see.

Ole Maggie laid the baby on her breast.

Sadie didn't want to look. She didn't want to touch. She didn't want to know.

She felt his soft breath on her neck. She closed her eyes.

Sweet Jesus.

15

February 2, 2012

Wherein Martin is hopeful he has found his place.

FOUR STORIES BELOW THE STREET quivered with activity. It was a beautiful day after several days of cold, wet rain. All kinds of people were making the most of it. They lingered in front of shop windows, popped in and out of buildings, flagged down bright yellow taxis, or sauntered along the sidewalk clutching a takeout coffee in one hand and someone's arm in the other. Down at the corner, a Guatemalan food stall was doing brisk business, with a straggly line of hungry people waiting to buy spicy plantain tamales. After days of gloomy, cold weather, Martin imagined no one minded standing that long in the sunshine.

It seemed everyone had a purpose, somewhere to go, something to do. Martin studied the scene with such intent that his eyes began to burn. He blinked a few times and then checked the clock. In about 45 minutes he might know whether he would once again join their ranks. It had been more than three months since he'd told Jake to take his job and shove it.

After making that huge first step toward changing his life's purpose, his days had taken on a rather aimless quality. Thinking back he could see it was as if he was going through a kind of detox. Every day he vowed to be more purposeful, but his good intentions would vanish if someone called with tickets to a game, or wanted to get a pizza and a couple of pints. He did a lot of sleeping in too, which made it even harder to get anything done.

Although his mom had told him to take his time, he could tell she was starting to wonder when he would end his "vacation". She knew he was spending a little bit too much time having fun instead of buckling down. Given the pace he'd been keeping over the last six years, it wasn't all that surprising. He assured her that he would begin making plans in earnest.

And that day had arrived about a month ago when he'd engaged in that Googling marathon on homelessness. Today he was meeting a real estate agent to check out possible locations for his drop-in shelter for the homeless and down and out. He'd spent four weeks organizing funding and he was surprised at how good he was at that. Guess all those years pitching story ideas had honed his powers of persuasion. He'd managed to talk a couple of his dad's old business buddies into backing him, and he'd applied for the *Doors Opening* grant as well as a couple of others he'd heard about. He'd also made arrangements to tap into some of his inheritance money if he needed it.

The first location on the agent's list was a shuttered restaurant a few blocks away from his condo. Not the best part of Beale Street, but Martin couldn't afford anything too splashy. And besides, he realized it would be better to locate in a less popular area of the street. After all, he didn't want his clients 'bothering' anyone and he wanted to ensure the location made his clients feel comfortable.

Martin finished getting ready, then headed out twenty minutes early so he would have a chance to see the place before his agent arrived.

In his excitement, he walked right by it. He laughed to himself as he backtracked half a block. He couldn't believe he hadn't noticed the big, overhead sign. From the outside at least, the building certainly looked promising. It was large and didn't seem to have too much wear and tear. He tried to peek through a hole in the paper covering the windows, but couldn't see much beyond a jumble of tables and chairs.

He stepped back just as a petite young woman with Asian features walked up.

"You must be Martin," she said.

"I am," he replied. "Celeste?" He was a bit taken aback by how young she looked. And she was so tiny. She only came up to his chest. He gave her a quick smile, hoping he hadn't seemed rude.

She smiled back and extended her hand. "Yes, it's me, in the flesh. It's really great to meet you."

From her voice on the phone he'd guessed she was probably a newbie, but to see her in person, he thought she looked like she was barely out of high school. He hoped she knew her stuff.

"Yes, good to meet you, too." He shook her hand and was surprised by her firm grip. She looked him right in the eye, too.

Well, maybe she does know what she's doing, he guessed hopefully.

She unlocked the door and motioned for him to go ahead. "Please. After you."

He smiled again and stepped over the threshold.

Celeste watched Martin enter, took a deep breath, mouthed the word, 'Wow!' and followed him inside.

16

August 11, 2012

Wherein Jacob receives another rude awakening.

He could not tear his eyes away from the confounding box up on the wall opposite his bed. The people inside of it were like enchanted miniatures! Who or what was making the music? Where were the voices coming from? And, what in God's name were those horseless objects racing down the sides of mountains like they had invisible wings?

Jacob could only assume he was witnessing evidence of the supernatural. His eyes narrowed.

The witch. This must be her sorcery!

Attempting to sit up a little more he discovered his arms were tied to the bed railing.

"What the devil?" he muttered and yanked fruitlessly at the straps. "They've tied me up like some kind of criminal!"

A burst of music drew his attention back to the box. Female acrobats—nearly naked ones at that—were running at top speed, twisting and turning again and again, before landing gracefully on their feet. Jacob had seen slaves turning cartwheels and flipping head over heels, but never like this!

A sign flashed across the front of the box underneath a young Negress, beaming from ear to ear: 'Gold medalist'.

"What?" He croaked. "Her?"

And then he beheld several beautiful young mulatto women sitting on a couch.

My God. Those temptresses are looking straight at me!

He leaned forward as far as he could against his restraints to get a better look at them.

Now, why do they have peaches in their hands?

A sign appeared above their heads: The Real Housewives of Atlanta.

"Mr. Williams?"

The women vanished and were replaced by a crowd of scruffy looking white men laughing and holding up glasses of ale.

"Mr. Williams? How are you feeling today?"

Jacob slowly pulled his eyes away from the box to see the doctor standing beside him. The doctor nodded and gave him a small smile.

"I'm not sure if you remember that we had to give you a tranquilizer yesterday. You became quite, ah, upset while my colleague and I were talking with you."

Jacob stared at him blankly, then something stirred in the back of his mind; he did recall a bit of commotion. That fat female darkie—the one who was about to poison him. Most likely the witch's accomplice.

He shrugged. "I do."

"We had to move you, Mr. Williams, as we couldn't have you disturbing the other patients."

Jacob's eyes slid around the room for the first time. He was alone, away from prying eyes. His mouth twisted into a half smile, and then, remembering his restraints, said angrily, "Did she do this?"

"She?"

Jacob frowned. "That woman."

"Mr. Williams, I assure you, it was for your own good."

"My own good!?" Jacob sputtered. The sound of trumpets drew his attention to the box again.

"What in God's name is that?" He said, pointing.

"That? The Olympics? Didn't you know they were on?"

"Olympics? The name of that box is Olympics?"

"Box?" said the doctor in surprise? "That's just the TV. Is it disturbing you? I can turn it off."

"Yes, it most certainly is. I am certain that witch, er, I mean, that female acquaintance of yours must have something to do with this handiwork of the devil."

The doctor pressed a button that made the box go dark and silent and then gave Jacob an odd look. "'Handiwork of the devil'? Well, I've heard TV called many things, but that's a first."

"Don't mock me, young man."

The doctor pressed his lips together and crossed his arms. "I assure you I am not mocking you, Mr. Williams. Now I need to ask you another question."

Jacob sighed. "If you must."

"What year is it, Mr. Williams?"

Jacob's eyes lifted again to the box and then he frowned. "Well, it's 1837, of course."

The doctor raised his eyebrows. "Is that so?"

Jacob picked nervously at his restraints. "Although everything appears so strange, so very different. And yes, even at my plantation—it was... well, it was so very odd. Strange looking people had invaded my home and were behaving as if it was their property." He gave a slight shudder at the memory.

The doctor was quiet for a moment. "I recall you said you were a plantation owner. And you have slaves."

"That is correct. And, so?"

"So, it's the year 2012, Mr. Williams. All the slaves were emancipated in 1865."

Jacob's mouth dropped open and then snapped shut. His eyes narrowed as he looked at the box again and then back at the doctor.

"That's simply not possible," he said.

The doctor gave him a quizzical look. "What do you mean?"

"I know you are lying!" Jacob sputtered. "On both counts. Without slavery the economy would collapse!"

The doctor gave a quick laugh. "Really, Mr. Williams?"

"Yes, indeed, doctor. And not only that, slavery is how barbaric countries become civilized."

The doctor gave a quick laugh. "It is? How very interesting, Mr. Williams."

Jacob frowned. "I warned you before. Do not mock me!"

"Mr. Williams, I can assure you Emancipation did happen and it is most definitely the year 2012. You can Google it, if you don't believe me."

"Google? What is Google? Oh, blast it. I simply—"

His eyes shifted to the box for a moment then swiveled back to the doctor. "Someone is playing an evil trick on me and whoever it is will be sorry they thought they could toy with Jacob Williams. Now, I want to go back to my plantation. I wish to be released at once."

The doctor shook his head. "Sorry, I can't authorize that. Dr. Shields has ordered that you remain here at least until tomorrow. However, if that's what you insist, then I can't stop you. Do you have anyone who can come pick you up?"

"Pick me up? How do you mean, Doctor?"

"Well, come to the hospital and get you."

Jacob looked down. After a few moments of silence, he uttered, "No. It seems... well it seems I have no one."

The doctor stared at him for a few moments and then patted his arm. The man was an intriguing mystery, he had to admit. He wished he could convince him to stay put, but the man seemed determined.

"I see," he said at last. "Well, then. Before you leave, wait for me to come back with some information that might help you on your way. I wish you the best of luck. And I hope things begin to make more sense for you very, very soon, Mr. Williams."

17

August 11, 2012
Wherein Patrick has a revelation,
which he is quite reluctant to accept.

HE STROKED THE BUSINESS END of a rawhide whip as a white man trembled in front of him. When he raised his arm to strike, the man screamed and tried to flee, but his legs were buried up to his shins in the ground. "Please! Don't hurt me! Please! Please!" the man shrieked. "I'll go with you, Patrick. Put the whip down! Please! Take me wherever it is you wish to go."

A bell tinkled in the distance. Patrick hesitated and looked behind him.

The man whispered, "Hurry!"

The bell grew louder.

Patrick's eyes opened.

Alarm clock.

His fingers groped for the button and gave it a smack.

Wow, he thought. That was one hell of a dream.

He rubbed his eyes and yawned.

Now, who the heck was I going to whip? Oh, I know... it was that guy from the plantation! But, why the hell would I want to do that?

Straining to remember the dream before it disappeared, he recalled his intent to take the man somewhere. But where would he take him? And why?

The alarm rang again. He gave the snooze button another punch so he could snatch a few more minutes to process his dream before getting ready for work. His thoughts returned to the day of the field trip. That guy—the re-enactor playing Mr. Williams—had charged down the stairs waving a fireplace poker around like he wanted to take someone's head off. Why? And what if he hadn't collapsed? One of the kids could have been hurt! Christ, I don't even want to go there. Now think. Staff said the guy was a re-enactor, but it seemed to me like he was overacting. Ha. Make that "over re-enacting". Huh, no doubt the real Jacob Williams would have had a heart attack too if he saw 30 uninvited black kids in his front hall.

He sat up.

"Holy shit."

Then he laughed. You think a plantation owner decided to come pay us a little visit all the way from the 1800s? Get a grip, man.

He stared at the abstract painting on the wall over the dresser. His wife's choice. Never really liked it, but he put up with it to keep the peace. But he had to admit, all those shapes and colors were somehow kind of relaxing to look at.

His eyes widened.

The bed in the plantation. It had been messed up like someone had slept in it. And, the guy had been wearing a night robe.

"No. No. No. That's just not possible," he muttered dragging his hands through his short fro. "There's no way."

He checked the clock. If he didn't get a move on he was going to be late. He glanced at the empty pillow next to him. If Janice were here she'd be asking a million questions about what was bothering him, which he just didn't have the answers for.

As always he marveled at her discipline. Up at 5:45 almost every day to hit the gym, and then off to work for 7:30. He'd never been a morning person. Just trying to get to school by 8:15 was tough some days.

He climbed out of bed and headed over to the washroom.

If I get a chance at lunch, I'll call the plantation to see whether they've heard if the guy's ok and find out what else they know about him.

As he waited for the water to heat up in the shower, he thought again of the scowl on the man's face while he'd been resuscitating him.

Paramedics said I saved his life. Told them I was happy to help.

So why did it seem like he hated my guts?

18

August 12, 2012

Wherein Jacob is mortified to acknowledge that the road back to his past is fully dependent on the charity of the present.

I, Jacob Williams, the richest man in this entire region, cannot pay my hospital bill. With nary a friend, family member nor servant living in what they claim to be the Year of Our Lord Two Thousand and Twelve to come to my aid, I have no choice but to rely on the hospital's charity care to pay my debt.

I've been cooped up here only a few days, but it feels so much longer. Time is certainly not on my side. My efforts to convince the doctor that I am the rightful owner of the Williams Plantation failed. His notion that something altered my brain during my heart attack is nonsense. I know exactly who I am. But, how I got here remains a mystery to me.

The doctor would have liked me trapped inside these walls longer, but today I leave. I signed my name on a paper that says I am of sound mind and that I have released myself against doctor's orders.

I had been brought here in my nightclothes, but now a stranger's hideous clothing is on my back. The garments are far too loose, but again, I must rely on charity. How shameful that I, master of the largest plantation in the county, am reduced to wearing hand-me-down clothes.

All of my possessions fit inside one small paper bag: my nightclothes, a water vessel made from a sort of flexible glass, and an egg sandwich ensconced in filmy see-through material. In one of my trouser's pockets are directions to a 'shelter'. The doctor had returned to my room to give it to me, along with a note instructing to go there if I needed assistance. In my other pocket is an envelope containing a twenty-dollar paper bill. A veritable fortune! Kindly given to me by the same doctor. My eyes widened when I saw the portrait of Andrew Jackson—my President– gracing one side of the bill. I wanted to return it to the doctor, as it shamed me to have to accept his charity. But then, I swallowed my pride. How was I to manage without money? I folded the bill and hid it on my person.

I have no intention of looking for the shelter. If I am to return to the year 1837, which is where I belong—where whites are the masters and Nigras are still in their power then I must go back to my plantation. I am certain the key to how I arrived here in the future—and how I will find my way back—is there.

Now, after negotiating endless bewildering corridors, I have located the hospital's entrance lobby, but I find myself hesitant to go further. My senses are assaulted: squealing children, people jabbering in unfamiliar languages, black faces everywhere I look.

A glass door, opening and closing through yet another form of sorcery, is all that stands between the outside world and me. I pause a few feet away, transfixed by the strange and chaotic scene on the other side. I see oddly dressed people of every shape and shade imaginable: white, black, brown, yellow. How scantily dressed the women are! All those bare legs and midriffs. And there are some wearing trousers that end well above their knees.

Many people balance dark spectacles on their noses, others wear ridiculous hats—they look like overgrown, waddling ducks. Some men shuffle along with hands in their pockets as they stare at the ground. Others carry small cases and stride past or into the hospital with more purpose. I am at a loss to understand why so many people are pressing small objects against their ears? Some appear to be talking, but to whom? They are alone. Others cradle little boxes in their hands and poke at them with fingers or thumbs as if they have nervous tics. And what are those long white strands sprouting from their ears?

One or two women push small contraptions with wheels, which I surmise are prams; I see a child in one. There are leashed dogs pulling their masters along. What could they be tracking?

Beyond them all, many rolling contraptions like those I saw on that box—more than I can count. They race by at unbelievable speeds. There are much larger ones as well, with garish lettering painted on their sides.

For the life of me I can't imagine what has happened to the horses and wagons. Did a terrible plague kill off all the horses?

So many questions, but, if I am able to return to my plantation and find my way back in time, I will have no real need of the answers.

I lift my chin and straighten my shoulders. There is no other choice it seems. I must be strong.

I walk through the door.

19

August 12, 2012

Wherein Patrick calls the Williams' Plantation, and then starts a list.

AFTER THE LAST STUDENT DRIFTED OUT OF HIS CLASSROOM, Patrick pulled out his cell phone and punched in the number he'd looked up earlier.

"Williams' Historic Plantation, how may I help you?"

"Hi, Patrick Monroe here. I brought my class by on opening day and I was just wondering—"

"Oh, Patrick! Hello! So nice to hear from you! This is Louise. I met you in the Great Hall. Thanks again for all your help. I don't know what we would have done without you! We've been meaning to call, but things have just been so hectic."

"Uh, thanks. I can just imagine," Patrick answered thinking, now there's an understatement. "I've been wondering how the re-enactor is doing?"

"Well, as far as we know, he's ok, but it seems there was a bit of a mix up. In fact, it's all kind of strange."

"Really? How so?"

"Well, evidently, he wasn't the re-enactor after all."

Patrick's heart skipped a beat. "He wasn't? So, who was he?"

"Well, we don't really know. He didn't have any ID. We were thinking of charging him with trespassing and attempted assault, but given the fact he suffered a heart attack, well, we didn't feel right about that. And we didn't want the bad publicity, if you know what I mean."

"I understand." replied Patrick. "So, no ID. Is he still in the hospital?"

"I'm pretty sure he was released, but I have no idea where he'd be going. The real re-enactor," she laughed, "now that sounds a little bizarre, doesn't it? – turned up after your class left. Said he was having one of those days – car trouble, phone battery died – that sort of thing."

Jingling the coins in his pocket Patrick thought for a moment. "So, I'm assuming the re-enactor looks like the guy who had the heart attack."

"Yes, he certainly does. That's why we were confused."

"And does the re-enactor look like the plantation owner?"

"Yes. That's why he got the part. Didn't you see Mr. Williams' portrait when you were here? In the parlor?"

"No, I didn't get a chance. I seem to recall one of the parents may have taken the students in there while I was outside talking to a paramedic. Wish I'd seen it."

"If you like, I can email you a photo of it."

"I wouldn't want to trouble you."

"No trouble at all. I have a jpeg of it that we're using for our promotional literature and website. We were so busy getting the house and property ready for opening day, the marketing materials were put on the back burner for a bit."

"Thanks, I'd appreciate that," Patrick said and took a quick look at the wall clock. "Louise, I won't keep you much longer. I just need to know a couple of more things."

"Don't worry, I'm about to go on my break. Fire away."

"Just curious if you happened to notice anything kind of odd about the guy?"

"Odd?" she chuckled. "Other than the fact that he tried to attack us, not really. Did you?"

"Yes, I believe I did."

She was silent for a moment. "How so?"

"For one thing, he was wearing a night robe."

"Really? Wait a sec, come to think of it, you're right! We figured he must have somehow gotten into the house the day before and decided to crash in one of the rooms. It just so happened that he picked Jacob's. Maybe he found the robe in the bedroom closet. Our goal is to make the plantation as authentic as possible, right down to the clothing in the wardrobes."

"So, no security alarm?"

"It wasn't completely up and running until the next day," she replied sheepishly.

Patrick glanced at the time. "Just one more thing and I'll let you go. Did you notice how it seemed like he was kind of hard to see at first? And hard to hear?"

"Hard to see?" She paused for a moment. "Well, I had my back to him so I didn't notice him until we heard him yelling from the landing. In fact, my colleagues and I were facing the opposite way—

toward you and the students—so he caught us completely off guard. And as for hearing him, well, I couldn't really understand what he was yelling at first, since I was pretty focused on you and your class. Still gives me the willies to think about it."

"Sorry, I didn't mean to bring up bad memories."

Patrick glanced at the clock again. He had to pick up Janice in 25 minutes so she could get her car from the mechanic's.

"Thanks so much for all the information, Louise. I look forward to receiving that photo when you get a chance. And I hope everything goes smoothly for you and the staff from now on."

Patrick pressed end on his iPhone, popped open his MacBook and found the Word program. Starting a new file he quickly typed:

An Unusual Incident at The Williams' Plantation

What I Know So Far:

1. *The man was NOT the re-enactor.*
2. *No ID. No one sure who he is.*
3. *Possibly in the house overnight or early in the morning.*
4. *Wearing a night robe.*
5. *Yelling at us to get out.*
6. *About to attack us with a brass fireplace poker.*
7. *Looks like Jacob Williams—owner of the plantation.*
8. *Had a heart attack.*
9. *I revived him.*
10. *Seemed to hate my guts.*

20

May 1837

Wherein a woman realizes she might be better off without her husband.

SHEILA LOOKED THE OVERSEER UP AND DOWN as she tapped her open palm with a lace fan. She abhorred having to deal with the man. She knew only too well he provided Jacob with his house girls.

"No, I haven't seen the Master at all today," she said and turned away from his gaze. How dare he look at her in that manner! "I haven't laid eyes on him since last evening," she added through clenched teeth.

The overseer gave a little grunt and looked over his shoulder at the drive, as if willing Jacob to appear. "Well, if Master Williams turns up, remind him we have a meeting. Had a meeting," he corrected.

He tipped his hat, smirked, and then clumped down the front steps.

She closed the massive door, leaned her back against it and vigorously fanned herself. How she hated that man!

Her lips pressed together in a tight straight line. She could just discern the edge of Jacob's portrait in the parlor. He'd disappeared before, but this time seemed different. Usually somebody knew where he'd gone.

Where are you Jacob? How could you do this to me?

Governor and Mrs. Jackson were scheduled to arrive for dinner the following day. She had been planning the event for months.

Sometimes it was hard to imagine she had ever loved her husband. Back when they first met, before his father died, he was different. He seemed to really love her too. Or, so she thought. And then Old Master Williams passed and Jacob took on the job of running the plantation. She had been excited and thrilled to be the wife of a man who was in charge of the largest plantation in the region. Certainly, the task wasn't an easy one for Jacob as there were so many decisions to make and keeping the slaves in check could be a challenge at times, but he had been groomed for the role. Though he seemed a little reluctant to take over the reins, it wasn't long before she began to suspect that the power had gone to his head. And then, his interest in the slave women, which she'd noticed even before his father died, became more blatant with each passing year.

She scowled as her thoughts switched to his latest harlot who had run away a couple of days ago. She'd been absolutely furious when she'd found out about her. Last night, she had a row with Jacob about the wench after dinner. How dare he continue to satisfy his disgusting urges that way! He had promised her that after that bitch Suzanne there would be no more.

Oh, I'm going to kill that man!

She heard faint crying upstairs. Baby Chloe was awake. In just moments, the crying escalated into pitiful wails.

Where in heaven's name is that nurse? Lord, has everyone gone missing in this house?

"Carolyn!" she called. "Carolyn! Baby Chloe needs you!"

She snapped her fan shut and crossed the hall to the staircase. Pausing on the first step, she stopped short. A dastardly thought had occurred to her—something downright wicked, but she had to admit, pleasing to think about.

Who even needs this beast of a husband? I am certain my life would be far better off without him.

A smile softened the lines that had begun appearing on her face, despite her best efforts to ward off the hands of time with various expensive ointments she ordered from Memphis. Ignoring Chloe's cries, she considered the delicious prospect of running the plantation under her rules. She knew she was more than capable. First order of business: she would fire the overseer.

"Well, then," she said under her breath as she began mounting the stairs. "I hope you never come back, Jacob Williams."

21

August 13, 2012

Wherein two doctors set up a meeting to discuss their mysterious patient.

ROGER POKED HIS HEAD INTO DR. SHIELD'S OFFICE.

"Got a minute, Abby?"

Without looking up she replied, "Ah, sure Roger. Just need to finish this email and I've got rounds soon, but yeah, I have a few minutes for you. Grab a seat."

Roger eased his lanky frame into one of the chairs in front of her desk. As her fingers flew over the keys he eyeballed her tidy office.

Don't know how she does it, he thought. My office is a mess. Piles of paper everywhere, books and research documents piled up all over the place. Everything's neat and tidy in here. There's cool art to look at, a snazzy mirror and a vase of flowers on a shelf that looks like it's floating in mid-air. And I like that mint color she's painted the walls. Geez, what does she think of my office?

With a final tap on the keyboard and a last click of her mouse, Abby had a swallow of her tea and then gave Roger a smile.

"So Roger, what can I do for you?

Roger blinked. She sure had a great smile. Those dimples. God.

"Uh, our 'plantation owner'. Can't stop thinking about him."

"Ah, yes. My favorite patient," she sniffed. "Wasn't too sorry to see the last of him, that's for sure. I hope he doesn't have a relapse."

"He certainly was a handful, wasn't he?" Roger chuckled.

"Handful?! He was a righteous pain in the ass, and then some. And there was something about his eyes that kind of gave me the creeps."

Roger drummed the armrests of his chair with his fingers. "But, wasn't he fascinating?"

She shrugged.

"Well, you have to admit there was something about him that was out of sync. Maybe it was a form of amnesia, but I can't help but wonder if it was something else."

"Something else, what?"she asked lacing her fingers together and resting her chin on them. She gave him a long look.

"I have my suspicions." He peered at her closely. "You won't think

I'm crazy if I share them?"

She dropped her hands to her desk and chuckled. "Excuse me, Roger, but you're a shrink. It's a given."

"Very funny."

"So?"

"So, in my mind he seemed convinced he was what he kept saying he was."

"A plantation owner. Like I said before, that's possible. But not from now."

"Oh, come on," she laughed.

"Hey. You have to admit he was reacting strangely to everything," Roger reminded her.

"True. But that could have been the amnesia."

"What about his reaction to the nurse?"

"Ok, so he was a bigot with amnesia."

"The day before he left, I got a chance to talk to him again—alone."

"And?"

"He thinks you're a witch."

"What? Oh, that's ridiculous."

"I kid you not. And, I think he was serious."

"Oh, good grief."

"And he said Eloise was your accomplice."

She shook her head. "Oh boy."

"True. You should have seen him watching TV. It seemed to me like it was his very first time."

Abby's brown eyes widened, then she waggled a finger at him. "Roger, I think you believe him."

Roger leaned closer and lowered his voice, "He nearly had me convinced."

"Time travel's impossible, Roger."

He gave her a quick smile and glanced at his iPhone. "Look, I know this is not the best time. Can we meet later to properly discuss our mysterious Mr. Williams?"

Reaching for her lab coat on the back of her chair, Abby said, "Well, I might have a few minutes this afternoon."

"Great." Roger pushed himself up out of the chair and ran his hands through his hair.

"One more question."

"Fire away."

"How does that shelf stay up?"

Without missing a beat, she said, "Magic."

He gave a snort of laughter. "Of course."

"Roger?"

"Yes, doctor?"

"Your hair."

He turned to the mirror. One side of his head looked it had been licked by a large animal.

"Oops!" He sheepishly patted his thick curls back down, gave her a lop-sided grin and dashed out of her office.

She smiled to herself. Roger certainly could be adorable in his own lost puppy kind of way. Then her brows narrowed. That annoying man called me a witch!

22

June 23, 2012

Wherein Celeste attends a momentous opening.

MARTIN HAD CERTAINLY GIVEN HER A BIG REQUEST: find a downtown commercial location with floor space large enough to comfortably feed and accommodate at least 100 people, plus staff, with room for a large kitchen, washrooms and offices. To top it off, he didn't have a big budget. He told her he wanted to give down-and-out people—especially families—a safe place to congregate where they could put some good food in their bellies and feel like someone really cared about them. She could feel the passion in his voice.

Celeste was a sucker for people with big hearts. She vowed to find something Martin could afford. And, she'd done it. The very first location he'd looked at. It was almost like it was meant to be. And today was the grand opening.

Taking care not to drop the huge African violet she'd purchased on impulse, Celeste hoisted up a bag of groceries, took a deep breath and then pushed through the front door of *Sanctuary*, the aptly named homeless day shelter Martin had created.

In her heart flickered a tiny flame, which had nothing to do with whether the shelter would prove a success, although she sincerely hoped it would, of course. Something else had ignited it that first afternoon she'd laid eyes on Martin in person. That man was the whole package: skin the color of pulled taffy, chiseled jaw with a just a bit of a cleft in the chin, gorgeous soulful green eyes, close-cropped nappy black hair, slim but buff, oh yeah, he was virtually irresistible. And when he smiled—wow. And then there was that great, big heart.

Celeste's eyes darted around the spacious and inviting main room, which, if all went well, would soon be crowded with hungry but hopeful folks. In fact, after listening to some of Martin's shocking stats on homelessness in Memphis, she wondered if there might even be a line-up to get in.

A knot of people stood off to one side. She spotted the broad V of Martin's back. It seemed he was listening intently to someone. At the door closed behind her, he turned and beckoned her over with his 100-watt smile lighting up his face She hoped she hadn't been staring at him too hard.

She made her way across the room.

"And here she is," Martin announced to the group with a flourish, "Celeste, my realtor extraordinaire! And look, she's brought supplies!"

"Not to mention an African violet," Celeste laughed and then found herself blushing as she deposited everything on a table.

Oh God, she said to herself. An African violet! What was I thinking? Well, hopefully he doesn't know what it's called, or doesn't know anything about plants, and if he does, he won't think I'm being—What? Insensitive? Good grief. Calm down girl. You're reading too much into this.

She looked up into Martin's face and saw with relief that he was beaming down at her. She gave a tiny gulp and smiled back.

"Celeste, I believe you've met my social workers Howard, Adele, and Douglas, before. I'd like to now present Julia and Patricia, head and assistant cook—man, what they do with a few chickens and vegetables is epic, Brenda, my fearless administrator slash manager, Chris, my shrewd keeper of the books, and Don, my "can-fix-anything-you-throw-at-me" maintenance guy."

"Very pleased to meet y'all," said Celeste with a laugh, shaking everyone's hand and noting that Brenda was giving her a very thorough once over, "I'm so excited for you. I can't believe how great this place looks."

"None of this would have been possible without you, Celeste!" Martin said. "I mean it."

"Oh, well—"

"Ok, group hug everyone!"

Martin's team gave a little whoop and then crowded in. Martin stretched out one long arm to pull Celeste into the throng. Drinking in the warmth and happiness palpable in the circle, she also noted with pleasure Martin's aroma of cinnamon, coconut and something else a little edgier that she couldn't quite put her finger on.

"Ohhhhhh, Martin! This is fantastic!"

Celeste peeked over Martin's arm to see his mother maneuvering a huge bouquet of flowers through the front door. He called over his shoulder, "Mom! Welcome! C'mere and meet the gang!"

Celeste had met his mom when Martin had asked to see the location a second time; he had brought her along for feedback. Celeste had liked Charlotte right away. She was no nonsense, but very warm. As she'd observed the dynamics between them that day, Celeste had gotten the distinct impression Martin was a bit of a momma's boy. But not in a clingy, wimpy kind of way—more of a respectful, adoring, dutiful son kind of way.

"Everyone!" Martin said, "This here's my beautiful mom, Charlotte.

"Hello troops! Glad to meet y'all," she said treating them with a lovely, red-lipsticked smile. She did a slow spin to survey the room then turned to her son. "Oh, my Martin, you've done well! This is very impressive. I am so proud of you! So proud! In fact, I almost forgive you for not letting me in here during the last phase of renovations!"

He squirmed slightly. "Sorry about that, Mom. But I really, really wanted it to be a surprise."

She patted his cheek. "It's all right, dear. I'm just teasing. Now where's that kitchen again? I'm dying to see how it turned out."

He pointed toward a set of swinging doors and she strode toward them.

Celeste touched Martin's elbow. "Well, I'll leave you to it. I have a showing to get to."

"I hope you come again, Celeste. Whenever you like."

"Thank you. I would love to see how things are going."

She turned to the group. "Congratulations everyone! I wish this worthy venture every success."

Martin walked her to the door to say goodbye. As she shook his hand, she noticed his mom step out of the kitchen. Celeste got her attention and gave her a little wave. Then she looked back up into the rainforest of Martin's eyes and added, "I hope y'all have a fantastic first day."

She floated back to her car. As she started the engine, she gave a little laugh when she heard the song *Love fool* pouring out of the car speakers.

23

August 14, 2012

Wherein Patrick's students absorb a very important lesson.

"FEAR FROM MORNING TILL NIGHT: LIFE OF FIELD SLAVES ON A COTTON PLANTATION."

The horn blows an hour before daylight. The slaves wake up, eat breakfast as fast as they can, fill their water gourds and wrap their dinner of cold bacon and corn cake in a cloth. They hurry off to the field. Anyone found at the slave quarters after daybreak gets a whipping. Near the end of August the cotton-picking season begins. The cotton grows up to seven feet high, each stalk having many branches, shooting out in all directions. Sometimes slaves pick down one side of a row and back along the other. Usually, there is one on either side, gathering every blossom and leaving the unopened bolls for another picking.

The first time they go through the field, the slaves must try not to break the branches off the stalks. The cotton will not bloom upon a broken branch. The overseer will whip anyone who breaks one.

When the sack is filled, it's emptied into a basket and stamped down. A day's work for one slave is usually two hundred pounds of cotton. When a new hand, unaccustomed to the work, is sent into the field, they are first given a whipping. Then they are told to pick as fast as they possibly can. Their fingers must learn how to pull the cotton boll gently and quickly, without being pricked by the sharp stamens.

After their long day in the field, the slaves worry about what will happen when they get to the gin-house where the cotton is processed. There may not be enough cotton in their baskets, or there will be too much, and then they will be expected to pick the same amount the next day. If they don't pick enough, they get a lashing.

Except for fifteen minutes at noon to eat their dinner, they are not allowed to rest one moment until it's too dark to see. When the moon is full, they might work until the middle of the night. They don't dare stop—even at dinnertime, or return to their quarters, however late it is, until the slave driver shouts, 'Halt!'

After the weighing and the whippings, the baskets are hauled to the cotton house; all hands are sent in to tramp the cotton down. If the cotton isn't dry, instead of taking it to the gin-house, it's spread out on platforms and covered with boards. This is all done by torchlight.

Each slave must then do chores. One feeds the mules, another the pigs, another cuts the wood, and so on. Finally, they reach their quarters, sleepy and exhausted by their long day. Then a fire has to be kindled in the cabin, the corn ground in a small hand-mill, supper prepared and eaten, as well as dinner for the next day in the field. All that is allowed them is corn and bacon, which is given out at the corn-crib and smokehouse every Sunday morning, the day of rest. Each slave receives, as his weekly allowance, three and a half pounds of bacon, and a basket of corn. That's it. No tea, coffee, sugar, and except for a little sprinkle now and then, no salt.

There is no time left to wash their bodies or their clothing. When they finally lie down on their beds—a plank twelve inches wide and ten feet long with a stick of wood for a pillow, the bedding a coarse blanket—they are filthy from the day's work and the day's before that. They fear they will oversleep in the morning.

And then, much too quickly, the horn blows an hour before daylight."

The student looked up from his paper and glanced at Patrick, who nodded in approval. The boy returned to his seat.

"Thank you, Lawrence. Very good work," Patrick said marveling how a 15-year-old had managed to paint such a vivid picture. He felt such pride in his student's work combined with the familiar pang of outrage at the life his ancestors had endured. And for a moment, he'd glimpsed the Williams' re-enactor's face with its mask of disgust and hatred. He forced the disturbing image into the back of his mind.

"All right," he said. "Comments? Questions?"

Several students raised their hands.

Patrick pointed at a girl in the front row.

"Esdee?"

A nervous smile flitted across her face as she rose to her feet. Esdee was one of his most sensitive students. Since the start of the year she had often reacted passionately to the subject matter being discussed or assigned as homework in his class on slavery in the United States. Patrick nodded his encouragement.

"Ok," she said sounding a bit out of breath. "I thought your presentation was really good, Lawrence. Like, I really felt as if I was there."

He smiled. "Thanks."

"My question is," she continued, her voice quivering. "Why weren't the slaves given money to help them when Lincoln emancipated them?"

Several other students immediately piped up. "Yeah! Why not?"

"An excellent question, Esdee," said Patrick. "Lawrence, your thoughts?"

"Yeah, I wondered about that too," he said. "So I Googled 'money for freed American slaves'. It's called 'reparation' not compensation.

Esdee blinked and then gave her head a quick nod.

"Lincoln wanted to give freed slaves land and mules," he went on. "But when he was assassinated at the end of the Civil War in 1865, the next president got rid of the plan. Former slaves were pretty well left to fend for themselves. Lots ended up working at," he held up four fingers to represent quotation marks, "'slave-wages' for the people who'd been their masters."

"Wow. So nobody else bothered to help?" she asked.

Lawrence shook his head. "Um. I don't know."

Patrick interjected. "Esdee, there was so much resentment toward emancipation in the South the interest in helping the freed slaves just wasn't there. And, after the Civil War ended there wasn't the money."

"But still, that's... that's so wrong!" she fumed.

Patrick lifted his shoulders. "It does seem that way, doesn't it? But, you have to understand—the southern economy was in ruins. The truth is there was more interest in helping the slave owners."

Esdee shook her head.

"And, as Lawrence said, a lot of freed people ended up in refugee camps, which were often the very slave pens they'd been held in before being auctioned off to their former owners. Hundreds of freed slaves died of disease or starvation in these camps. Others who did find work had no choice but to become poorly paid sharecroppers for their slave masters."

A profound silence enveloped the class. Then a student began to chant. "Justice. Justice. Justice!"

Moments later the entire class was chanting with him and pounding desks with their hands.

"All right, people!" said Patrick. "We don't want the principal in here!

Surveying the young, outraged faces in front of him, he wondered if he'd unleashed a monster. They were all so young and apparently very sheltered. He sighed. What would happen when he gave his lesson on the Black Panthers? Despite worrying that he might be stirring the pot, he threw caution to the wind and went on.

"We are going to explore this further in our next class, but in a nutshell, here's what happened after the war: there was a period of something called Reconstruction to help the South get back on its feet. But, it failed. Meanwhile, the Ku Klux Klan got its start."

Hearing the collective intake of breath, Patrick added. "I promise we'll talk more about that in another class. Anyway, Reconstruction was followed by a period called Redemption, which was when white-dominated state legislatures enacted Jim Crow Laws. Anyone know about these laws?

Patrick nodded at a boy sitting in the middle row, whose hand was waving. "Yes, Max?"

"Um, weren't they about how blacks had to be kept separate? Like, having to drink out of 'black-only' water fountains and not being allowed to sit at the front of buses? Oh, and only being allowed to go to 'black' schools?"

"You got it, Max. In other words: Segregation. And because of it, discrimination against blacks went right across the country, but it was worst in the South. The Civil Rights movement of the 1950s and 1960s fought it hard. Things did get better, but the effects of Segregation are still with us."

Patrick glanced at the clock. "All right. We have fourteen minutes before the bell. So let's talk about justice. I can certainly appreciate why you are asking for it, but what does it really mean? What can be done now, 147 years later? Many generations have come and gone. I'm sure if you took a poll, most people—white and black—would say it's too late."

"Money!" exclaimed Esdee. "Like, it's so simple. The descendants should all be given money."

"Nice thought Esdee, but, unfortunately, it's not that simple. First of all, how to tell who is a descendant and who isn't? Records from those days are hard to find and sometimes the slaves were known only by their first name. There were no computers of course."

Benjamin shot his hand up. "And how much money would be enough? I think that would be really hard to decide."

Esdee looked chagrined, but then brightened. "Well, what if each black American born in this country was given $20,000. It wouldn't really make up for what happened to the slaves, but it would be something. Right?"

Patrick walked to the blackboard, picked up the chalk and printed 40,000,000. Turning back to the class he said, "That is the estimated number of descendants of American slaves living today."

Esdee's eyes widened.

Then he added x $20,000.

"All right. Who can do the math?"

Benjamin thought fast, "That's $800 Billion! Wow."

"Right," said Patrick. He added that figure to the board and underlined it. "And who would give the money? Should it be the government?"

"Huh, I think so, but that's a lot of money," admitted Benjamin.

Patrick smiled. "And you may not realize it, but that would be taxpayers' money. I can tell you that the majority of them would not be happy about their money going to the supposed descendants of slaves almost 150 years after Emancipation.

Benjamin nodded. "And what about the blacks who are well off? Look at Oprah. She's one of the richest people in the world. She sure doesn't need the money."

A hand fluttered in the back row. Patrick nodded his head at a girl who rarely participated. "I heard that Oprah's ancestors went to that country the slave days' government made up in Africa to get rid of free blacks. 'Cause people said they were lazy, useless and trouble makers."

"Correct, Leisha. It's called Liberia." Patrick was surprised she had this kind of knowledge. She was one of his most uninvolved students, rarely taking part in class discussions, preferring to draw in her book or stare out the window.

He continued, "And that's a whole other can of worms. Hopefully, we'll have time to discuss it in a future class. Ok, everyone. Any other thoughts?"

Lawrence stuck his hand in the air. "What about all the poor blacks trying to get ahead, but don't have enough education? And all the blacks in prison? My dad told me that the prison system is about making money and now the number of black men in jail is more than the number of male slaves before the Civil War!"

Patrick gave a nod, his face grim. "And, believe it or not, after the Civil War, slavery was abolished for all except anyone convicted of a crime. The Slave Codes were rewritten as Black Codes which criminalized legal activity for African Americans. Standing in one area of town or walking at night became "loitering" or "breaking curfew" for which they were imprisoned. That meant a huge increase in the number of black convicts."

Lawrence shook his head. And then Leisha's hand went up.

"I think college should be free."

"That's an idea," said Patrick.

The girl went on. "Like, even in 2012 it's hard for blacks to get a good education—the kind that will give us good jobs. It's kind of still like the way slaves were kept ignorant on purpose. I think if more blacks were educated they will stay out of prison."

She has been paying attention, Patrick thought. "Well, there are government grants for low income students. Hundreds of thousands of young blacks have gone to college as a result. But it's still very tough getting into the top-ranked schools because of tough competition. And SAT scores from lower-income students tend to be less than scores for richer students."

"But if higher education were free—" Leisha reiterated.

"Even if there was free tuition, residence, books, supplies, food and so on, add up," Patrick explained. "An extra $15-$20,000 a year."

The girl's face fell.

It was Patrick's turn to shake his head. "I know. Doesn't seem right, does it?"

"There must be something that can be done," sighed Esdee.

Patrick had a momentary vision of Jacob Williams sitting in his class, listening to this discussion. Now wouldn't that be something?

The bell rang.

"Ok," said Patrick. "Tomorrow we divide up into groups to see what we can brainstorm. Class dismissed."

24

May 1841
Wherein Sadie wonders if it's time to return.

When the sun comes back and the first quail calls,
follow the drinking gourd.
For the old man is awaiting for to carry you to freedom,
if you follow the drinking gourd.
The riverbank makes a very good road,
the dead trees show you the way,
left foot, peg foot, traveling on, follow the drinking gourd.
The river ends between two hills, follow the drinking gourd.
There's another river on the other side,
follow the drinking gourd.
Where the great big river meets the little river,
follow the drinking gourd.
For the old man is a-waiting to carry you to freedom,
if you follow the drinking gourd.

SADIE HURT FOR HER KIN. Her Mama. Her Pa. Her three brothers and three sisters. They never escaped her mind's eye. She could see their faces during her long busy day scrubbing laundry. And when she lay her head down on her pillow at night, there they were—so close it seemed she could reach out and wrap her arms 'round them.

Four years had passed since Sadie had escaped the plantation and the clutches of her master, Jacob Williams. The days of freedom with her precious son Henry in their own little house brought such joy. But, the nights were a different story. She always prayed sleep would not be disturbed by memories of what Henry's father had done to her: the ugly look on his face when he'd surprised her in the parlor, the nasty feel of his rough fingers as they roamed over her body, the hot liquor breath on her neck when he trapped her hands behind her back and covered her mouth with his hand. And then the pig grunting sounds he'd made when he'd yanked her legs apart and started thrusting inside her privates. Her body had ached for days.

Other memories gave her bad dreams, too—the memories of the nights and nights of running for the Promised Land with only the stars, the moon and the animals in the woods to give her company.

The times she was almost caught during her journey were especially awful. The first close call was the day she'd been dozing in a big ole hollow tree. She'd been woken up by voices. She carefully eased her head out of the tree a ways and saw two old white men with fishing poles headed straight at her. She'd pulled herself back in quick and hid as best she could. When they got closer she'd held her breath until they passed by without discovering her trembling on the other side of the rotting bark.

Another close call happened later in her journey. She'd stolen some food from a cabin and then, since it was starting to get light, climbed a nearby tree. After devouring the food, she'd tied herself to one of the branches so she could sleep without falling out. The sound of someone giggling woke her up a little while later. She peered down through the leaves to see a young man and a young lady sitting in the shade of the tree. They were kissing and petting something fierce. Then, someone started hollering in the distance. The two got up and hurried off.

Sadie couldn't even guess how many times she'd gone to sleep hungry on her journey. Far too many, that's for sure. The small sack of rations she'd taken from the plantation had lasted only a few days. How she'd kept the babe growing in her belly was a downright miracle.

She'd run off on a moonless night. The moon was full for the second time when she finally reached her last stop—the Ohio River.

And now, the longer she lived in *Harmony*, the stronger her yearning to see her kin. She tried not to think about what may have happened to them the morning she was found missing, but she couldn't stop herself from fretting. How were they punished? There would have been whippings, but had her family been torn apart by being sold to different masters? She longed to send word that she was alive and well, and maybe get word back from them and know what happened. She hoped and prayed they were all right.

During Sadie's years living in freedom, she'd been squeezing everything she could into her head about somethin' folks called the Underground Railroad. First of all, it wasn't even a railroad. And it didn't have trains. Its 'railways' were back roads, swamps, caves, forests, rivers and streams with secret safe houses to rest up in.

If only she'd known about the railway before she ran. She'd used the land and the sky to lead her north, like Ole Tom told her to, but a roof over her head, a hot meal, a kind word, a bed to sleep in now and then? Well, that would have been such sweet pleasure.

Missus Margaret was what people called an abolitionist. Turns out she was an agent on the railroad, too. Every single day she sent Joe and a few other helpers to the shore of the Ohio River in the hopes of rustling up some hungry and desperate brave souls fleeing the bonds of slavery.

Sadie knew the Lord was watching over her the morning Joe had discovered her. To have been found alive just when her strength was near worn out was a miracle.

After Henry was born, Sadie stayed on with Missus Margaret for a few months longer. When she moved into her own little place, Sadie started earning a bit of money by taking in white folks' laundry. Felt mighty good to be paid for her labors. And, she could keep an eye on her baby boy at the same time.

Now Sadie knew a home was somewhere safe, where a person could rest up and keep clean, where there was plenty of good food to eat, where no one hurt you, where nobody forced you to work for free.

Henry was now a sturdy little boy. One night as she was tucking him to bed after prayers, she found herself thinking again about her brothers and sisters. They would be getting so big now. She brushed away the hot tears that spilled onto her cheeks when she realized she might never see them again. Was it time to act on a notion that had been swirling in her head for the last few months? She'd told herself she was a darn fool to think about it.

But, as she gazed down at her son who had fallen asleep the instant he'd laid down, she could see herself going south. She could see herself finding her family. She could see herself setting them free.

And after she'd done that, her life would almost feel complete.

25

August 13, 2012

Wherein two doctors have a meeting of the minds about a most unusual patient.

ROGER GRINNED AT ABBY as she glided toward him, balancing a cup of coffee, her clipboard, and her bulging briefcase.

She sank into the seat across from him. "Whew. That's better. What a week."

He'd found a booth in the hospital cafeteria that offered a smidgen of privacy. He'd heard that her mother was unwell, so he wasn't certain if she would have time to meet that day. Apparently, she would stop by her parents whenever she could to check on her mom.

Abby took a sip of coffee and closed her eyes. "Ahhh, good. Needed that."

He nodded. "Coffee, the wonder drug. So, here we are. Two doctors flummoxed by a patient like no other."

She smiled. "I'll say."

Roger took a swig of his own coffee, looked around the room for a second, and then blurted, "OK, I know you're going to think I'm crazy, but I definitely feel there's more to this guy than meets the eye."

"I know you're crazy, Roger," she teased. You're a shrink. And you're a poet too, but...."

"Don't know it. Yeah, very funny. But c'mon, don't you think he's more than just odd. Get this: when he was watching TV, he said that your sorcery had something to do it."

"With what?" And then she burst out laughing. "Omg. TV?"

"Yeah. Well, I don't really know. He didn't explain himself. Believe me, I was having a hard time not laughing at him. And we know he wouldn't have liked that."

Still chuckling, Abby dabbed her eyes with a paper napkin. "No, that's for sure!"

"OK, now listen to what he said when I asked him about his plantation and his so-called slaves."

"This I gotta hear."

"He said, and I quote: slavery is how barbaric countries become civilized."

She stared at him. "What? But, that doesn't even make any sense."

"Well, it appeared to me that he thought it did."

"Oh, my. Talk about delusional thinking."

Roger stared at the dregs in his cup for a moment then lifted his eyes to Abby's. She tilted her head expectantly.

"Listen. Abby, the more I think about it, it seems to me like this guy was absolutely convinced he was a plantation owner. From... before."

Abby said nothing. Then she looked around for a moment before saying in a low voice, "Which means, he time traveled, Roger. And we know that's impossible."

"Or is it?"

Her eyes widened. And then she shook her head. "No. Not possible. No!"

His eyes burrowed into hers. "Don't you ever think about the things that happen that can't be explained?"

She said nothing.

"Like how about the fact that ancient civilizations on other sides of the planet have inexplicable commonalities?"

"Not really," she shrugged.

"Or..., ok... whatever. Let's just say that I do. And I took an hour last night to do some research on time travel."

She gave a little snort.

"Look, if you had time to go on-line, you'd find an incredible array of stories about people who claim they've gone backwards or forwards in time. It's quite fascinating."

She laughed again. "Please—"

"Bear with me, OK?"

She nodded and tried to look serious.

"So, the more I read the more I started to feel that maybe something did happen to Jacob. I even stumbled on what are most likely conspiracies about governments participating in time travel experiments, but they were quite amazing accounts. In fact, one lawyer claimed he was part of the government's time travel experiments when he was a kid."

"A lawyer, huh?" she snickered. "And lawyers never lie."

"Yeah, I know, I know. OK, better example. I read that some inventor from 1906 came up with the idea for the cell phone. There are even old newspaper clippings about it; people think he must have come from the future because how else would he have had that idea?"

"Uh huh..." murmured Abby as she sipped her coffee and rolled her eyes.

"Oh, and speaking of cell phones," Roger continued, "there's a scene in Charlie Chaplin's 1920s movie, The Circus, where a woman looks like she's talking into one. I spent some time checking out the footage on YouTube and I gotta admit, it does look like she's talking into something."

"Oh yeah, I think I heard about that. I thought it was proven she was using some kind of old fashioned hearing aid?"

"But, there was no one next to her. If she was alone, who was she talking to?"

Abby grew quiet and took another sip of her coffee. Had he managed to convince her even a little?

Her eyes darted around the busy cafeteria and then looked sideways at him. "You know, Roger, I have to admit that this patient was different. I had it drilled into me to believe only what science has proven to be true. I've had patients with all kinds of personalities and idiosyncrasies but, I have to admit, Jacob Williams was unlike any other patient."

She polished off her coffee and started tearing the cup's rim into bits. "Listening to you, I have to admit my gut is whispering, 'maybe just once something impossible could be possible'."

"Well, well, Dr. Shields," Roger said as he leaned back and folded his arms across his chest. "Good to see there's a human being in there after all."

She made a face. Lowering her voice, she added, "So, let's you and me pretend that Jacob Williams is who he says he is and that he did, in fact, time travel from the year 1837, well before the Civil War. From that point of view, I have to admit his reaction to blacks and women, let alone technology, all makes sense." She shook her head. "Jesus. I can't believe I just said that."

"So you do think there's a little more to this world than we've been led to believe, huh, Doctor?" replied Roger with a wink.

"Well," she said slowly, "I guess the way he behaved when Eloise was trying to give him his meds wasn't just because he was a paranoid bigot with amnesia. And, he actually thought she was my accomplice?"

"Did I hear my name?"

A nurse was standing beside their table, smiling down at them.

"Oh, hello, Eloise!" said Roger wondering how much she'd overheard. "Yes, yes, you did. Abby and I were just talking about a recent patient. That fellow who needed to be sedated when you were about to give him his meds."

"Oh, that guy?" she shrugged. "Believe you me, it's not the first time something like that's happened, Doctor."

"Oh, is that right?" said Roger.

"Oh, yes, some white patients still don't like black nurses and doctors helping them," she said, crossing her arms.

"Sorry to hear that, Eloise," said Abby frowning. "It's 2012 for heaven's sake. That's ridiculous."

"Ridiculous it may be, but this is still the South, Dr. Shields. Believe it or not, certain attitudes have not changed all that much."

"I'm sorry to hear that, Eloise. Really, I am," said Abby, putting a hand on her arm.

"Thanks, Doctor. I don't like it one little bit, but I'm used to it. I had to get used to it." Eloise sighed and then looked at her watch. "Whoops. Got to get back. Nice talking to you both."

Lost in thought, Roger and Abby watched her stride briskly away.

"Well," began Abby, "That was an eye opener. Hard enough being female in the medical profession, even in 2012. I've been so wrapped up in, well... everything, I hadn't realized bigotry was still that rampant." She gave her head a slow shake.

"Yup. Hard to believe, isn't it?" agreed Roger. He reminded himself that she hadn't been a surgeon for that long, so her time in the "real world" of medicine in Memphis, Tennessee was pretty minimal. Not surprising that she would come across as a tad naive, even though she acted tough.

"In my practice," he explained, "I deal so often with hate issues that sometimes I wonder if intolerance and hatred is built into some people's genes. But then I remember what Mandela said: no one is born hating another person because of the color of his skin, his background or religion. People learn to hate and if they can learn to hate, then they can learn to love, for love comes more naturally to the human heart."

"I like that Roger," she said and gazed at him in admiration. "Now if only more people believed it."

I could lose myself in her eyes, he thought. He pulled his gaze away and checked his watch. "I know you've got to get going in a couple of minutes. What do you think we should do about our Mr. Williams? If we can find him, that is."

"Good question, Roger. Guess we should have been a little more pro-active and tried harder to keep him here. So, you don't have any idea where he is?"

"Well, I imagine he's trying to figure out how to get back to his plantation. That's the only place where he would feel grounded. And who knows? Maybe he thinks that since it's where he came in to our time, it's where he'll go back to his."

Abby crumpled the remainder of her cup. "That actually makes sense."

"I figure he's probably still roaming around the city somewhere," said Roger. "I'm sure he hasn't gotten too far yet. Even though he's not exactly what'd you call a nice person, I felt a bit sorry for him. He has no one here, he's completely out of his element, and he's lost his status and wealth. I gave him a little cash so he'd be able to get something to eat at least."

Abby's phone beeped. She clicked off her alert and then gave him a quick, dimpled smile. "Aren't you a softy? Look, I've got to go get prepped for surgery. You thinking you might try to find him? If so, your best bet would be to check the shelters."

"Yeah, good idea," Roger said as he watched her rise and gather her things. "Park benches aren't all that comfortable, or safe. I'll start checking the downtown shelters tomorrow, if and when I get some time."

As Abby turned to leave he thought of something else and touched her arm. "Let's keep this between us for now. All right with you, Doctor?"

"Absolutely. Keep me posted Dr. Eaton," Abby called over her shoulder as she rushed off toward the elevators.

As Roger watched Abby weave through the maze of tables, he said under his breath, "Thank you, Jacob Williams. Even if I never find you, you've given me an excuse to get better acquainted with a certain charming doctor."

26

May 1841

Wherein Sadie visits Missus Margaret to ask a favor, one she will likely never be able to repay.

WITH HENRY'S SMALL HAND TUCKED IN HERS, Sadie set off for Missus Margaret's house. It was a fine spring morning, but she hardly noticed. She'd had another restless night. When she woke up that morning, she'd told herself it was time. She was going to go get her kin. If Missus Margaret could help, of course.

As she fretted about what her friend would say, Sadie's brow furrowed. It was so much to ask of someone.

Missus Margaret's sipped her tea as she listened quietly to Sadie's plan. When she finished talking, the old woman placed her teacup in its saucer and gave a long sigh.

Sadie's heart sank.

Margaret lined face looked grim, but then she gave her a little smile. "My dear, I understand you miss your kinfolk terribly. It must be dreadfully hard for you to continually wonder about them, but, you do know how very, very difficult this will be, don't you?"

Sadie looked down at her hands, still wrinkled from being plunged all day in hot water scrubbing laundry. Then she glanced at Henry who was happily playing with a small wooden horse on the floor next to the bay window. She managed to put a tiny smile on her face before turning back to her friend.

"Yes, Missus Margaret, I know it. I'm pretty ashamed of myself coming here like this to ask for more help when you've done so much for me, but, well, you see, I... I just didn't know what else to do."

Missus Margaret folded Sadie's small hands between her soft crooked fingers, looked into her eyes and said, "Now don't you fret, my girl. I was expecting one day you would come to me with an idea like this. Of course, I'll help you, Sadie."

Sadie whooped and threw her arms around the old woman. "Oh, thank you, thank you, Missus Margaret! You are my angel right here on this earth, I swear!" Tears of joy sprang into her eyes and started streaming down her face.

"Mama, Mama! Why you crying, Mama?" Henry had abandoned his toy and had laid his head on Sadie's arm. He looked up at her, his angelic little face puckered with concern. "Please, Mama. Don't cry, Mama."

"Oh, my darlings," laughed Margaret rubbing Sadie's back and stroking Henry's soft curly hair. "Somehow we will do this. Just give me a little time to see what kind of plan I can hatch."

Sadie bent down to kiss Henry's forehead. Wiping her eyes she looked into her friend's face. "Thank you, Missus Margaret. I know this world is a battleground between good and evil, but I gotta hope that good will overcome. At least some of the time."

Meanwhile, back down on the Williams' plantation, Sadie's family had been secretly plotting their escape for over a year. They'd been spared the torture of being split up and sold to different owners, but almost all had paid a price when she disappeared. Sadie had been careful not to reveal her escape plans to a soul, especially to her loved ones, but Jacob and his overseer assumed they had known and abetted her. Lashings were doled out to every family member except one—Little Jenny, who was only a few summers old.

Everyone in the quarters knew that comely young girls suffered in the Big House at the hands of Massa. Sadie had been so ashamed about what he'd done to her she couldn't even tell her mother. And when she finally did, her mama had looked at her with big, sad eyes and shook her head. Then she said that Sadie just had to bear it.

Soon, talk passed from the house slaves to the field slaves that Missus Sheila hated Sadie. She knew something was going on between Sadie and the Master and she was getting madder and madder about Jacob's 'habit'. One of the parlor maids heard her telling a lady who had come over for tea how she couldn't wait to punish Sadie. The Missus wanted her beaten and locked up in a shed. Sadie heard other whispers too; that Missus wanted Sadie branded.

On the morning the family awoke to find Sadie missing, the news of her disappearance spread like wildfire. Massa was mad as a bull, but Missus was a puzzle. Nobody could tell for sure if she was happy or angry, but every time Missus looked at her husband, her eyes could freeze water.

Since she hadn't been hauled back to the plantation, Sadie's family believed in their hearts that she had made it to freedom. It was too painful to think otherwise—that she'd been captured or had passed into the Lord's hands. It was because of her that their daily longing for freedom began to feel like more than just a dream. If only they could find out where she was, then they could send her a message that they too were hoping to follow her path.

And maybe, just maybe, she could help them.

27

June 30, 2012

Wherein Martin's new enterprise is an immediate success, but he's not really sure if he's happy about that.

WITHIN A WEEK OF THE SHELTER'S OPENING, there was a line snaking down the sidewalk before they could unlock the front door in the morning. *Sanctuary* was not only a hit, it was a necessity.

For Martin, watching people from every stratum of society stream in and out through his door felt almost like being an eyewitness to the decline of civilization. From the information gleaned from his intake forms, he learned that many of his clients coped with homelessness by sleeping on friends' couches or hunkered down in their cars or vans. Otherwise, it was over-night shelters—if they were lucky enough to get in. A few desperate souls took their chances and stayed out on the streets.

Listening to their stories he was struck by their similar refrain: homelessness could happen to anyone. Estelle lost her apartment after her hours had been cut at her job; George was a former car salesman who now lived in his car; Grace worked in television, got sick and didn't have enough insurance to cover her medical bills; Tony was a musician and a carpenter, but when his hands were injured in a car accident, he was out of a job. There were Iraq war vets with post-traumatic stress disorder, women running from abusive husbands, teens kicked out by parents for being gay, or who had grown too old for foster homes and had nowhere else to go.

Martin's expectation that the majority of clients using his shelter would be African American was a given. His "assessment of need" research before *Sanctuary* opened had revealed black unemployment during the recession—especially for women—had skyrocketed.

Blacks lucky enough to have jobs were usually paid less than their white counterparts and were having trouble making ends meet. Those who had gone to college were certainly not grads of the expensive Ivy League schools, which still made a huge difference on resumes, especially when competition for good jobs was as fierce as it currently was. Added to the mix: countless high school dropouts with just about zero odds of getting work—even just flipping burgers.

So a high priority for Martin was to provide job training. He hoped to organize classes in food prep since the shelter ran a professional kitchen. For now, Martin and his team provided free counseling, free vitamins, one free local and long-distance phone call per day, free books and donated clean clothing. His next big goal was to find a way to offer affordable housing.

Martin had made sure to install lockers in his shelter. Having a safe place to store their belongings was a huge advantage for the homeless. Otherwise, they had to drag their stuff everywhere they went. Stowing their belongings in a locker meant they could go to doctor's appointments, job interviews, and check out places to live unencumbered. And another plus: they wouldn't instantly be labeled as homeless.

All Martin asked in return was that everyone pitch in: help in the kitchen or serve meals, and clean up afterward. And, he had clear rules: No Booze, No Drugs, and No Attitude. If anyone violated these, they were out.

Opening his shelter made Martin aware of just how lucky he was. In fact, he realized more than ever that he'd lived a charmed life. His family was well off due to his dad's business success. His mom didn't have to work and had devoted a lot of time to Martin and Solomon when they were growing up. Everything had come easy for him, but Martin had nearly taken all that for granted.

His encounter with his dead brother was always at the back of his mind. He hadn't heard from him again and he wondered if he ever would. He still didn't completely understand what had happened that morning, but was grateful for the experience.

A couple of weeks after *Sanctuary* opened, the young panhandler Martin had seen twice on the street showed up with his wife and baby. The family paused on the threshold, looking a bit unsure whether they should come in. Martin spotted them from across the room and strode over to greet them. "Welcome! How nice to see you."

He shook their hands and took a peek at the baby.

"Sweet little thing. A girl?"

"Yes," said the mother, shyly. "Angela-Maureen."

"Lovely name. My name is Martin." He said with a smile and then nodded at the father. "I believe we've met before."

The man's eyes widened, and then he gave a slow nod of comprehension.

"Oh, wow. It's you."

Martin smiled. "Yes. It's me. What's your name, bro?"

"Micheal. And this is my wife, Jacqui."

"Please, come on in."

28

August 13, 2012

Wherein Jacob's return to his plantation is interrupted by a disturbing discovery.

He took a deep breath and stepped through the enchanted door to emerge into an alien world: the City of Memphis, 2012. Squinting from the harsh afternoon light—so painful after days trapped indoors—Jacob fought the impulse to retreat inside. The noise, the smell, the non-stop motion were almost too much to bear.

He spied a bench a few yards away. He moved over to it and lowered himself onto the hot metal slats. For several minutes, he sat without moving, his head lowered and with his hands over his ears to muffle the din. When he dared lift his eyes to peer around—his nose twitching from the acrid smell emanating from the road, the array of four-wheeled contraptions of all shapes and colors whizzing along alternately bewildered and fascinated him. He wondered again about the fate of the horses.

At least I won't have to worry about treading in manure, he thought, and in spite of his discomfort, gave a weak chuckle.

It soon occurred to him how much busier the road was than the slab of light gray stone upon which the oddly garbed people walked. Occasionally a horseless contraption stopped to discharge one or two more upon the slab, swallow up others and then tear away.

Gazing at all the activity on the street was making him slightly dizzy. Lowering his head again, he pondered what to do … which way to go.

How he detested this state of indecision. It was so unlike him. But it was painfully clear his options were limited. He watched the feet walking past and noticed most were going left. Should he follow their lead?

He lifted his head and stood up. Taking care to avert his eyes whenever he saw a black face, he began his trek. All too soon his steps slowed.

"Damnation," he muttered.

A seemingly impenetrable flow of contraptions was speeding past him at a crossroad. He stood rooted in place wondering how he would get to the opposite slab alive. After a few minutes of watching the ebb and flow, he discerned a yellow box on the other side of the road seemed to be in command. When it revealed a tiny red hand, the contraptions began to move past him while the people waiting on the corner with him stayed still. Then, when a white walking figure replaced the hand, the contraptions stopped and people on his slab and opposite him began to cross the road.

The third time the walking figure appeared he gathered the courage to take a step forward. A sharp horn sounded. He yelped and jumped out of the path of an enormous black horseless contraption. He could see the driver shaking his head. Several anxious moments later, he reached the opposite walking slab, his heart was knocking so hard inside his chest he feared he might have another attack. He stumbled over to a building to rest. Slouching against the wall, he closed his eyes and took in several deep breaths until he felt better.

Pressing on he successfully navigated several more intersections. Though his confidence as a pedestrian increased, he found himself becoming more anxious … not a single building was familiar to him. His eyes swept over shop after shop, tavern after tavern, eatery after eatery, but failed to find one structure from his own time that would give him a sense of hope.

Then he noticed a statue ahead. Drawing close he discovered the stone likeness of a handsome troubadour playing a sort of oversized lute. A cluster of white women surrounded the stone man. A pair of them pointed little boxes at him while the others placed flowers at his feet. Then she straightened up, her mouth vigorously chewing away at something while she stared with longing at the stone man. "I miss you, Elvis," she said and blew it a kiss.

Jacob's curiosity was piqued. He tentatively approached her. "Excuse me, madam. Who might this man be?"

She gave a little snort and then laughed right in his face. He could see a white wad of something glistening on her tongue. He took a step back in revulsion.

"You don't know who the King is?" she said.

"The King?" he said, squinting up at the statue's face. "Is this the king of England?"

"Hoo boy! That's a good one. Where'd you come from? Mars?" She looked at her friends. "Hey girls, believe it or not, this guy doesn't know who Elvis was!"

"What? Y'all kidding, right?" hooted a rotund young woman. "Everyone knows that!" She looked Jacob up and down. "Where you been hiding?"

"I've not been … Now listen here, I will not be mocked!" said Jacob.

"Mocked?" she laughed. "I ain't mocking you. C'mon, everyone knows who Elvis is."

The chewing woman turned around to look this way and that. "Hey!" she cried. "Is there a camera hidden around here some place?"

"Ha! Maybe we're on 'Candid Camera'," laughed another one.

"I've had just about enough," Jacob said and strode off. "Disgusting creatures," he sputtered.

As he carried on his way, it occurred to him that he felt almost like a blind man, groping along in the dark; he didn't really know where he was going, but he felt compelled to move. Then, as he averted his gaze from yet another black face, a different thought entered his mind: while he was attempting to avoid the darkies, it seemed that everyone was avoiding him. Men, women and children brushed right past him. Others, with their eyes fixated on those infernal little boxes or with them pressed to their ears, veered away from him at the last second. No one took a moment to nod or give him a greeting. What did those boxes contain that was so damn mesmerizing? If not for the occasional beggar rattling a paper cup for coins, he was an invisible man.

He was reminded anew of that terrible day when he'd awakened to find strangers in his home who at first behaved as if he didn't exist.

He gave a long sigh. How he longed for his plantation. It made him who he was. But he was far too proud to ask for help. He would find it. Himself.

A glimmer of water at the end of a street caught his eye. His heart quickened.

Was it the Mississippi?

Tens of thousands of bales of cotton from his plantation were shipped down the Mississippi River every year. Perhaps there would be a boat that could carry him back to his land.

The water drew him like a winking beacon, but when he arrived at the riverfront his heart sank. Instead of a scene of bustling maritime activity, only a few oddly shaped crafts floated on the murky water. A smattering of people strolled the shoreline while a few souls occupied the small park next to the river. Supremely disappointed, he decided none-the-less that he should take some time to rest in the park. He spotted an empty bench under a tree and headed straight for it.

How good it felt to sit and rest his feet. With his elbows planted on his knees he dropped his head down to stare at his ugly shoes. His hand slowly moved up to his face to rub the whiskers he'd missed when he attempted to shave with the so-called razor he'd found in the hospital washing room that morning.

His stomach gave a twinge and then emitted a faint growl.

"Am I ill?" he murmured. He'd never felt this sensation before. Was it due to his heart attack?

Then he gave a rueful laugh. "You're hungry, Jacob."

Remembering the sandwich given to him in the hospital, he fished it out of his paper bag of belongings. Though slightly crushed it smelled quite acceptable. As he wolfed his food down, he stared at the river and contemplated his next move. Resuming his march seemed his only option. And finding something to drink would be wise, as he had drained his vessel of water some time ago.

An unearthly racket erupted behind him. Over his shoulder, he saw a trio of youngsters, including two pickaninnies, headed in his direction along a smooth stone path that snaked down to the river. They were balanced on short, wheeled wooden boards. He took hold of a large stick that lay near his feet.

"Keep away!" he warned.

To his relief, they sped up as they passed him by. He put the stick down on the bench in case he might need it. He was growing increasingly tired of feeling nervous about everything around him. The box he had looked at in the hospital room came to mind again, but he pushed the memory aside. He refused to think about neither the witch nor that Negress winning the tumbling contest.

However unpleasant the recollection, it did remind him of the doctor … the one person who'd been kind to him. He checked his pocket to ensure that the money the doctor had given him was still there. He must avoid pickpockets at all cost.

The smell of the river cheered him a trifle. As he looked at its rippling gray surface, an idea began to percolate. His plantation lay due south from Memphis about ten or so miles away. Perhaps he could walk along the river to his home?

A terrible din above his head made him flinch.

"What the devil?" he cried.

He wondered if he was about to be attacked. An enormous dragonfly was hovering over him a few hundred feet up.

With a yelp, he dove for cover under the tree next to the bench. Keeping a wary eye on the thing as it dipped and buzzed overhead, he concluded it wasn't a giant insect at all … it was another mechanical monstrosity that could somehow fly above this strange city of the future. A few moments later, he watched it roar out over the water and then disappear.

He trudged back to the bench to wearily contemplate his next move. Could he indeed walk to his plantation? Of course, if he did get there, since it was no longer his, he might not even get in. The presence of the strangers on his final day there made sense to him now. They had taken over his house because he was dead, as were his family, his friends, acquaintances, and every last one of his slaves.

He heaved a sigh. How could it be possible there were no Williams' descendants running his plantation?

He mournfully stared up into the branches of the tall oak tree next to him. Might it have been a seedling when he was alive?

His vision grew bleary. "Good Lord. I'm weeping." He quickly rubbed the tears away.

He might never know—let alone understand—why he'd been chosen for this maddening journey nearly 200 years into the future, but for whatever reason, it had occurred. Despite how miserable he felt and even though his plantation was no longer legally his home, he had to return there. Besides the river, it was all that he knew.

"You must keep moving, Jacob," he told himself.

He pushed himself off the bench and plodded down to the waterfront and turned south. Maybe, if he were lucky, he would stumble upon a ferry.

A building up ahead caught his eye. It was emblazoned with the words 'Cotton Exchange'. He hurried toward it, but his steps slowed when he saw it was no longer operating as an exchange. It had become a museum.

"What on earth happened to the cotton industry?" he moaned. A stout man passing by gave him a curious look. Jacob stumbled over to the iron fence that ran along the river. Gripping the railing, his head slumped to his chest, he closed his eyes and wished for the hundredth time that this were all a fantastical dream he would wake up from and he would be in his own home, in his own time.

But it was not a dream. When his eyes blinked open, nothing had changed. A little ways away, he noticed that the stout man had stopped and was looking at him. What does he want? he wondered.

Jacob turned away to toss the see-through pouch from his lunch at some seagulls roosting on the rocks near the water. They eagerly poked at it until a trio of others gulls wheeled down and squawked furiously at them. They flew off, and then fearlessly dove back into the fray, trying to reclaim their find. He had to admire their spunk. They didn't give up, so neither should he.

He licked his dry lips. Well, Jacob, he thought, if you're going to attempt this journey, you must find water.

Looking about in the hopes of spotting a well, he noted that the man that had been watching him had moved on. He was a little disappointed, as perhaps he could have asked him where to find water. Then his eyes fell upon a thick newspaper sticking out of a rubbish bin a few feet away. The portrait of a man on the cover seemed familiar to him. He pulled the paper out of the bin and shook it open. Under the banner Memphis Daily News, the headline shouted, *Trump Still Questions Obama's Place of Birth!*

The artist was highly skilled, he thought.

There were in fact, two portraits. The first was of the man who looked familiar—a pompous looking fellow with fleshy, pursed lips and an odd growth of straw-colored hair piled on his head. He appeared to be scowling at something or someone.

My stars, he looks very much like the planter just east of my plantation. Could this be his descendant?

He peered closely at the other portrait.

This must be his slave, likely a runaway. But, no, that's not possible, is it? The doctor told me the slaves had been freed.

Jacob's eyes had grown weaker in recent years. Holding the paper at arms' length, he scrutinized the words below the illustrations for a few moments. Then he gasped and dropped the paper as if it had been set alight. Giving it a vicious kick into the river, he fell onto his knees.

"Christ in Heaven!" He began beating the ground with his fists. "A goddamn nigger is president of the United States of America!"

29

August 14, 2012

Wherein Patrick receives an important clue that the impossible might in fact be possible.

"Um, Mr. Monroe, we were wondering if you noticed anything, um, like, unusual at the plantation?"

Patrick looked up from the paperwork on his desk to see his student Esdee standing in front of him, along with her classmates Benjamin, Lawrence, and Leisha. He wasn't overly surprised by their presence. After all, the discussion about post-emancipation days in the U.S. and the fate of millions of freed slaves had been thought-provoking and emotionally charged.

Esdee twirled a strand of one of her long, skinny braids as Benjamin piped up, "Before that crazy white guy came charging down the stairs at us."

Patrick raised his eyebrows at him.

"Um, well, you know... that re-enactor," Benjamin said quickly.

Patrick nodded. "Define 'unusual'," he said.

The students looked at each other and then Esdee leaned in toward Patrick to blurt, "Well, it seemed like one second there was nobody on the landing and the next second, there he was! I mean it was as if the guy just popped up out of nowhere."

"No, not exactly 'popped'. More like he came into focus out of nowhere," added Benjamin and then gave an embarrassed grin. His voice was changing and had cracked on the word 'focus'. "You know what I'm saying?" he continued. "Sort of like, there was nobody there, then there was a hazy image of a body, and then there he was."

"Definitely," Lawrence agreed. "Like he came into focus."

"Like an old-fashioned Polaroid photo," Leisha added.

Patrick gave them a hint of a smile. His speculation about whether anyone else had seen anything strange that day had just been confirmed.

"Did anyone else notice anything 'unusual' that afternoon?" he asked.

"Well, a few of the other kids thought they saw something, sir," Benjamin replied with a shrug of his shoulders, "But not like we did. Most of them were busy checking out the paintings and antiques and stuff.

"I got a picture of him," announced Leisha, a grin lighting up her face. "I took it just after we heard him on the landing yelling at us to get out. Here. See?"

She held up her iPhone. Patrick peered at the screen and there he was, the stranger who had been haunting his thoughts, the man who apparently despised him even though he'd had saved the man's life.

He swallowed hard and then flashed her a smile. "So you did."

Esdee was studying Patrick closely. "So, you saw something too, Mr. Monroe?"

"Yes, I believe so," he admitted. "And I've been wondering about that slept-in bed."

"Yeah! That was weird!" agreed Leisha.

"Look," Patrick said, "I'm glad you all came to talk about this with me today, but let's keep this between us for now. Ok? We can talk some more in a day or two."

The students glanced at each other and then nodded their heads, except for one.

"What about you, Leisha?"

"Oh, yeah, sure," she said and then looked down.

"Ok, everyone. You're going to miss your lunch. Thanks again for coming to see me about this."

Patrick checked the clock as he watched them file out of the room. Good, I've still got 20 minutes.

He pulled his lunch out of the bottom drawer of his desk and popped open his computer.

So, Leisha had managed to get a shot of the guy. He gave a chuckle. Patrick, c'mon. Almost all the kids carry smart phones or cameras these days. At least one of them would have taken a photo of the guy.

Considering she'd been at least 25 feet below him and had to blow it up to see his face, he thought Leisha's shot was surprisingly clear.

He opened up his email and found a message sent by Louise from the William's Plantation. She'd attached the jpeg of the plantation owner's portrait as promised. One click later and the painting from nearly 200 years ago of a middle-aged man with cold green eyes filled his computer screen.

"Holy shit," said Patrick under his breath. The resemblance to the man he'd revived was uncanny. "I don't believe it. Wow, oh, wow.

This is crazy!"

The same green eyes. The same—everything!

It seemed the impossible had actually happened: the man whose life he'd saved last week was Jacob Williams, a cotton planter from the 1800s and master of hundreds of slaves.

30

June 1841

Wherein Sadie and Margaret board a 'train' south to collect some precious cargo.

THANKS TO MISSUS MARGARET'S UNDERGROUND RAILROAD contacts in the Williams' plantation area, Sadie received word that her family had not been separated. And Margaret had also managed to pass along to Sadie's kinfolk the miraculous news that not only had she made it to freedom, she would be coming for them later that year.

On a windy, moonless night in early summer, Sadie's family gathered up their few belongings, some precious bundles of food and then crept out of their cabin. Silently praising God that the blowing wind covered the noise of their many pairs of feet, they stole through the darkness towards the woods. Upon reaching the cover of the trees, they headed toward a shallow stream they'd been told was just a short ways in, trying their best not to stumble in the darkness.

With Little Jenny on Jeremiah's back, the family eased into the shallow water. After wading upstream a ways, Jeremiah passed the little girl to his wife Ellen as he and his two youngest sons climbed onto the opposite bank. They took a few steps over to a large spreading tree looming in the darkness where Jeremiah put the smaller boy on his shoulders and whispered to him to wrap his arms high up near the branches. Then father and sons walked backwards in their tracks to the river and re-entered the chilly water. Jeremiah hoped these actions would confuse the hounds—who would soon be on the chase—into believing the family had taken cover in the tree, but then seemingly disappeared.

The fugitives turned and splashed along the stream in the opposite direction about twice as far as they had already come. When they found the tall white tree that served as a marker, they clambered up onto shore and then tramped a fair ways through the woods to a road. Jeremiah and his wife breathed sighs of relief when they spotted the faint outline of a covered wagon awaiting them. The family clambered up into the back and disappeared under piles of empty cotton sacks, which served to dry their wet clothes.

The wagon creaked along the road in the velvety darkness. Some time later it pulled up to a safe house where another wagon awaited.

Figuring Massa would do everything in his power to find them and haul them back to the plantation, Jeremiah and Ellen felt they had no choice but to split up their family and had requested the extra wagon. Not only would this make them harder to find, the chance that at least some of the family making it to freedom was greater. Jeremiah took the boys with him in the first wagon and his wife kept the girls with her in the other.

It was getting light when Ellen and the girls arrived at the next safe house. Their grief at leaving Jeremiah and the boys behind was nearly forgotten when they saw Sadie standing at the door. She raced to their wagon crying tears of joy and relief.

Sadie had left her little son Henry back in Ohio with trusted friends and was posing as Missus Margaret's lady's maid while they traveled, with Margaret's helper Joe acting out the role of their driver. Before they had to press on, she and her family were allowed to rest for a while and get to know each other again. Ellen's hair was cut in an effort to alter her identity. She cast off her worn and torn slave apparel and gratefully changed into more respectable clothing, as did her daughters. Then their journey continued in the light of day with Missus Margaret now posing as the mistress of five slaves: Sadie resumed her role as lady's maid, Ellen and the girls pretended to be house slaves, and Joe again held the reins to the horses.

Their wagon had departed about an hour after Jeremiah's had left the other safe house. His head had been shaved bald in an attempt to modify his appearance, but because of his size he was still easily recognizable. A decision was made that he would continue the next phase of the journey hidden under the cotton sacks. Several bags of freshly picked cotton were stacked into the back of the wagon to serve as a wall that would block prying eyes. His three sons were stowed in the back too, but unhidden for they were pretending to be the young slaves belonging to their "master"—a white farmer/underground railroad agent named Edward, who continued driving the wagon.

Everyone was well aware slave traders and bounty hunters would be hot on their trails, and though more than four years had passed since her escape, they would still be on the look out for Sadie. Prior to leaving Ohio, she had altered her appearance by changing her hairstyle and finding the largest bonnet she could.

All the escapees had adopted aliases. They had been trained to repeat their new names on command, recite that they belonged to Missus Margaret or to Massa Edward, recount what they did for them, what their "owners" did for a living, and where they lived.

Despite this cunning subterfuge—complete with counterfeit ownership papers—there were many close calls for Sadie and her group during the journey. Occasionally, their wagon was stopped and the occupants questioned by sentries or bounty hunters encountered along the road. Sadie, Missus Margaret and Joe held their breath while the children were interrogated. To their great relief and pride, the youngsters always acted out their roles to perfection, even Little Jenny, who, although too young to really understand where they were going and why, held her big sisters' hands to keep from getting scared by the strange white men.

One morning, as they rolled down a bumpy road after getting some rest at a safe house about twenty miles from the border of Ohio, two particularly nasty bounty hunters halted their wagon. Brandishing guns, the pair ordered Margaret to show her niggers' papers. After these were scrutinized the men studied Sadie and the others' faces closely, comparing them with a clutch of slave runaway posters. Fortunately for Margaret and her charges, there had been an upsurge in escapees, resulting in an overload of wanted posters. Those advertising their plantation's runaways hadn't been widely circulated yet and the bounty hunters hadn't received them. So, having no hard evidence, they reluctantly allowed Margaret and her party to move on.

The frequent detours down back roads toward the beacons—usually a single candle burning in a window signifying a safe terminal—pushed the runaways off the beaten path at times. But these side trips were necessary so that everyone could rest, eat and receive a short respite from the fear of capture.

When Little Jenny suddenly took sick, Missus Margaret and her charges were delayed almost a whole day. The owner of the last safe house was a doctor so they decided to backtrack several miles hoping he could take a look at the little girl. Happily, the problem stemmed from the fact that Jenny's eyes had been bigger than her stomach. The rich cocoa cake the doctor and his wife had served them had been too tempting. It seemed she had eaten three extra pieces when no one was looking.

Over a fortnight passed since the whole family last saw each other. Jeremiah and the boys had been transferred several times to other wagons along the way, which further helped them elude detection. They were the first of the two groups to arrive at Harmony.

After devouring some food, the boys decided to keep on the look out for the other wagon, even though their elders advised them it could be days before it showed.

When they spied it creaking up to the sentry stationed at the entrance of the community a short time later, they let out a big whoop. Jeremiah came running—his long legs a blur. He helped his wife down and hugged her so hard she had to tell him to stop, as she couldn't breathe. When he let her go, she dropped to her knees to kiss the ground.

Witnessing this joyful reunion was a pure tonic for Missus Margaret who was thoroughly exhausted. The months of planning and the long, harrowing journey south and then north again had been an epic struggle, but watching their happiness made her efforts so worthwhile.

Here in Margaret's little community of Harmony, Sadie's kin would be split up once more, but now by only by a few yards instead of many miles. They would be sheltered in two homes until a sufficient dwelling could be constructed to house them all.

They were all safe and sound.

At least for the time being.

31

August 8, 2012
Wherein Martin gets a talking to.

WHEN HIS REALTOR CELESTE called one day asking how things were going, Martin was pleased he could tell her better than expected. Then she asked how she could help his cause. "Well, that's awfully nice of you to ask, Celeste," he said, "but, would you have time?" He assumed she was far too busy with her job.

"I'll make time, Martin."

When his mother Charlotte popped in to the shelter later that day, he casually mentioned the offer as they were having a cup of tea.

She wasn't surprised in the least. "She's got a thing for you, Martin," she said and then blew on her tea.

"A thing?" he laughed. "C'mon. No, she doesn't."

"Darling. Open your gorgeous green eyes. I suspected it when I met her that first time, and then, when I saw her at your opening, she looked like she definitely wanted to be more than just your real estate agent. I'd say she's positively smitten."

He rolled his eyes. "Smitten. Now there's a word you don't hear too much nowadays."

"Don't roll your eyes at me, young man. It's a perfectly good word. And that's what she was," Charlotte replied with conviction. "Smitten."

"Well, she's never given me any clues that she's 'smitten'. She's always seemed 'all business' to me."

"That's because you just haven't been paying attention, Sugar. You've had a few other things on your mind, haven't you? I guess she gave up waiting for you to make the first move."

"Well, yeah. I have been a little distracted," he laughed. "But trust me, I usually notice when someone's interested in me. I guess I've been so focused I missed it."

"Unh huh. Well, I'm a mother. We notice things like that. Now, if I were you, I would make a little effort to get to know her better. She seems like a fine young lady."

He smiled. "Yes, she is a very fine person."

"So why don't you ask her out for lunch, Martin?"

"Hm. Well, I don't know. I'm really busy. And I like to eat lunch at the shelter—"

"Good grief, Martin. Ask her to lunch. I command you." Then she gave him that look.

Shit, he thought. There's no way I'm going to win this one.

"Look, Martin. She's smart. She's kind. She's beautiful. And she's smitten. And I want grandchildren before I'm an old lady. Ask her to lunch.

He gulped down some tea and then gave her a slow nod. "All right, Mom. I'll call her. Tomorrow.'

She smiled sweetly and patted his hand.

It's just lunch, he told himself. It's not like I'm asking her to marry me, or anything.

32

August 14, 2012
Wherein Patrick vows to find Jacob Williams.

HE PUT DOWN THE TESTS he was marking and looked at the print of Jacob's portrait for probably the 100th time. Those eyes were unmistakable; he would never forget their intense look of hatred at the plantation. Earlier that day, when Patrick had concluded that mysterious angry man had time traveled, he'd conducted a bit of research on the subject. While he'd never given time travel much thought before, although he had enjoyed H. G. Wells' book, The Time Machine, when he was a kid and he'd loved the classic movie, Back to the Future, he was soon mesmerized by the avalanche of information he found on the web. There were countless books and legends about it, not to mention droves of people claiming to have slipped forwards or backwards through time, or to have encountered supposed time travelers. Tearing himself away from the computer to mark tests had been a challenge.

One story was particularly riveting: the tale of Rudolph Fentz, a man who had supposedly vanished in 1876, then reappeared 74 years later in New York City. According to the Fentz urban legend, at approximately 11:00 p.m. on a June night in 1950, at an intersection near Times Square in New York City, a police officer spotted a strangely dressed young man standing motionless in the middle of the street. The officer approached him to offer assistance, but then the light at the intersection changed and the man walked toward the sidewalk, straight into oncoming traffic. He was struck by a taxi and killed.

No one at the scene could explain where the man came from, or how the hell he'd ended up in the middle of the busy intersection. He had stood frozen to the spot, until he had made his fatal mistake. And this is the point in the story where things became really intriguing. When police and paramedics arrived, they were perplexed by the man's appearance. He looked like he'd stepped right out of the 19th-century: thick mutton chop whiskers, a tall silk hat, buttoned cutaway coat, checkered pants, buttoned shoes. And when they searched his pockets, they found old coins and banknotes—none minted after 1876—and all almost in perfect condition. There was also a letter sent from Philadelphia dated from 1876 and some business cards for one Rudolph Fentz, presumably the deceased.

The case was considered an unsolved mystery for over 50 years until somebody found out it had been lifted from a story written by Jake Finney, best known for his book, Invasion of the Body Snatchers.

Maybe, thought Patrick, the plantation owner was Memphis's very own 'Rudolph Fentz', but in this case, he was the real McCoy?

He glanced at Jacob's portrait for the 101st time.

I wonder what happened at the hospital when he realized where he was? Did he go nuts?

He could just picture Jacob yanking his tubes out and yelling his head off.

And what about the staff? Did they suspect anything?

He gave a little snort. Let's face it, that's a busy hospital. Most likely they didn't have time to think much about Jacob. If they had, they may have figured he was a bum, 'cause he wouldn't have had any money. And if anyone had suspected something, wouldn't I have heard about it by now? Hell, the media would have a field day with a story like this.

Patrick linked his hands behind his neck and settled back into the couch.

The guy was like a modern day Rumpelstiltskin, he thought, but instead of waking up and discovering he was 20 years older, Jacob had opened his eyes just a day later, although, in reality, he was almost 200 years in the future.

Man, I can't even begin to imagine what it would it be like to go from horses and buggies when you fell asleep to wake up to cars and planes. It just boggles the mind. Of course, everything would be foreign and unfamiliar to him—not just cars and planes. The guy would be confronting buses, trucks, motorcycles, television, electricity, cell phones, computers, sky scrapers, strange looking clothing—you name it. Wow. The ramifications of a time traveler from the past stumbling around in the 21st century were pretty mind blowing. And this was a planter with hundreds of slaves who couldn't hide his loathing of black folk. Jacob's wealth and luxurious lifestyle were literally built on the blood, sweat, and tears of generations of black slaves. How could the man even wrap his head around the fact that they'd been freed?

And then Patrick threw his head back and roared with laughter.

Holy shit. I'd give up a month's salary to see Jacob's face when he found out a black man was running the country!

"What's so funny?" called his wife from the kitchen.

"Ah, nothing really, Janice," he said. "Just a silly thing that happened at school."

He was still reluctant to share his revelation about Jacob with her.

"Well, it must have been pretty funny. What was it?"

"Well," he thought fast. "It's kind of hard to explain. It was something pretty stupid that somebody said in the staffroom. One of those things where you had to be there."

"Huh. Ok, then. Sounds like your workplace is a barrel of monkeys."

"Yup. At times."

"Dinner will be ready soon. Don't go anywhere," she warned.

He had a habit of disappearing into the garage or his study just when it was about time to eat.

"Nope, I won't. Promise."

His mind returned to the puzzle of Jacob Williams.

If I were Jacob Williams, where would I go? Hm, that is, if I'd managed *not* to suffer another heart attack when I found out about President Obama.

Patrick heard his wife pull the roast out of the oven. His stomach instantly started growling.

"Smells great, baby!"

Home, he thought. Where else would Jacob go? That plantation was where he felt he belonged and was all he knew. I bet Jacob is trying to find a way to get back there, probably thinking he can find the wormhole or portal, or whatever it was he'd fallen through to get here, so he could go back.

Patrick dashed up to the study and fished his MacBook out of his briefcase. He pulled up his list:

"An Incident at The Williams' Plantation"

His fingers began tapping the keyboard.

Conclusions:

No. 1 Jacob Williams has traveled forward through time from the 19th century.

No. 2 His photo was taken just as he emerged into the 21st century. He paused for a moment and then typed:

No. 3 THE REASON HE HATES ME IS BECAUSE HE IS A SLAVE OWNER AND I AM A BLACK MAN.

Patrick stared at his computer absorbing the full implication of those last words. Why would a man, who had never laid eyes on him before, hate him so much? Of course, the fact that in Jacob's world, Patrick was a "nigga". And for Jacob, nigga = inferior being.

But to outright despise Patrick at first sight? His mind raced back to that fateful day. What had Jacob seen before he'd come charging down the stairs? What could have set him off?

He closed his eyes and thought.

Let's see: a black man had walked in, been introduced to some white folks and shaken their hands. Yes, that would have definitely been a shock. In Jacob's world blacks had to be inferior to maintain the status quo; masters literally whipped their belief system into them. So, he had probably thought to himself: 'well, look at that. Down there's one uppity nigger who hasn't had the program beaten into him yet. Boy's way too big for his britches.'

And then... oh, wow. Patrick's students had come in. But those weren't just any students entering Jacob's precious home. Those were 30 black kids standing in his front hall like they had every right to be there. And on top of that, there were three black parent volunteers.

Yup, that was a lot of black.

And to top it off, when Jacob had come to and seen his black face hovering just a few inches above him, well that would have about done him in!

Patrick amended his list:

No. 3 THE REASON HE HATES ME IS BECAUSE HE IS A SLAVE OWNER AND I AM AN UPPITY BLACK MAN.

He sat back and studied the screen. Then his fingers started flying:

Just what am I supposed to do with this information?

Am I supposed to look for him?

And, if I find him, then what?

He pressed the heels of his hands into his eyes and thought.

The dream.

I was about to whip a white man. A man who looked like Jacob.

An outrageous possibility came into sharp focus: Revenge? Was that it? To exact some kind of revenge in retaliation for the centuries of injustice borne by the black race at the hands of their white masters?

He had to admit the idea was certainly tempting. But no, that wasn't his style; he was an avowed pacifist. If he did manage to find Jacob, he needed another strategy.

But what?

"Hey up there. Dinner!" his wife called from downstairs.

Already? he thought. It seemed like he'd only been upstairs for a few minutes.

He saved and closed the word file and shut his laptop. He had an impulse to talk to Janice at dinner about his revelation about Jacob. But would she believe him? She was not the most open-minded person. And, after all, for most people, time travel was strictly a science fiction concept.

His mind contemplating the fickle notion of time, Patrick hurried down the stairs. His concept of time was so different now. It seemed the instant his eyes had locked on to that face in Leisha's iPhone photo at school, his whole concept of it had undergone a paradigm shift. That old movie cliché of a sequence of fluttering calendar pages depicting the passage of time popped into his head; it was like the pages were slapping him upside the face.

He smiled sheepishly at his wife as he slid into his seat at the table. "I know. I did it again. Sorry Janny Jan."

"Patrick Henley Monroe," she said with a stern look that he knew was just for show. "What am I going to do with you?"

"I think I'm hopeless, baby."

"Mm hm," she said. "Well, tomorrow, you cook."

"You know I can't cook, babe."

"Just make my favorite thing for dinner: reservations."

He laughed. "All right. I can do that."

As he bit into the delicious roast, Patrick's mind twigged on to one additional detail from the dream: the man had been pleading with him. He'd said: 'Take me wherever it is you wish to go.'

"Huh," he said. He glanced across the table at his wife who was giving him an expectant look.

"Absolutely delicious, babe," he said hurriedly. "You did it again."

She smiled back. "Uh huh. You're a lucky man, you know that?"

"I know it," he chuckled. "Believe me, I know it."

As he brought the first forkful of roast to his lips, Patrick had a revelation about what he should do with a time traveling southern plantation owner named Jacob Williams. Patrick was a teacher. Therefore, he would "teach" Master Williams a thing or two about humanity.

But first he had to find him.

33

July 1847

Wherein Sadie and Henry prepare for an important visitor.

"AND JUST WHERE DO YOU THINK you're goin', young man?"

The back door banged shut. Over his shoulder, her boy said, "I was just going to look at the stars, Ma. There's no moon tonight so I'm thinking maybe I can see the Milky Way." He turned to look at her and then hung his head a little bit. "Sorry about the door slamming, Ma."

"Huh. You turning into a stargazer now, Henry? You think I can't see with my own two eyes you trying to sneak out that door to do who knows what? Well, unh unh, you're not."

She rapped her wooden spoon on the kitchen table.

"Get back in here young man. I need you to peel these here spuds. Then I need you to go fetch some more wood for that stove. And then we'll see if you do any star gazin' tonight."

Henry turned on his heel and walked past her to the kitchen table, sighed and plunked himself back down on a chair. Sadie crossed her arms and stared at his mournful face.

"C'mon, chile! Those spuds ain't going to peel themselves!"

He picked up the knife and commenced peeling.

She watched him work. Guess the boy's decided the best way to get outside was to get a move on inside, she thought. He's got a bit of the devil in him, that's for sure. Now that he's getting older, I'm going to have to keep a close eye on him.

She gave a little chuckle. She had to admit though, he'd piqued her curiosity, as he so often did with all his ideas and notions.

"What's a Milky Way, Henry? Someone up there milking the cow that went and jumped over the moon?"

She knew Henry was trying hard not to roll his eyes, but he managed to keep a poker face, fearing she'd heap on more chores.

"No, Ma. The Milky Way is a great big band of white light that spreads clear across the sky. Best time to see it is when there's no moon and the night sky is darker than usual. Teacher started talking about it in her astronomy lesson last week."

"That so? Astronomy? My, oh my. Isn't my son all Mr. Smarty Pants, now? All your mama knows about is the North star."

Her beautiful green-eyed boy grinned and ducked his head.

"Aw, I'm not so smart, Ma. Just finding it interesting is all. I can show you if you like."

Sadie felt her heart melt a little. She reached out to stroke his cheek, marveling once again how the color of his skin reminded her of a cinnamon stick. She loved him so much it felt like her heart might crack in two.

Her mind rolled back to the morning when he came into the world. Her first impulse was to reject her newborn on account of who his father was and what he'd done to her. But how could she do that? Henry was just an innocent baby! He couldn't help who his daddy was. And besides, she didn't have any other kin here in those days. He was all she had. And, he was part of her.

"You know we got Missus Margaret, Joe and Mr. Douglass all coming over after church tomorrow. So we won't have no time to be peeling and shining and getting this place spic n' span before we leave in the morning."

Henry nodded his head. "Sure, Mama. I know how you like everything to be pretty as a picture."

"Well you better hurry on up and maybe you can see those milky stars before you head on to bed. Hm. Maybe I'll step out there too."

He grinned and set back to work. She left him to it and stepped into the parlor.

How Sadie loved her little house. The long wait for one of the other families to move out when a larger home had been built for them was well worth it. This house was perfect for the two of them—a simple place where she could raise her precious baby and live close to good people who looked out for them.

She gave a little start. Has it already been nine years? she thought. Time sure do fly.

She surveyed the small parlor room and smiled.

Huh, not too bad at all. Got that wood on the mantelpiece shined up real good, and the two oak chairs gleaming too. I sure hope Mr. Douglass will be comfortable here. Huh. I still can't believe that such a famous man as Frederick Douglass—author, speaker and escaped slave all in one—accepted Missus Margaret's invitation to come all the way to *Harmony*.

She gave a little gulp

And I can't believe he's gonna talk to me and some of the others who don't mind sharing stories about our lives before we got here and how we made our escapes. I still don't like to remember those times, but I promised Missus Margaret I'd be strong.

Her eyes focused on the rug.

Wish I could do something about this here ole carpet! It's so thin the pine floor peeks through. That old settee's seen better days too. Got a sag on one end where the spring's busted—little bit tough for some folk to heave themselves up out of there.

The corners of her mouth twitched and then she shook with silent laughter as she remembered when the preacher and his wife had come for tea.

Preacher I like just fine, but that wife of his… hoo boy, she's got some airs! She sure made that settee groan when she sat her hindquarters down on it. Didn't have a chance to seat her somewhere's else so I kept my fingers crossed she wouldn't bust right through it. Her husband had a good ole time helping her up outta there.

Sadie shifted her gaze to the fireplace where her looking glass sparkled above the mantle. It had cost her hours and hours of scrubbing laundry and a couple of her famous pecan pies in trade, but it had certainly been worth it. She loved how it brightened up the room, even on gloomy days.

She thought back to the morning when she and Henry finally moved into the house. She had held his little hand and announced to the walls:

"No more darkness for me. Unh unh. No siree. This house is going to be bright and shiny and full of light, full of love, full of goodness, full of music, full of peace, and full of joy."

Henry had looked around, and then tilted his head up. "Who there, Mama?"

She'd laughed and said, "Oh, don't mind your Mama none, Henry. I just knows we are going to be so happy here, that's all."

He had laughed too, and then clapped his chubby hands together.

"Me happy too, Mama!"

34

August 14, 2012
Wherein Jacob receives a sobering lesson about inflation when he looks for a place to lay his head.

He stopped walking and scanned the river. A deep frown unfurled across his brow.

Christ. The river's turning north! I'll have to retrace my steps. Oh, what a damn waste of time this has been.

Reversing his direction he realized with a start that the sun was on the decline.

Good Lord. Where will I sleep tonight?

At this fresh worry, what little strength he had in reserve seemed to fade away. He reluctantly studied the towers bristling over the small park.

I simply must find somewhere to rest. I will renew the search for my plantation tomorrow.

He leaned against a tree for a few moments trying to gather his wits. Hopefully, he could find lodging before the streets grew too dark to see.

His money! He hadn't lost it, had he?

He frantically searched his pockets. His hand found the bill.

Thank the Lord. At least I shall be able to find a suitable lodging house, enjoy a hearty dinner and down several whiskeys at a tavern. I could certainly use a drink after the day I've had. It's been almost a week since I last had one! And just think, I will still have a tidy sum left over.

Once again he marveled about why the doctor had bestowed such a generous gift.

He looked back at the city towers and spotted a shining golden sign: *Holiday Inn.*

That could be just what I'm after, he thought. Now then, if all goes well, before I know it, I will be slumbering in a soft bed. I'm certain things will seem better in the morning.

Summoning power he didn't know he still possessed, he set off toward the golden beacon, his mouth watering at the prospect of a tumbler of whisky.

When he finally reached the inn he eagerly entered the lobby and approached the reception desk. His relief that a young white man was at the helm was palpable.

The man looked up with a smile. "Good evening, sir. May I help you?"

"Ah, yes, my good man. I'd like to book lodging for the night.

"Yes, sir. Will that be cash or credit card?"

"I don't believe I understand. Credit card? Cash? I will pay with good American currency thank you."

Giving Jacob a bit of an odd look, the man said, "Ah, thank you, sir."

Jacob watched curiously as the man's fingers began striking tiny letters on a board on the desk in front of him. Peering at a thin black box that lit his face with a soft glow, the clerk smiled, "You're in luck, sir. We still have a few rooms available tonight. For one person our standard room rate is $168 plus tax."

Jacob was speechless for a few moments.

"I beg your pardon?" he gasped. "How much did you say?"

"A standard room is $168 plus tax."

"I am sure you must be mistaken, young man. That is an incredible sum."

The man's eyebrows lifted and he gave a brief pause before adding, "Well, sir, it is high season but since you are paying cash I may be able to discount this a little. Let me see what I can do." He began tapping the letters again.

A wan smile returned to his face. "Ah, yes. I can do something a little better for you. $142 for the night."

"This is absolutely preposterous." Jacob sputtered. "A room should cost no more than $1. What you are asking of me is... well, it's highway robbery!"

A woman appeared in a nearby doorway. "Is everything all right here, Tim?"

"NO, everything is not all right!" Jacob retorted. "Your man here is demanding an exorbitant amount of money for one night's lodging!"

"Tim? Can you explain please?"

"Well, yes, I think so," the clerk replied nervously. "This gentleman asked for a night's stay. I quoted him $168 and then discounted it to

$142 since he's paying cash, but he said it should only cost $1. And I did tell him it was high season," he added hastily.

"$1?" The woman said with a laugh. She moved over to stand beside the clerk. "Perhaps you should try somewhere else, sir. Please don't think me impertinent, but if you are low on funds you could stay in the men's shelter."

"What? How dare you insinuate that I, that I am—"

But words failed him. He could feel his cheeks flushing. The pair looked at him then spoke to each other in low tones. Jacob was rooted to the spot, unsure of what to do next.

"Well, then," he finally said when he had regained some composure. "I will make my leave. I would not stay here for all the tea in China!"

He stalked out.

To his chagrin, Jacob quickly learned this was not an isolated incident. After humiliating himself two more times, it became clear the princely sum of $20 would not even pay for a cot. It seemed he had no choice. Reaching into his pocket he retrieved the directions for the shelter provided by the good doctor. Finding an illuminated shop window by which to read it, he experienced a new surge of panic.

"How on earth will I find these streets?" he groaned.

He scanned his environs, trying not to panic. After several agonizing moments of indecision he determined his best option was to head further away from the river.

He trudged off down the street. When he neared the corner, he discovered—much to his relief—a map that appeared to be glowing from some hidden light source. It was displayed on a low board firmly planted into the gray walking slab. A small red arrow bearing the words "You Are Here" indicated a round spot on the map.

"What the Devil? How does the map know where I am?" He looked around to see if anyone might have been speaking to it about him, but there was no one in sight.

Oh, this is a strange and bewildering world, indeed, he thought.

He turned back to the board and examined it closely. With intense concentration, he was able to match up the streets to those on the doctor's note.

After another hour of wandering along the walking slab, peering up at street signs on one corner after another, he managed to locate the shelter. He stood frozen on the threshold wondering if he should flee. The place was crawling with darkies.

"Good evening. Can I help you?"

An older white gentleman had appeared before him. Jacob could barely speak—he was so disgusted and so dogged tired.

"Are you all right?"

"No, I am not," replied Jacob in a weak voice.

"Are you hungry? Dinnertime's over, but we've got some leftovers. Why don't you go sit at a table and I'll bring you a plate?"

Jacob looked around and saw that most of the niggers were playing cards, looking at newspapers or books, talking or just staring into space. He took a deep breath and slouched over to one of the tables. He found a spot next to the wall, with his back facing the room.

Fortunately, he didn't have long to wait. The white man reappeared with a plate of food and cutlery, which he placed in front of him. A few seconds later, he was back with a glass of water. "Sorry, we ran out of milk."

Jacob assumed a tumbler of whisky was out of the question.

"Thank you," he murmured.

"My name's Larry," he said, "And you are?"

"Jacob."

"Nice to meet you Jacob. After you eat, we can get you registered. You're in luck. Usually we're full by this time but we've still got a couple of available bunks."

Jacob nodded his head and picked up his fork. He was ashamed to be reduced to this level—to have to rely on charity, but he was ravenous and thirsty. There was a piece of chicken, some carrots, beans, rice and a bun. He began to eat. The food disappeared in a flash. It seemed he had never eaten anything quite so delicious. He was tempted to lick the plate.

Larry returned and told him where to place his dishes. Then he led Jacob to his desk where he took down his name and age. He wasn't surprised in the least when Jacob explained he didn't have an address or a social security card.

It was getting late so Larry pointed to the washing room where he could clean up and then directed him to the sleeping area. Inspecting a piece of paper on the wall, he pointed into the room, "There are two empty bunks near the middle. You can take one of those."

Jacob's eyes followed his finger. Most of the men were getting ready for bed or already lying down. He quickly looked away. How was he going to sleep amongst all these stinking baboons?

"Do you have a sleeping bag or some blankets?"

Jacob shook his head.

"Well, I might be able to rustle up some bedding for you. Lights out at 10:30," he continued. "Breakfast from 7:30 to 8:30. Here's a toothbrush. Soap's in the washroom. Come back to the desk when you're cleaned up and I'll give you some blankets if I can find any. Feeling better?"

Jacob nodded. He did feel slightly better now that he had received nourishment and a roof over his head. But mostly, he felt exhausted and full of dread thinking about the long night ahead of him.

He shuffled into the washing room to clean up and change. He was still not accustomed to toilets and running water, let alone using a brush to clean his teeth, but acknowledged to himself they were marvelous inventions indeed. He fished out his nightclothes, which he'd carried all day in the bag provided by the hospital. He was surprised and actually gratified to discover they'd been cleaned.

And then it was time. He couldn't delay the inevitable any longer. He trudged back to the front area and picked up a roll of bedding. Taking a deep breath, he walked down the brightly lit hall to the sleeping area. The large room was filled with rows of metal beds stacked in twos. Head down, he slunk into the middle section and managed to find a lower bunk that was still empty. He wedged himself in, pulled the covers up over his head, closed his eyes and gave a silent prayer: Dear Lord, please help me get through the night and when I wake up tomorrow, may it be the year 1837.

35

June 1850
Wherein Missus Margaret has no choice but to deliver terrible news to the people of Harmony.

"OH, DEAR GOD. NO...NO!" Margaret plucked the spectacles off her nose and then nearly broke her teacup as she put it hastily into the saucer. The news she'd been dreading for months was too utterly painful to continue reading. Her eyes found the man's portrait in the oval frame on the opposite wall. "Albert, it's happening!" she cried. "How will I explain this new madness to our flock?"

Her husband's beatific smile did not alter.

How Margaret hated to read the newspaper. So often it contained such terrible tidings: captures of escaped or even worse—freed slaves—and the wanted posters of runaways were so very disturbing. But she had no option. In order to stay abreast of current events, be apprised of who might turn up near the river and require rescue, and to determine which inhabitants of her little settlement were in the most danger of being kidnapped, she was compelled to sift through these reports.

Though Ohio had been a free state for almost 50 years, the designation had only meant that its citizens were not allowed to own slaves. Perversely, whites were mandated to turn in any and all runaways, and were prohibited from harboring them. Pro-slavery factions waited like cobras to pounce on any colored face in all the villages, towns and cities.

And now she had just learned that the horrible rumors were true: the nightmarish Fugitive Slave Act would become law in less than a few months. And it was much more brutal and insidious than the first Slave Act enacted some 50 years ago. All too soon, escaped and even freed slaves anywhere in the United States could be captured and arrested, jailed, and returned to their former owners. They could also be sold to the highest bidder, as if they were no better than beasts of burden. And those who aided runaways faced fines or even imprisonment.

It was almost too much to bear. She willed herself not to cry. She must be strong. The people of Harmony depended on her. And she knew they must depart very soon, before it became too risky to move.

Releasing a very long sigh, she again regarded her husband.

"Why, oh why, is mankind so wicked, Albert? I simply cannot understand it."

She studied her husband's earnest, sensitive face. How fortunate that despite years of protestations he'd finally agreed to sit for a portrait. After he passed, she still felt his presence. Looking at his image always gave her strength.

"I know you wish you were with me still to share my burden, dear one. Somehow, I will endure it."

Margaret and her husband Albert had been intentional lawbreakers; they had purposely done everything within their power to protect and help the brave souls who had risked everything to escape the hell of slavery. As Quakers their belief system of brotherly love embraced all—regardless of race or color.

Margaret had not only preserved their unique community of *Harmony*—the product of a Utopian vision she and Albert had shared and then managed to found in order to nurture and lift up the Negro—she had continued, against all odds, to expand it after he passed. The years had been rewarding but oh, so very difficult.

Keeping out ruthless and greedy bounty hunters trolling the state for escaped slaves was a never-ending struggle. Margaret, Joe and all the inhabitants could ill afford to let their guard down for, in an instant, all would be lost. Sentries were posted at each entrance of the small community and every inhabitant kept a close eye on the wooded areas to ensure vigilantes weren't sneaking through the fields. A tower had been constructed to allow a broader lookout. There had been several close calls over the years, including two attempts to burn down the community. Several times bounty hunters had almost infiltrated *Harmony* but had been thwarted in time. A simple but effective warning system based on whistles and bells had saved the day.

Without Margaret and Albert's pedigree and wealth, their unique settlement would not have been possible. Sheltering the runaways and providing them with a chance at freedom in their own simple but sturdy homes—hand-built by members of the community—the couple also strove to empower the residents through the gift of knowledge.

A school had been established where children and adults alike could learn to read, write, do figuring and nurture their creative sides. A church was built where all could worship and make joyous music. A system of trading had been developed which encouraged the manufacture of goods and production of agriculture so they need not rely on the outside world for food and other necessities, excepting the occasional luxury item, such as the looking glass Sadie so cherished.

Harmony would soon celebrate 15 years. During the community's eighth year, Margaret's husband had died. Despite her grief, she had taken the reins and continued to deal with the constant backlash from those opposed to their radical experiment. From time to time, other Quakers who shared her convictions lived amongst them in *Harmony*, and she welcomed their support and strength.

In a sense the inhabitants of *Harmony* lived in a fortress; only a few of the biggest and strongest men could venture beyond its boundaries due to the genuine risk of capture and repatriation into the bonds of southern slavery. And they had no choice but to arm themselves in the event of an attack.

Margaret rubbed her gnarled fingers. They were bothering her more than usual that morning. The knuckles were swollen and red. Perhaps a storm was brewing?

With a rueful smile, she said aloud, "Yes, a storm is on its way, isn't it Albert? Hopefully, with God's help, we can all weather this latest assault."

She dropped her eyes back to the pages on the table. Her stiff fingers slowly folded up the paper and pushed it aside. She gazed again at her husband's face.

"I know. I mustn't complain, Albert. Somehow I will summon the courage to tell them. I know it's best just to come right out with it, and the sooner the better."

She sighed again. She could foresee no other choice for any of *Harmony's* denizens.

"How I shall miss them. Especially Sadie and young Henry."

She shivered to think about the packs of salivating "Christian" wolves counting the days until they could legally swoop down on the inhabitants of *Harmony* who, through a simple twist of fate, had been born the "wrong" color. And she knew that her days here were numbered as well. Despite her advancing years and deep roots in the region she would have little choice but to find a new home, and more than likely, not in the United States of America.

Margaret's attention was drawn back to Albert's portrait. If he were here, she knew he wouldn't waste another moment. Without hesitation, she summoned Joe and asked him to request that everyone congregate at her home as quickly as possible for an important meeting.

He nodded and hurried off.

She folded her aching hands to say a quick prayer. As she awaited everyone's arrival, she tried to shake off the disturbing notion that she might soon be mistaken for the grim reaper.

36

August 15, 2012

Wherein Jacob receives yet another rude awakening, then relives a distant memory.

SOMEHOW, HE MANAGED TO SLEEP. It was not a pleasant slumber for it was frequently interrupted by the snores, groans and whimpers of the men around him. And it seemed every time he fell back under, someone climbed down from a creaky bunk to stagger off to the washing room.

And then, all too soon, the night had turned into day; the room was bright with artificial light. Jacob opened his eyes to see the bottom of a mattress a few feet above his head and a pair of legs walking by. He uttered a low curse. He was still in the wrong time and the wrong place.

He remained where he was, gloomily staring at the mattress bottom as he waited for things to settle down. Then he swung his legs over the side of the bunk and eased himself up. He groaned. His legs and lower back ached from all the miles of walking the previous day. Kneading his lower back muscles, he reached down for his things and wandered off toward the washing room.

"Morning, man," a darkie said, rinsing his hands at the sink.

Jacob ignored him.

The nigger was studying him.

"Saw you come in late last night. Where you from?"

"If you only knew," Jacob muttered.

He performed his ablutions and drifted into the main area of the shelter to discover a raggedy line of men shuffling alongside a table. Clutching bowls and spoons they stopped at a big pot where a dour young woman was doling out steaming mush. Then the men plucked some fruit from several large platters, filled cups with milk or coffee and preceded to one of the long tables.

The gruel smelled good. Ravenous yet again, Jacob moved into line and picked up a bowl. The queue moved slowly but steadily and eventually he received his share. He glanced about for somewhere to sit. There were a few white faces in the room, but the vast majority was black.

Ha, he thought. So much for emancipation! This lot has evidently not accomplished much, which is not surprising, given their inferior brains.

He spotted an almost respectable looking white man. He walked over and settled down beside him. The man looked at Jacob and nodded. Jacob returned the nod.

The man sighed. "Wish they had molasses. Been a long time since I've had any."

Jacob's spoon paused halfway to his mouth as another breakfast table from a very long time ago came into sharp focus. He was nine years old. The Reverend had joined his family for their mid-morning meal after church and had just given the blessing. Jacob noticed his father frowning at their servant, Dinah, who was pouring molasses on Jacob's younger sister's flapjack.

"Too much!" his father roared, and then rose from the table to give Dinah a beating. When his hands hurt too much he removed a shoe and beat her with its heel until she could no longer endure the blows without screaming and raising her elbows to ward them off.

Jacob's father bellowed for one of their largest male slaves to come hold Dinah's hands behind her back and then continued her punishment. Though she collapsed onto to the floor screaming in agony, he continued the beating.

Finally, his father tired. The punishment stopped. Dinah pulled herself up and staggered outside so she could wash off the blood. She hobbled back in while the family was still at the table. Her face was an almost unrecognizable mask: lips, chin, nose, cheeks swollen twice their normal size. She re-commenced serving them.

When Dinah left the room once again, she bowed and thanked his father—her master.

Yes, Dinah had certainly been taught a lesson that day.

Jacob returned to the present. "I don't care much for molasses," he said to his neighbor, and then put his spoon of oatmeal into his mouth.

While he filled his belly, Jacob noticed the manager moving about the crowded room. Had he slept there as well?

I must speak to him after I break my fast to see if he can help me find the plantation, he thought.

He looked at the long, curved yellow fruit on his plate, unsure what to make of it. He watched how his neighbor peeled his before taking a bite of the white inner meat. Mimicking his actions, Jacob was surprised by how soft and tasty the curious fruit was. When he finished the last bite, he pushed back his chair and walked toward Larry.

Someone touched his arm.

"Hey, man. You're supposed to put your dishes over there in the dish bin."

Jacob glanced down at the hand on his arm. It was brown. He slowly looked up into the face of the darkie from the washing room.

"Get your cotton-pickin' hands off me," hissed Jacob.

"Motherfucker," said the nigga and made a move towards Jacob and then thought better of it when Larry strode over.

"Hey, what's going on, guys? Is there a problem here?" Larry asked.

"There most certainly is," Jacob replied struggling to keep his voice level. "This impertinent nigga had the nerve to tell me what to do."

Larry glowered at Jacob. "Hey, man. We don't tolerate that language or that kind of attitude here! Whatsoever. You will have to leave. But first, apologize to Rodney."

His lips pursed tightly together in disgust, Jacob glanced around and noticed a sea of menacing black faces staring at him. He turned back to Larry and the nigga who was waiting expectantly.

Jacob gulped and then straightened his shoulders. "Apologize? To him? Ha! I'll do no such thing!"

He snatched up his bag, and stormed out of the shelter.

37

August 15, 2012

Wherein Patrick begins his search for a man lost in time.

HE PULLED UP HIS LIST OF MEMPHIS HOMELESS SHELTERS on his Mac. It had only been two days since Jacob had been discharged from the hospital; he couldn't have made it far. There weren't many so Patrick hoped it wouldn't be difficult to learn if Jacob had turned up at any of them.

After three attempts, he hit pay dirt.

"Yes, there was a man by that name here."

Patrick noted some irritation in his voice.

"There was?"

"Yes," the man said a bit curtly. "He left this morning."

"Any idea where he went?" Patrick crossed his fingers.

"No. He didn't say. He was asked to leave. Right after breakfast."

"He was? Why, if you don't mind my asking?"

There was a pause. "Are you a relative or a friend, sir?"

"Neither. I just met him recently. I'm hoping to track him down. I, uh, need to give him some important information."

The man cleared his throat. "Well, if you must know, he made some racially inappropriate comments."

"Oh. I'm not surprised. Um, I mean, I'm very sorry to hear that. But, the truth is, he really can't help himself."

The man gave a snort of laughter. "Really. And why would that be?"

"Well, it's a long story. Which relates to why I need to find him. Did you happen to notice which way he went?"

"Yes. I wanted to make sure there would be no further trouble so I watched him. He headed north.

"Thanks very much for your help."

Patrick hung up and pondered his next move. It was only 9:45 am. Jacob was probably still wandering around trying to figure out how to get to his plantation. Then he would be looking for some lunch. If he tried another shelter, they probably wouldn't take him in. After the kind of behavior that got him kicked out he'd certainly be blacklisted.

He smiled as he considered the irony inherent in that word.

"Hunh," he said out loud. "I guess Master Williams is finally getting a taste of his own medicine."

38

August 15, 2012

Wherein Jacob's chance discovery gives him hope.

HE SLUMPED AGAINST THE WALL, his head bumping a little against the rough bricks. His eyes stared off into the distance, but saw only a foreign place that he loathed. His breakfast lay in his belly like a lead weight.

Rubbing his stomach he tilted his head back and watched a bird soaring high up in the sky. But, no... It wasn't a bird. It was some otherworldly contraption that could fall down to the earth at any moment. How could it possibly stay up there?

"I have been kidnapped," he muttered. "Taken against my will to this hell on Earth."

He looked at the busy road and grimaced.

How I hate this world with all its noisy contraptions and ridiculous laws. Who would curse me in this way? All men are 'free and equal'. Bah. That goes completely against the natural order of things.

A young couple strolling past caught his attention. Even though the man was black he was holding the white woman's hand. Jacob resisted the urge to lunge out at them and wrench their hands apart. Instead he hocked up some phlegm and spit it on the grey slab after they passed him by. A pair of women walking past gave him a wide berth. He gave them a glare and they hurried off.

"Ha," he said and rubbed his mouth with the back of his hand, and then squeezed his eyes shut. How much more of this world can I bear? he asked himself. He felt such despair. He knew that even if he did find his plantation,would he possibly find his way backwards in time?

He thought of his children. With a start he realized he longed to see them again. Usually, they were more of an afterthought for him.

Do they miss me? he wondered. Do they even know I'm gone?

He blinked back tears as a new and terrible insight occurred to him: If I can't find my way back I may very well have only one choice left to me—I will take my own life.

Suddenly, he was doubled over in pain. Porridge and fruit splashed onto his shoes. A voice laughed.

"That'll teach ya, motherfucker!"

Jacob lifted his head a little to see a darkie walking backwards away from him. He was gesturing with his middle fingers.

"Bastard!" Jacob croaked, struggling to straighten up. He recognized the nigger from the shelter he'd confronted earlier. "Wait until I catch you!"

His breath had been knocked out of him. People stepped away as he lurched along holding his aching stomach. Far up the street he could still see the back of the nigger, but he soon disappeared from sight.

Jacob's steps slowed until they stopped altogether. He stood motionless in the middle of the sidewalk with his head bowed, hands limp at his sides. He noted how much uglier his shoes were with bits of his breakfast stuck to them.

"You all right?" said a voice.

Jacob slowly looked up. An older white man was standing beside him, looking concerned.

"You ok?" the man said.

"OK? I don't know what you mean," said Jacob and then looked the man up and down. He didn't especially like what he saw. He was thin—too thin—and his clothes were dirty. He carried a bulging dark green bag over his shoulder.

"Just thought y'all could use some help, is all," continued the man.

"No! I am perfectly fine," said Jacob walking away as best as he could. He certainly did not wish to associate with a person of no means.

He noticed a crowd about hundred yards down the street. Though his stomach still ached he found himself mildly curious. He cautiously headed in their direction, but as he drew close, he hesitated. There were too many black faces in the mob for his liking.

A fence separated the mob from a cluster of people standing on the steps of a fortress-like building lined with immense columns.

That could have been built in my time! he thought.

Curious, he moved toward the barrier, taking care to stay clear of the darkies. On the other side of the fence stood a row of stern officers of the law, garbed in black from head to toe, batons in hand. He was astonished to see the vast assortment of weaponry hanging from their belts. The word POLICE was stamped on the clear shields propped in front of them.

He took a nervous look around. Was a war about to erupt? Where could he go to take cover? He turned back to stare at the officers. Would they protect him? He was not heartened to see two niggers in their midst.

Jacob caught his breath. On the steps behind the officers, scrawny white youths with shiny, bald heads were waving placards bearing the words *White Power*.

"My God," Jacob murmured. "I don't believe it! Perhaps I am not alone, after all."

Figures in flowing white robes topped with pointed hoods stood above them. Other figures—clad entirely in black like the officers—waved large flags, some adorned with three black letter Ks.

A robed figure raised a large white horn to its mouth. As if by magic, his voice reached Jacob's ears.

"We, the KKK, hold this rally to protest the change of the Nathan Forrest Park name. This park honors the memory of the great Confederate hero, Lieutenant General Nathan Bedford Forrest, the Klan's first Grand Wizard."

"White power! White power! White power!" chanted his colleagues.

Boos and catcalls erupted from the people crowded on Jacob's side of the barricade. They outnumbered the small group on the steps by at least five to one.

A tall Negress with frizzy long hair cupped her mouth with her hands and screamed, "How come there's no park for Martin Luther King?"

The dark mob began to chant, "M L K! M L K! M L K!"

Ignoring their bellows, Jacob elbowed his way closer to the fence, his face joyous.

If I'm unable to return to my time, he told himself, I now have an option besides death. I will take up with the KKK!

39

August 15, 2012

Wherein Martin meets his realtor for a quick but memorable lunch.

CELESTE RIFLED THROUGH HER CLOSET. What to wear? What to wear? Martin's lunch invite to discuss her volunteer role at his shelter was today. At last. He'd told her the restaurant was her pick, so she'd suggested a fun sushi place a short drive from his shelter. It had a huge bar encircled by a little stream of water with tiny wooden sushi boats floating on it. Whenever something caught your fancy, you simply grabbed a plate off a boat.

Finally, she settled on a sleeveless electric blue jersey dress with a cowl neckline and a red belt that showed off her long straight black hair. Then she stood on her tiptoes to pull down a box from the shelf above her head. She didn't have an opportunity to wear these babies very often: fire-red Manolo Blahniks. She normally wore low heels for work because she walked so much. She brushed some specks of dust off their toes. Blahniks were basically a waste on her "on again, off again" boyfriend Shayne, but she had the distinct impression Martin was a legman. Turning this way and that in front of the hallway's full-length mirror, she nodded at herself in approval. Oh, yeah. These will do nicely. The pumps added a good three inches to her height and accentuated her calf muscles. She'd been training for a half marathon over the last couple of months, but hadn't realized she'd added that much muscle.

It looked like rain, so she grabbed an umbrella and headed out. She was always punctual, but this time she wanted to make sure she was at the restaurant nice and early, well before Martin got there.

The place was hopping, which was surprising given that it was early for most people to have lunch. She was irritated with herself for not making reservations. Luckily, she spotted a couple of empty stools by the sushi bar. As she settled in she realized she was a tad nervous, which was unlike her. Her rule was not to drink at lunch, but after she settled onto her stool, she ordered a sake to calm herself a bit and soak up some liquid courage.

The server smiled as she set down the drink in front of Celeste. Then she cocked her head to study her.

"Wow, girl. You look hot."

Trying not to grin, Celeste sniffed her sake and took a sip. "Mmm. Thanks, Doris."

"Meeting Shayne?"

"Ah, no. A client. He should be here any minute." Celeste made a show of checking her phone. Shayne was a friend of Doris's.

Doris arched an eyebrow and walked away.

Celeste took another sip of sake and looked at her phone again. It was a few minutes past twelve. What if he doesn't come?

Jesus, Celeste. Get a grip! He's a good guy. He won't stand you up—unless maybe something happened at the shelter?

Her worrying was interrupted as Martin strolled into the restaurant and scanned the busy room. She gave a little wave and he started toward her, his arms swinging gracefully, making his shoulders roll from side to side in a way that made her breath catch in her throat.

Oh, yeah, arriving early was definitely worth it.

She swiveled her stool around to say hello. His black curls were sparkling with raindrops.

"I guess it started raining," she said. "Or you just got out of the shower?" she winked.

"Ha, it's pouring, actually." He gave her a subtle once over. She saw his eyes widen when he spied her shoes.

I knew it, she told herself triumphantly.

He pulled out the stool next to her and sat down.

"Wow. Boats."

She laughed. "Thought you might like to do a little fishing."

"Ha! Last time I did any fishing I was a little bitty boy. Thought I caught a big one, but when I pulled up my hook, a beat-up old umbrella was hanging from it."

Celeste laughed as she imagined an adorable, little Martin staring in dismay at his big "catch".

He glanced around the room for a few seconds then trained his luminous green eyes on her. "Sorry I'm late. Had to stop to take a call. There was a bit of a kerfuffle at *Sanctuary*."

"Oh? How so?"

"Not much to tell, really. Just that we received a call from one of the overnight shelters to keep an eye out for a certain person. Seems he doesn't like black people a hell of a lot and isn't shy about showing it."

"Rcally? I gather he appeared."

"Yup."

"So what happened?"

"My manager didn't want him to stay, but I told her to give him a chance, but to keep a very close eye on him."

"I hope everything goes ok."

He nodded. "I'm thinking maybe he was just having a bad day. Sounded to me like he was a pretty typical client. Hungry, tired, a little paranoid—she said it seemed like he just wanted to get out of the rain and be left alone."

Celeste smiled. Martin really did have a heart of gold. Or maybe, he was just incredibly naive.

He regarded the flotilla of Sushi boats. "M m m! Haven't had Sushi in ages, and I do love it," he remarked as he grabbed a plate of rainbow roll. "This looks delicious." As he gobbled a piece down, his eyes closed with pleasure. "Can't believe I've never been here before."

Doris appeared at Martin's elbow to take his drink order.

"I see your client's arrived, Celeste," she said with a nearly imperceptible wink. "Welcome to Quick Sushi, sir. Would you care for a beverage?"

He flashed his dazzling smile at her. "Well, normally I don't drink during the day, but beer is certainly tasty with Sushi."

"Shall I bring you a Sapporo then?" she said, grinning from ear to ear.

Aha, Celeste thought. She's under his spell.

"Perfect."

Doris hurried off to fill his order. Martin turned to Celeste and lifted an eyebrow.

"What?" she said.

"Something I should know about?"

"Oh, don't mind Doris. She, ah, likes trying to stir things up a bit."

"I see." He chuckled and tucked into his sushi.

A few moments later, he gave her a searching look. "So, I hope you don't think I'm being rude or presumptive or anything, but I was wondering something."

"Oh? What would that be?"

He flashed another killer smile and her heart skipped a beat.

"Are you from around here?"

"Yes, and...?"

"Well, I've been trying to figure out something. Is your background Japa…"

"Ha! Nope."

"Chinese?"

"Nope."

"Vietnamese?"

"Nope."

"Ok. I give up."

"Malaysian."

"Really? A Malaysian in Memphis. Hunh. Has a nice ring to it."

She chuckled. "Thanks. I think."

Doris returned with Martin's beer and neatly poured some into his glass.

Martin thanked her and raised his glass to Celeste. "Cheers."

She raised her cup and gave him a big smile. "Cheers to you."

He took a swig of his beer. "Ahh. Tastes so good." He smacked his lips a little and then gobbled down another slice of sushi.

"You certainly enjoy your food," she said.

"Oh, yeah. Definitely," he replied with a wink. "Especially sushi. Great choice of restaurant, Celeste."

She caught herself staring at his eyes. That color! She'd never seen anyone with eyes like his before. Then she looked at his mouth. Such nice full lips. She could feel her cheeks reddening as she realized her imagination was running away with her.

C'mon, girl, she told herself. Get a grip!

She swiveled her stool to face the sushi stream, hoping he hadn't noticed her pink face. She busied herself choosing which plate to pick up next.

When she turned back she saw him staring at her.

He blinked and then said. "You have really nice hair."

"Why, thank you," she said. "I've grown pretty attached to it."

He chuckled. "So, you were born here, Celeste?"

She closed her eyes for a moment. Sometimes, it was hard to remember that she had lived anywhere else. When she opened her eyes, she found Martin staring at her shoes. "Uh, well," she said, a bit thrown off, but pleased nonetheless. "I was born in Malaysia, but we moved here when I was a little girl. You see, Mom's a huge Elvis fan. When my dad wanted to emigrate to the States, she voted for Memphis."

"Elvis? Interesting."

She gave a little laugh. "Well, she's got Dad wrapped around her little finger so here we are. Ta da. Mom goes to Graceland all the time."

He paused for a moment as if considering something, then gave her another lightning fast once over.

"Well, I for one am certainly glad your mom got her way."

Celeste's heart did another little flutter. She tilted her head a little and smiled. "Why, thank you. And speaking of fish," she said. "Sometimes I do feel a bit like one—a fish out of water, that is. Our community is pretty small."

"Have you ever been back to Malaysia?"

"A couple of times." She poured herself some more sake. "Kind of feel like a fish out of water there too." With a twinkle in her eye, she added, "I hope you don't think I'm being rude or presumptive or anything, but I imagine you were born here?"

"And why would you think that?" he answered with a mock frown.

"Um, no reason," she grinned and snatched another plate off a boat.

"Well, good guess," he said with a laugh. "My family's from the country. Not too far away. My grandparents have a small farm, but my mom decided city life fit her style better. After she met my dad in college and they got married, they decided to move to Memphis."

"Good thing. Somehow I can't picture you riding a tractor."

"You'd be surprised," he said with a grin, his long brown fingers expertly nabbing another piece of sushi with his chopsticks.

"You're pretty good with those."

"Thanks. Haven't lost my touch," he winked. "Used to eat a lot of sushi and Szechuan in my college days. Anyway—tractors. I go back to visit my grandparents when I can, but I feel kind of bad 'cause it's been a while. I've been so damn busy. Anyway, when I was about 13 my grandpa taught me how to drive one. Mostly I just helped him haul things around. They don't work the farm anymore. They've got a little veggie patch and that's about it."

"Sounds nice. What crops did they used to grow?"

"Cotton, corn, and tomatoes."

"Cotton? Wow. I didn't even know that was still grown around here."

"Yup. There's still an industry, but not like in the good ole days."

He furrowed his brow and grew quiet. She sensed something was bothering him.

"They were slaves, you know. My grandparents' great grandparents, that is."

Celeste looked at him. "Really. Here in Tennessee?"

He nodded.

"Wow. That's crazy. I mean, um—" She looked down and smoothed the napkin on her lap, hoping that she didn't sound stupid. She knew almost zilch about slavery and she'd never met anyone who was a descendant—or if they were, they hadn't talked about it. "Do you know much about what life was like for them?"

"Not a whole lot. My grandparents told me a couple of things, but I felt like it upset them, so I didn't pester them too much. And my parents, well, whenever I tried to ask them about those days, it seemed like they just wanted to forget. They were involved in the Civil Rights movement. Lost a couple of friends during a protest."

Celeste gave a little gasp. "Oh, I'm sorry to hear that."

Martin's phone buzzed. His eyes narrowed as he checked the call display.

"Damn. It's the shelter. I told them to call only if it was urgent. Hope you don't mind?"

"No, not at all. Go ahead."

He slid his finger across his iPhone. "Yes, Brenda."

Celeste noted a frown feeling its way across his smooth forehead as he stared at the uneaten sushi on his plate.

"Oh, really?" he said. "Ok, I'll get back as fast as I can."

Pocketing his phone, he looked at Celeste and said with reluctance, "Hate to do this to you, but I've really gotta get back to the shelter."

"Oh, that's all right," she said, hoping to sound convincing. "Hope everything's ok.

"Hope so, too," he said as he stood up. He quickly fished out his wallet. "Here, I hope this covers lunch." He put $40 on the table.

"I think that's too much—"

"Don't worry about it. Let's do this again next week."

Her heart leaped. "Um, sure… I would love that."

"Good. I'll call you. Promise. We didn't even get a chance to talk about what you can do for us at *Sanctuary*!"

He flashed another movie-star smile and then she was treated to the delicious view of him walking away.

40

August 15, 2012
Wherein Abby and Roger formulate a plan for if and when they find Jacob.

ROGER LEANED AGAINST THE DOOR FRAME of Abby's office, watching her rifle through charts.

"How's the hunt going?" she said, pulling out the one she needed.

"Nothing yet, but I think I'm getting close. I had given him directions to one of the overnight shelters. Sure enough he'd been there."

"And?"

"They kicked him out."

"Damn. Well, I'm sure they were happy to see him go," she said with a shrug. "So, what now?"

"Well, I'll check the other shelters, although it's likely he's been blacklisted and they may not let him in."

"Ha. That's a good one," observed Abby.

"What?"

"Blacklisted?"

"Oh, yeah. Ha. Guess that is kind of ironic considering how 'tolerant' he is of people of color."

"I wonder what he did, or said," Abby murmured as she wrote something in her chart.

"I'm sure it wasn't pretty."

"No doubt."

Roger linked his fingers and stretched his arms above his head. He hadn't been getting to the gym lately and he was beginning to pay for it. His upper back was tightening up from all the computer work he'd been doing.

"So, I can't see where else he'd go besides another shelter. Unless he somehow made his way back to his plantation?"

"Yeah. Maybe. Or maybe he's dead,"

"My, my, aren't we cheery?"

"Let's face it Roger," she said, pushing her glasses up onto to the top of her head and kneading the spot where they'd sat on her nose, "Memphis isn't exactly Mayberry, RFD, you know."

He chuckled. "That's certainly the understatement of the decade. Well, if he is still drifting around somewhere the fact the media hasn't found him yet means he's blending in. Somehow."

"Just another lost soul on the streets of Memphis," she surmised.

Roger shrugged. "Yeah. I'm sure if anyone actually talked to him, they would probably think, 'well, here's a homeless person who's not right in the head. Better stay clear'."

"Which is why most people pretend they don't see them."

"Time travelers?"

She giggled.

"Oh, right," he winked. "Homeless people."

"Figured out yet what we're gonna do when we find him, Roger?"

"Not exactly, although I definitely would love to question him about life back in his day."

"I still almost can't believe it," she said in a near whisper, as she closed her chart. "How could someone from 1837 be wandering around in the 21st century? In Memphis of all places."

"Well, it apparently did happen. And I can't wait to find him."

"God. I can't imagine what it would be like to be stuck in time," she mused. "What else in life would come close to that?" She drummed her fingers on her desk, lost in thought, looked at him and said, "Being left behind in the space station after it was mothballed?"

"Hm. No, not quite." He stared at his shoes and ran his fingers through his mop of hair. "I've got it," he said and gave her a triumphant smile. "There's this isolated island off the coast of India. The people are still living in the Stone Age and want no contact with the outside world. They're pretty hostile to outsiders. In fact, they try shooting them with bows and arrows. I think getting stranded on that island would be the closest thing to it."

"Wow, how fascinating in this day and age," she nodded, her eyes wide. "Yeah. I think that's close to what Jacob's going through, except, of course, he's gone the other way in time."

"Indeed, he has. Although sometimes I think our civilization is still in the Stone Age about certain things," he said with a little smile.

And then his smile faded. "You know, when the press gets wind of our time traveler, all hell will break loose."

Abby stood up and grabbed her lab coat. "You're right, Roger. We need to find him and tuck him away somewhere safe. For his own good."

As she put her stethoscope around her neck, she noticed Roger had a strange look on his face.

"You kind of look like the cat that ate the parakeet."

"Canary."

"Right."

"Do I?"

"Come clean, doctor."

He opened his mouth, but before he could say anything she said, "Wait. I think I know what you're going to say. And we can't do that, of course."

"Of course."

"No matter how tempting it would be to be the ones—"

"Who introduce a time traveler to the world?" he whispered.

Abby gathered her charts in her arms and flashed a vivacious smile. "But it is certainly food for thought, Roger."

He grinned. "And speaking of food, what are you doing for dinner tonight?"

"Um, well, I was supposed to go to my parents for dinner, but I begged off. I just couldn't do it tonight. Said I was busy. But I wasn't. Don't tell."

"Well, now you don't have to feel guilty. You'll be busy having dinner with me."

"Well, I have a policy not to go out with work colleagues, but—"

Roger grinned. "That sounds like a 'yes' to me. I'll pick you up at seven. If you'll give me your address, that is."

She laughed. "I will. But later. Gotta fly."

He stepped aside as she passed through her office door to begin her rounds. He breathed deeply as she sailed by.

Mmm… flowers.

41

June 1850

Wherein Sadie frets about her mother's haunted memories, and then is summoned to a troubling meeting

WAKING UP WAS STILL A WONDER. For the first few moments she would lie in bed wondering where she was. And then a smile would light up her face for she was safe in her very own house. And when Sadie thought about her family her smile would widen for they were safe and sound too, and just down the road.

Before rising to start breakfast, she usually allowed herself a few more moments to revel in the joyous knowledge that she'd done it. She had set them all free—with the help of Missus Margaret, Joe, and many good souls all the way south to Tennessee and back up to Ohio. Every member of her close kin had been rescued and brought up to Harmony. Gone for good was the deep, dark pool of sadness that once troubled her day and night, tormenting her with doubts as to whether she would ever see them again.

Giving her arms and neck a good stretch, she said aloud, "Yes, Lord. It seems anythin's possible, if you put your mind to it."

Then her face clouded. Sometimes when she would walk down to her parents' house, she'd find her Ma or Pa looking at nothin', but their bodies would be shaking like they were staring at somethin' awful.

The first time it had been her mother. Sadie had rushed to her side and placed her hand on her forehead to see if she had a fever. "Mama, y'all right?"

Her mother's head had jerked, then her eyes shifted to Sadie's face, but to her horror, her mother stared at her like she didn't know who she was.

"Mama?" Sadie had cried. "It's me, Mama!"

Her mother kept on staring, and then said, "Who?"

"Sadie, Mama! It's me, Sadie! I'm right here, Mama."

With an odd little smile, her mother had said, "Oh, Sadie, yes, there's my honey chile."

Sadie hugged her with relief.

"Oh, my. I sure feel strange sometimes," her mother said, kneading her forehead with bent fingers. "I still see pictures in my head from..." she'd hesitated, and then sighed, "from before. They sure are somethin' terrible. When they gonna go away?"

"Mama, hush now," Sadie murmured, kissing her on top of the head.

The terrible things her Mama and Pa had seen, the lashins and other punishments they'd suffered during their long years of bondage, had marked them with the kind of scars no one could see.

Sadie had spent fewer years in chains than they, but she too had sometimes felt so sad and shaky she could barely think. When it happened, she wanted to lie in bed all day, but she would get up because she knew her son Henry needed her.

Now that she'd enjoyed freedom for almost as long as she'd been enslaved, Sadie's "shaky fits", as she called them, were only just about gone.

She gave her mother a hug. "I don't rightly know how long it's gonna take, Mama. Fact of the matter is, them pictures may never disappear." Then she hastened to add, "But they do come less and less. Takes a bit of time before that'll happen. But it will."

Her mother heaved a sigh and whispered, "Y'all sure Massa won't get us up here, Sadie? Sometimes I feel like he's going to bust down our door and drag Pa, the children and me back down to hell."

"Oh, Mama. Please don't worry yourself about that none."

But it was almost impossible for them to shake off the nasty feeling their former Master was breathing down their necks. They had vowed never to speak of him, but Sadie guessed all the older family members worried he would send his men into their sanctuary to snatch them back down to his plantation.

Sadie gazed out the window at the cornfield that was just beginning to tassel. She could see her father's head bobbing up and down above the brilliant green stalks as he walked the rows picking off worms. Her little brothers trailed behind him.

Smiling at the sight, she stroked her mother's cheek. "Like I told you the last two times you asked Mama, we're all safe here in Harmony. He ain't never gonna get us."

"Sure hope so Sadie. I don't think I could bear it. No, I think I would die if Massa or the overseer showed up here."

Her mother turned her face to follow Sadie's gaze. She sat up a little straighter and sighed. "*Harmony* sure is a lovely place. I thank the

Lord every day he sent you back to get us."

"Me too, Mama."

"Now. Where did your sisters get to? We got to get some supper going—"

She pressed her mother's hand and gave her one more kiss.

"I just came over to pick some herbs, Mama. I'll leave y'all now."

Her mother stared into her eyes for a moment and smiled.

"You go right ahead, sweet."

Then she stood up and went over to the cook stove hollering, "Bonnilyn! Caroline! Supper ain't gonna fix itself!"

After that day, whenever Sadie went over to her parents she prepared herself for another scene like that. As time wore on, the spells didn't happen as much, but they were still a worry.

As she made her bed, Sadie decided she would go visit her folks later on that day, just in case.

After breakfast, Henry ran off to school and she got to work. Yesterday she'd been busy with her baking so she needed to catch up on the laundry she took in.

When she brought the basket outside to hang the wet clothes up, she was surprised by how hot the air was.

"Whew! It's a scorcher for sure. Laundry will be dry in no time."

Dropping the basket by the line, she straightened up and wiped the sweat off of her forehead. Her eyes latched onto the watchtower perched at the edge of the tomato field over by Missus Margaret's house.

Oh, Lordy, she thought. Soon my Henry will be old enough to start taking a turn in there.

It wasn't pleasant to think about, but they needed lots of eyes on the lookout for intruders bent on harming or stealing away the folks of Harmony.

She felt a shudder run up her backbone.

Sometimes I think we're still in bondage here, she thought. Anytime we step out of bounds without protection we can get snatched. We're worth a lot of money to them Christian wolves just itching for their chance to catch one of us and turn us in.

Her eyes darted around in search of something more pleasant to occupy her thoughts. A field of wildflowers over by Joe's house caught her attention. She drank in the riot of color and felt her heart quiet down as their calming beauty worked its magic.

She would never grow tired of looking at beautiful things, a pleasure denied her until she found the courage to break free of her shackles. How old had she been? Mama guessed about 16 summers, but since no one in her family knew how to count until they learned how in Harmony, she would never know for sure.

As she began to pin some sheets on the line, a flash of light caught her unawares. She looked over her shoulder to see a bank of dark, swirling clouds gathering from the south. They were moving fast. Crooked fingers of light stretched down toward a grove of distant trees as if trying to snatch them out of the ground. She shivered despite the heat.

She quickly unpinned the sheets and brought the laundry back inside. A few minutes later Henry rushed in.

"That was close!" he laughed.

She gave him a big hug, relieved that he was home safe. As they made supper the skies opened. Rain drove down in thick gray sheets while thunder cracked over their heads. Within minutes, the road had turned into a gushing rivulet. Sadie prayed that none of the Harmony houses would get struck by lightning.

The tempest disappeared as quickly as it came. Soon, the sun reappeared and water droplets glistened like babies' tears on the rose bushes next to her kitchen window.

No sooner had they put down their forks than Joe was outside the door, stamping his feet free of clods of mud from the wet road. Sadie always felt better seeing the "angel" who had scooped her up from the riverbed and carried her to Missus Margaret's so many years ago.

"Joe! Oh, my. Were you out in that storm? Come on in! Don't worry about your feet none."

"Can't stay Miss Sadie," Joe replied, removing his dripping hat and giving her a nod of his gray head. "Just came to tell you Missus Margaret wants you and Henry over to her house right away. She's got somethin' she needs to say."

She studied the man as he stood in the doorway catching his breath; he seemed agitated. She felt her gut do a little flip.

"Well, all right, Joe. Any idea what this is all about?"

"Can't say Miss Sadie, but Missus Margaret will tell y'all." He looked at Henry. "Son, can you please go up the road and tell your kin to come over to Missus Margaret's? I've got a few more other folks to rustle up."

Giving Sadie another quick nod, Joe took his leave as Henry raced off in the opposite direction.

Sadie put the dishes in the pan to soak and the cheese and milk under a wet cloth. Her mind worked at what the sudden invitation could mean. They had just had the weekly meeting a few days earlier.

Then she gave a little start. Missus Margaret's been looking a might worried these days,

Snatching her hat from the hook by the door she stepped into the parlor. As she pinned it to her hair in front of the looking glass, she noticed her eyes looked pinched and worried.

She bowed her head. "Lord, if you're listening, whatever Missus Margaret has to say, may we all have the strength to bear it."

She stepped back into the kitchen to see Henry had returned from his errand, his nose buried in a book.

She felt a catch in her chest as she gazed at him. She silently added to her prayer: Please, Lord, make it good news. Amen!

"You ready, perfessor?"

Henry stuck a bookmark to mark his spot and looked up at her with a half-smile.

"Yes, Ma'am."

She took his arm and they walked out into the cool, damp twilight.

42

August 15, 2012

Wherein Patrick follows his gut and is rewarded, two-fold.

WIPING HIS SWEATY HANDS ON HIS JEANS, Patrick hurried down the block. His nerves were on edge. He hadn't slept well after realizing he'd brought a slave-owning time traveler back to life. Drawing closer to the shelter he saw that it used to be a restaurant he'd been to a couple of times. He hadn't realized it had closed, let alone been reincarnated into a homeless shelter. Looking up at the sign, he got a chill. Jacob was inside the building. He didn't know how he knew. He just knew.

Pushing open the door, he saw a large, noisy room jammed with people. The scene looked chaotic, but then Patrick realized there was an order to it. Folks of all ages and colors were lined up for nourishment, others were eating, kids were running around or doing homework, and some people were on computers. As he took a couple of tentative steps in, his eyes darted around in search of Jacob. In this mob, he would not be easy to spot.

One or two faces turned to check him out, but since it was lunchtime, most people were preoccupied with getting food and finding somewhere to sit down to eat it. He was startled by how many seemed to be prosperous looking individuals.

But, of course, he thought. The Recession of '08. Memphis was clearly having a hard time climbing out of it.

Wading into the crowd, he didn't see any sign of Jacob. Was his gut wrong? Then, a fellow sitting by himself at the end of a long table caught his attention. The man turned his head. Studying his profile, Patrick felt a jolt of recognition.

A woman approached him. "Can I help you, sir?"

He quickly noted her name tag and gave her a smile. "Yes, Brenda. I've come to see one of your, er, guests."

"I see," she said pleasantly. "And who might that be?"

"I believe it's that man sitting over there, at the end of that table."

She turned to see the person he was referring to, and then looked back at him with an odd expression on her face. "Oh, I see. Well, Mr—"

"Patrick. Patrick Monroe."

"Yes. Well, you're welcome to come in and visit, Mr. Monroe, but—"

"Yes?"

Her eyes shifted to the man at the table and then back to Patrick. "I'm sorry. I'm not quite sure how to say this."

He gave her a quizzical look, though he had some idea of what she was trying to tell him.

"Well, you see, he's a bit, ah, touchy—especially regarding certain people." She blushed slightly. "And it seems like he wants to be left, um, alone. Sorry, I don't mean to be rude."

Patrick studied Jacob's rigid body. "Yes, it's pretty obvious. But, please, don't worry. I'm not insulted and I'm not concerned about his attitude."

He looked at Jacob again, and then added, "Well, not overly concerned, anyway."

She gave a little laugh. "Well, don't say I didn't warn you."

Before he could second-guess himself, Patrick threaded his way over toward Jacob. Then his heart began to pound. It was him. He resisted the impulse to back away. Instead, he gulped and said, "Excuse me. May I sit here?"

Jacob looked up, scowled, and then looked back at his food. "No, you may not."

Did Jacob recognize him? Well, no doubt he would say that to any black person.

"I know who you are. Jacob."

Jacob's fork paused a few inches from his mouth.

"And, I know what you are. I was at your plantation that morning."

Jacob slowly lifted his head, squinted at Patrick, and then frowned. "Were you? And just who might you be?"

"You don't remember me, Jacob? I'm Patrick. The teacher who brought the students for a tour."

Jacob pushed his plate away. His green eyes widened a fraction, and then narrowed to glittering slits.

"You."

Patrick tensed.

"You!"

"I can help you, Jacob."

He snorted. "You? Help me?"

Patrick noticed a few heads turning to regard them.

"Yes. If you'll let me," Patrick said quickly, hoping to avoid a scene. "Can we go somewhere and talk?"

"Absolutely not," snarled Jacob. "Why would I go anywhere with the likes of you?"

Brenda looked up from across the room, then signaled a co-worker to make a call. She hurried over to them. "Is everything all right here?"

Patrick shifted his gaze from Jacob to her and flashed a quick smile. "Ah, yes, Brenda. Everything's fine. We're just having a little—"

Jacob interrupted him. "No! Everything is not fine. Get this... this person away from me."

"Jacob. Listen to me, please! I just want to help you."

"Leave me be, you disgusting baboon!"

"Sir!" said Brenda in a stern voice. "We do not tolerate that kind of talk here. You will have to leave."

Forcing himself to remain calm, Patrick leaned closer to Jacob and said quickly, "Jacob, I can take you back to your plantation."

Jacob swiveled his head around and locked eyes with his. "What did you say?"

Encouraged, Patrick spoke fast. "I can take you back there, Jacob. But we need to talk first. There are some things I think you should know."

Jacob sipped some water. "And why should I listen to you?" He wiped his mouth with the back of his hand.

"You don't have to listen, Jacob. You don't have to do anything you don't want to do. But I think you might be better off if you do."

Brenda looked anxiously towards the door and then waved over a tall, 30-something bi-racial man who had just entered the shelter.

"Gentlemen!" he said as he approached, a broad smile accentuating his handsome features. "I'm Martin Willems, the founder of *Sanctuary*. Is there something I can help you with?"

Jacob turned to Martin with an annoyed look. Their green eyes met.

Jacob's mouth dropped open slightly.

Martin's smile wavered as he regarded Jacob.

And Patrick's gut did a little flip.

43

June 1850
Wherein Sadie, her family, and every other resident of Harmony migrate north.

"DON'T WANNA GO, MA. I like it here. Ain't fair."

Pausing from packing a bundle of linens, Sadie sat back on her haunches to regard her son.

"Henry. I thought they were teaching you proper English in that school."

He gave a little shrug.

"Now son, we hafta go. There's just no way 'round it."

He crossed his arms and looked out the window.

"Canada will be a whole lot better for us, Sugar Pie. You'll see."

"Ah, don't call me that, Ma."

She sighed and wiped the sweat off her brow with her sleeve.

"Now, all the folks are goin', Henry. You know you can't stay here by yourself. Please come on over here and help pack."

Once again, Sadie regretted not having a man in her life. Someone who could talk to Henry and set him straight. When he was a baby, a couple of the unmarried men in Harmony hoped to become her suitor, but Sadie just couldn't bear the thought of letting a man get close to her. And so, she had been left alone.

Sometimes, being both ma and pa seemed too much of a burden for her, especially now that Henry was growing up. Lately, he'd begun asking hard questions about his father. When he was little, she'd told him he was in heaven and that was good enough. But now he wanted to know who his father was. With Henry's complexion and green eyes, it was no secret the boy was different. She did take some comfort knowing he knew he wasn't the only one in Harmony with mixed blood.

There were times when she looked at his face and felt a little shock. Those eyes of his made her remember the man who'd sired him. But Massa's green eyes had been filled with lust while they slowly traveled up and down her body, as she stood trembling before him. But Henry's eyes were filled with motherly love. Unless he was being stubborn about something. That boy sure could be stubborn when he wanted to.

When she lay in bed at night listening to his gentle snores in the next room, she asked herself why she was so afraid to tell him who his Pa was. Yes, it was a lot easier to avoid thinking about the reason for his being here on this earth, but he had a right to know. Her parents and older siblings knew the truth; she was so glad they kept it to themselves.

She looked down at the bag she was packing and gave another little sigh. It was so hard having to leave so much behind, but they could only bring what they most needed. She gave a little shiver, thinking about the hard journey ahead of them.

Maybe when they reached Canada she would get the courage to tell Henry his father was the man who had enslaved and tortured her entire family, including hundreds of other men, women and children, because… well, because he could. There was just no good reason for it that she could see or understand. It just was. And Jacob Williams, like them other plantation owners, could put his cock inside any female slave he fancied without worrying about the law.

She heard a long sigh. Henry had turned from the window and was opening up his bag.

"That's my boy," she said.

Yesterday had been a bad day. When Missus Margaret told her flock how that Slave Act could put them all back in bondage, there was silence. And then people began to scream, no... no... no! Some of the women even fainted, including her Ma.

Missus Margaret had buried her hands in her face when she saw what her words had done. "I'm so sorry… I'm so sorry…" she said over and over until Joe came to her side and led her to a chair.

Sadie's Pa had caught Ma before she tumbled onto the carpet. As she fanned her poor mother, Sadie caught her breath at the sight of Pa's face. He looked bad. He was fretting, but she knew not just for them; her two oldest brothers had struck out on their own a few years back. But maybe they'd heard the news and were heading north away from danger.

She reached over and rubbed Pa's back. He seemed to not even know she was there.

At least the little ones didn't seem all that bothered by Missus Margaret's words. They wouldn't remember slavery life much. But the almost full-grown ones did. Their eyes were staring hard at the floral carpet like they were seeing it for the very first time. Some were trembling and rocking themselves.

Baby Adeline was the luckiest one in Sadie's family; she'd been born in *Harmony* just two years back. Sadie's sister Jenny, who everyone still called Little Jenny 'cause she never seemed to grow much, was bouncing Adeline on her knee.

Except for Adeline's giggles, a gloom had settled over the group. Finally, a woman named Sally lifted her head and looked close at Missus Margaret.

"Is it true there are black towns up in Canada, Missus Margaret? she asked at last. "'Cause that's what I been hearin'."

"Yes, Sally, 'tis true," Missus Margaret replied with a little smile.

Sadie could see she looked downright relieved to give them all some good news.

"A few years back, these towns were started up by escaped and freed slaves who had decided to keep going north."

"Well, that's where we're gonna go then," Sally responded and folded her hands across her stomach, which was big with child. Her husband placed his hand on hers. He smiled at his wife and nodded. "We best stick with our own kind. Oh, no offence Missus Margaret!" he said hastily.

Margaret gave a little laugh. "None taken, Casey." Then she let out a long sigh. "How I wish living in *Harmony* meant you really had lived in 'harmony' with those folks on the outside, but alas, that did not happen."

"Hunh. They don't know what they missed," said Henry.

"Very true, my dear," replied Margaret.

"True that," agreed several in the crowd.

"Now—" said Jeremiah, seemingly coming back to life. Heads lifted up as all eyes turned toward him. He'd become kind of the leader of the *Harmony* people not long after his arrival. He pushed himself onto his feet to tower above the faces that looked up at him hopefully.. "I've got somethin' to say."

He turned to Missus Margaret.

"At first this news was somethin' awful," he said, his eyes blazing.

"Un huh," murmured the crowd.

"And I was feeling low, mighty low. But now, this news is liftin' me up. Don' know about y'all but I am sick and tired of livin' like a scared rabbit. It's like the Lord has a plan for us—a good plan."

"Praise the Lord, praise the Lord!" chorused the assembly.

"This here news is like music to my own two ears. I think this is the chance we need—the kick in the behind to become truly free!" He smiled down at his wife who managed a weak smile in return. "Canada, get ready! We're a comin'!"

Then he picked up Adeline and spun her around, making her squeal with delight. Soon the other children were on their feet dancin' up a jig as everyone clapped out a rhythm.

And so, it was settled. The people of *Harmony* would make the long, hard journey north to Canada. And if they died tryin', well, death was better than life under the yoke of slavery. After tasting sweet freedom for so long, they would do anything to hang on to it. Living a peaceful life with their kind was possible, but besides Missus Margaret and a few of the other abolitionists that came to their community, they couldn't trust white folk.

Sadie looked forward to living somewhere truly free, but deep down, she was afraid. The bad memories of her run for freedom and then the tricky rescue of her family seemed fresh once more. It took all her strength to push those thoughts away and think instead about the good times waiting for them in Canada.

All too soon, it was leaving day. Sadie gazed at her image in her beloved looking glass one last time. There was no room for it on the wagon. She closed the door of her little home for the last time and saw her family waiting for her, along with Missus Margaret and Joe. Sadie rushed over to her angels, stood on her tiptoes to give Joe a big hug, and then wrapped her arms around Missus Margaret's thin frame.

"Oh, Missus Margaret," she said, a catch in her throat. "I sure wish you could come up with us."

"I know, dear heart," the old woman said as she patted Sadie's back. Missus Margaret's eyes were red and puffy from all the tears shed over the past few days. And now more began to spill.

"Oh my goodness," the old woman said in between sniffles. "If I continue to cry like this, I'll shrivel up like a prune."

In spite of herself, Sadie gave a little snort of laughter.

"I promise I'll do my utmost to visit when the time is right," Missus

Margaret assured her as she dabbed her eyes with a handkerchief. "I'm too darn old to travel all that way. And, I'm afraid I must go into hiding for a while."

Sadie hugged her a little tighter and then finally released her. Staring into her dear friend's eyes Sadie pulled something from the folds of her skirt.

"Missus Margaret, I want you to have this. Now don't look until we're gone, ya hear?"

She deposited a small wooden box into Missus Margaret's hand.

The old woman closed her hand around the box, nodded her head and gave Sadie a trembling smile.

The family clambered into the wagon, Jeremiah released the hand brake and they slowly pulled away. Sadie looked back until her house, Missus Margaret, and Joe had vanished from sight.

Margaret hadn't stopped waving until they were long gone. She rubbed her aching arm. She'd done her best to pave the way for the *Harmony* denizens, but she couldn't contain her worry; she was such a mother hen. Her contacts on the Underground Railway had already helped the smaller groups, unencumbered by young children, who'd gone ahead of Sadie's family.

Heartening news had drifted back south that the first group was almost in Canada. Safe houses were situated along the way every fifteen to twenty miles, which meant refuge was usually within a day's travel, and Missus Margaret's agents were also guiding travelers away from traps set by bounty hunters and slave traders.

"I can't believe everyone's truly gone," she sighed. Staring at Sadie's empty house she added, "*Harmony* is like a ghost town, now."

She stood with her arms limp at her sides. Joe scuffed the dirt with his toe, wishing he could think of some way to cheer her up. Then he brightened.

"What did Sadie give you, Missus Margaret?"

"Oh, yes. Let me see."

She carefully pried the cover off a hand carved box. Inside a small blue heart woven from dried forget-me-nots nestled on top of a delicate piece of dried moss.

Another tear trickled down Missus Margaret's cheek.

44

August 14, 2012

Wherein a student breaks her promise.

LEISHA'S INDEX FINGER HOVERED OVER HER MOUSE for a few seconds, then clicked, 'post'.

She'd done it. Her iphone photo of Jacob Williams was up on her Facebook time line.

Staring at his red, angry face gave her a momentary pang of guilt. She thought of her teacher's request to keep what happened a secret, but then she told herself, "Girl, when you've got a pic of a real live time traveler, you just gotta share it."

She typed in the comment box: "Hey y'all. Believe it or not, this Casper's a time traveler from slave days."

She smiled, took a sip of her Coke, and sat back to wait.

It didn't take long for her Facebook friends to notice her latest post. Joely was first. "Sure, Leisha. You on crack."

Leisha frowned as she typed: "Hey, I'm not the only one who saw him."

Joely: "C'mon. Was he wearing old timey clothes and riding a horse? Was he talking funny? Was he trying to whip you?"

Leisha: "Well, yeah, he was talking kinda funny, but mostly he was yelling. And he tried to hit us with a poker! Came outta nowhere. Mad as hell we were in his house. Was so upset had a heart attack right in front of us."

Her friend Maggie chimed in: "What u talking about? Time traveling? You cray."

Leisha: "Ain't. He looked just like the painting of the plantation owner hanging in the house."

Lenny: "So, where is he?"

Leisha: "Dunno. Last time I saw him he was getting put in an ambulance."

Robbie chimed in: "Hey, I was there too. The man ain't no time traveler. He's a re-enactor!"

Leisha frowned as she took a glug of Coke. Then she heard a ding. Her eyes moved down the screen. Esdee had just messaged her.

"Mr. Monroe is going to be so pissed."

She held her breath and then slowly let it out with a hiss. Her fingers flew across the keyboard, "Yeah, well, I don't care."

Esdee: "Leisha you need to shut up girl."

Leisha: "No one believes me anyway."

Esdee: "But still. We promised."

Leisha clicked the x on Esdee's pop up. Hmph. Think you're the boss of me?

There was another ping.

Brian: "Tell me more."

Finally, someone who believes me! But wait. Who is he? Don't recognize him.

She clicked on his name. Hm… friend of a friend.

Then she clicked on his "about" link.

Her eyes widened. Reporter for the Memphis Daily News

Grinning, she polished off the rest of her Coke.

45

July 1850

Wherein Sadie and her kin experience a close call on their trek to freedom.

THEY HEARD THE CHAINS BEFORE THEY SAW THEM.

"Quick now! Get in the woods!" ordered Jeremiah. "And hide yourselves good!"

Snatching up their bags and the blankets they'd been resting on, Sadie, her mother Ellen, the children and her Pa made themselves scarce.

They'd been walking that morning. Sometimes that happened when there wasn't a wagon ready to carry them from the last station on the Railroad. It made traveling a lot harder, but they didn't have much choice.

Before they set out before dawn, they had said a quick prayer that they would cross into Michigan before noon. That meant there wouldn't be too many stops to rest. But, with their turtle-like pace Sadie had worried they wouldn't reach their goal. Her legs and feet ached from carrying her load. She'd been so relieved when they finally moved off the side of the road to rest under some trees, drink some water and nibble a few victuals. The sound of the chains had broken her reverie.

Peering from her hiding place through the web of branches and tree trunks, Sadie held Adeline on her lap and whispered to her to stay as quiet as a mouse. Henry was crouched beside them. Then, Sadie stifled a gasp as a line of men, women and small children, chained together by their necks and ankles, shuffled into view.

A coffle!

Sadie's mother was squatted down on the other side of her, with her arms wrapped around Little Jenny. She kept one finger on her lips as a warning to be quiet. Sadie saw the fear in her eyes, and when she glanced over at her father and her little brothers, she noticed the muscles in her father's jaw were taut with fury.

To think these captured Negroes were being walked back south to slavery! Sadie had heard about these terrible things, but hoped she would never see one. She counted a dozen people going by. The stink of their unwashed bodies drifted all the way in to their hiding spot. The captives were weak, exhausted and could barely stand, their faces grim, without hope. Two white men on horses, brandishing whips and shotguns, guarded the front and back end of the line.

Sadie strained her eyes to see if anyone looked familiar, but as far as she could tell from that distance, they were all strangers. She felt ashamed at the sense of relief she felt. Her heart went out to those poor, lost souls. But she knew if they tried helping these folks escape they would put themselves in danger. They had no choice but to let them walk back down to Hell. Maybe further down the road, someone might chance a rescue.

The wretched group shambled out of sight. When they could no longer hear the chains, Jeremiah slipped back to the road to check if all was clear. He waved to his family hiding in the woods. They resumed walking in the opposite direction from the coffle. They walked faster now. To see first hand that slave drivers were still at work this far north was hard on their nerves.

Little Jenny whispered, "Mama?"

"Yes, honey chile?"

"Will we have to wear chains like them folks?"

Ellen quickly looked down at her, chucked her chin and managed a smile, "No, honey chile, we won't be wearing any chains. Don't you worry."

"I hope not Mama. Those people looked so sad."

Jeremiah squinted down the road and said nothing. He had Adeline on his back. She laid her little head on his shoulder, stuck her thumb in her mouth and closed her eyes.

The family had been on the move for almost a month. How many times had they nearly been caught and not known it, wondered Sadie. They had been hidden in cellars, barns, attics and even the haystacks belonging to 'conductors'—farmers and townspeople—who guided them from one Underground Railroad 'station' to another.

Weary of the snail's pace and the ever-present fear their tempers grew short; sometimes there were nasty arguments and the children would cry. Sadie often fought back her own tears. It took great will power to find the strength to keep moving. But they believed in their hearts that freedom was worth it.

One more hour of plodding, and then a shout from Henry. "There it is! The marker!"

Sadie's heart leapt. Michigan!

"Hallelujah!" cried Ellen, sinking to her knees. Sadie's father crouched in front of her and flung his arms around her.

"Come, mother, let us pray."

He helped her up and the family stepped through the trees, joined hands, and bowed their heads as Jeremiah began to speak. "Dear Lord, we give thanks for your help and guidance. Thank you for sending the sound of the chains to us in time so we could hide from the slave catchers. Thank you for giving our legs the strength to carry our load today. Thank you for delivering us to this last State before the Promised Land. Amen."

The family drank some cool water at a small brook, then, after making sure the way was still clear, struck out once more. Now there was almost a bounce in their step.

They had been told the stations on the Underground were more frequent in Michigan—every 15 miles instead of 20. If all went well, in about another week, they would be in Canada—New Canaan—The Promised Land!

After pushing a little further up the road they could see their first Michigan station, a neat, wooden farmhouse set on a little hill. They would rest here for the remainder of the day and stay for the night.

The farmer, his wife and four children greeted them like long lost friends. Soon the dining table groaned under a delicious bounty. There was water for bathing, and best of all, their load would lighten tomorrow—a wagon would be available for them.

Tucking Henry in for the night in the hayloft, Sadie bent and kissed his forehead. He didn't protest as had become his habit of late back in Harmony.

"Soon, Henry. Very soon, my son."

His green eyes glowed in the lantern light as he smiled up at her. Then, his eyelids fluttered, and he was fast asleep.

46

July 1850

Wherein Sadie and her kin are nearly thwarted from reaching the other side.

Seymour Finney smoothed his thick white mustache with a gnarled thumb. He could see how exhausted the family was. He was hesitant to tell them the bad news, especially after all they had been through. But he believed it would be best if they knew so they would be sure to be on the alert.

Seymour owned a livery, a tavern and a hotel in Detroit. For several years, his establishment had doubled as the terminus of the Underground Railroad in that part of the U.S. A short distance away from his property flowed a mile-wide river, the final barrier between refugees and the Promised Land of Canaan—Canada.

A long-time abolitionist, Seymour had taken on the role of conductor without hesitation and had helped many refugees successfully cross to freedom in Canada. He'd taken great pains to hide Sadie and her family in the top floor of his stable as soon as they'd arrived that day by wagon. For them to come so far only to be discovered was something he hoped to avoid at all costs.

"I'm afraid I have to advise you that bounty hunters are in the vicinity," he said at last.

Sadie began to tremble. Freedom was so close she could almost taste it. Was it about to be snatched away?

She reached over to Henry and took his hand.

He whispered, "Ow. Ma! Your nails are digging in to me."

"Oh, sorry, son!" She loosened her grip.

Sadie's parents leaned against each other as if to keep from collapsing to the floor.

"The men appeared a short while after your arrival," Seymour continued, "but I don't believe you have to worry."

Ellen asked in a quivering voice, "They say if they are lookin' for us?"

"No, my dear, they did not," he assured her.

She nodded and giving him a faint smile, reached an arm down to hug her two youngest tightly. Their heads drooped with fatigue against her hip.

"Ah, such dear hearts," Seymour said. "They have been through so much. I know all of you have."

"Yessir, we sure have," agreed Jeremiah. "What do we do now, Mr. Finney?"

Seymour smiled. "Please, call me Seymour. You wait. You eat some food and you rest."

Jeremiah nodded.

"The men are enjoying libations and will be sitting down to their dinner soon," Seymour added. "I shall see they become good and drunk and otherwise—" He winked quickly at Jeremiah. "—occupied. All they'll desire then is to fall into a soft bed. And when that happens, it'll be time for you to cross. You have my word on it."

Only a short while ago, Sadie and her family had been driven through the maze of Detroit's city streets. The sight of so many buildings, churches, people and carriages along the way had excited Sadie, but made her head ache.

They were in the loft of Mr. Finney's livery barn, a block from his hotel and he had just brought over dinner. It smelled so delicious it was getting harder for Sadie to concentrate on his words. As if reading her mind, Seymour glanced over his shoulder to see that his assistant had finished spreading out the feast on a blanket. He smiled and with a flourish, indicated that they should all sit down to enjoy it.

The young ones eagerly commenced eating as their elders thanked Seymour for his kindness and generosity.

"We are ever so grateful—" said Ellen, keeping one eye on the youngsters as they hungrily attacked the food. "How can we ever repay you?"

"It is nothing," Seymour assured her. "I am pleased to offer sustenance and help. Now, after your repast, please try to sleep. It's very likely you'll be crossing the river in the middle of the night. You'll need to rest up now while you have a chance."

With a cheery smile, he followed his assistant down the ladder and was swallowed up into the night. When they heard the latch click shut on the stable door, the family quickly joined hands. In a low, clear voice, Jeremiah prayed, "Dear God in Heaven, please don't abandon us now. We are so close. Please help this poor sufferin' family make it across Jordan to Salvation. Amen."

They all tucked into their food. When everyone had finished, Henry and the other children drifted off to sleep. Sadie made herself a little nest in the straw, but sleep would not come. There was a bit of starlight coming in from a couple of openings up near the roof. She looked over at where her parents were lying. She could see their hands were clasped and they were quite still, but she had a strong feeling they too were wide-awake.

She sighed and closed her eyes.

The next thing she knew Henry was shaking her arm and whispering in her ear, "Ma! Time to go!"

"Oh, my! Thank you, Jesus—"

With shaking hands she reached for her belongings, trying not to think about the terrible dream her son had woken her from. She'd seen the coffle again, but when she looked at the line of captured people, every face was familiar to her for they were all members of her family.

Seymour was waiting for them by the front door of the stable. He helped the family climb onto his wagon. He was nervous. The bounty hunters had asked him some pointed questions that evening. He was worried they'd gotten wind that some refugees were in hiding nearby. He didn't want to risk sharing his suspicions with the family for he knew how upset it would make them all. He prayed that all would go well.

The night was quiet. No one dared speak for fear of detection. Seymour flicked the reins and they began slowly rolling down toward the river.

A fingernail of a moon, a sprinkle of stars and an occasional gas lamp were all that lit the way. Sadie found her faithful guide—the North Star, after remembering it wouldn't be in its usual spot. They'd been told Canada curved below the U.S. at this spot, so they were headed south instead of north.

Their bodies swayed in time with the rolling wagon over the cobblestones. Sadie prayed the creaking wheels wouldn't wake anyone or cause suspicion. A dog barked as they passed through the ink-black streets, but not a soul emerged from the buildings or houses to follow their progress.

At last, she could see the sparkle of water and the dark shape of a skiff tied up at the river's edge. The wagon stopped and two dark figures emerged from the shadows to help the family off the wagon and into the skiff.

Breathing a sigh of relief, Seymour bid them all a hasty farewell and then the little boat shoved off.

Jeremiah and the two strangers pulled the oars with urgent but controlled strokes. Sadie trained her eyes on the few lights flickering on the opposite shore. Was that really Canada?, she wondered.

The river was as smooth as her looking glass; the only sound the rhythmic dipping of oars into the water. Her heart seemed to beat in time with every stroke. It wouldn't be long now.

The pounding of hooves cut like a knife through the still of the night. Sadie turned to see a pair of horses thundering down to the shore.

"Oh, God in Heaven! We're not even half way across!" she whispered.

Two men brandishing rifles sat atop the horses. "Damn it all," a voice slurred. "Them buggers are gettin' away, Fred! Whatcha think? Time for some target practice?"

Jeremiah barked, "Everyone, down!"

They all ducked as best they could. Sadie covered her head with an arm and nearly smothered Henry with her body as bullets whistled a few feet above them or ricocheted off the stern. Bent almost double, the oarsmen cursed as they rowed with all their might.

"Faster! Faster, Papa! Faster!" the children screamed. The little ones began to cry.

Laughter and bullets continued to ring out from the shore.

"Shittin' your pants yet, you black bastards?"

How did they find us? Sadie silently screamed. Please Lord! May they be too drunk to aim properly!

"Dear Lord God in Heaven, please help! Help us!" prayed her mother over and over.

The crossing seemed to take forever, and then, a bump. Sadie lifted her head a few inches. Land! Their boat had pushed through some bull rushes, and its nose was buried in a muddy riverbank. The two oarsmen leaped onto shore and quickly tied up the boat with the help of some folks, barely visible in the gloom, who had been waiting for them. The guns had ceased firing. But the voices, fainter now, but oozing with venom, drifted across the water. "Hey, you dirty niggers! You may think you're safe, but watch out! We're gonna come across and getcha tomorrow! Ha, ha, ha!"

"Oh, Lord Jesus!" cried Ellen. "Get us out! Get us out!"

"It's all right," called a kind voice through the darkness. "Don't you listen to them, now. You safe." Strong hands reached down to help the family scramble out of the boat. As soon as Jeremiah, Ellen and the younger children stepped onto the shore, Jeremiah fell to his knees and kissed the ground, choking back sobs.

Sadie was stunned. She had never seen her father cry before. She and her mother crouched down beside him. "It's all right, Pa," Sadie crooned, rubbing his back. "It's all right. We made it, Pa!"

Wiping his eyes on his shirt, he reached for her hand and his wife's. "Praise God! Thank you Lord for our safe passage!"

"Praise God!" his wife and daughter echoed.

"Grandma! Come over here!" said Henry. "Adeline's hurt bad!"

Ellen's head snapped up and she looked blindly around. Stumbling over toward his voice she found him and Little Jenny cradling Adeline. Ellen shrieked when she realized a large splinter of wood was sticking out of her baby's cheek; blood was streaming down her face.

"Oh, my poor, sweet baby!" She pulled the whimpering child into her arms to rock her for a few moments, and then tenderly handed her over to Sadie. Pushing herself up onto her feet, Ellen turned to face the opposite shore, her hands cupping her mouth.

"You dirty bastards!" she screamed. "I hope y'all rot in Hell!"

47

August 15, 2012
Wherein Patrick connects
the dots for Martin and Jacob.

THE DIN FROM PEOPLE TALKING and eating and getting in and out of squeaky wooden chairs faded into the background as the three men regarded each other intently. Finally, Patrick broke the spell. Sticking out his hand he said, "A pleasure to meet you, Martin. My name is Patrick Monroe."

Martin shook his hand absently. "Uh, yes. Nice to meet you too." He looked at Jacob. "And you are?"

With a tinge of reticence, Jacob replied, "I am Jacob Williams."

Patrick's head swiveled back and forth between the two faces.

"Have we met?" Martin asked Jacob.

"Absolutely not," Jacob sniffed.

Martin felt his blood pressure rising. "Well, you look a bit familiar to me. So, what can I do for you, sir?"

"Nothing. I came to eat. And I just wanted to be left alone, but then this man appeared and disturbed me," Jacob replied, glaring at Patrick. He hadn't intended to stop here. After failing to talk to any of the KKK people, he'd realized his stomach was growling from hunger and he remembered he'd lost his breakfast from the darkie's painful blow. He'd started walking again and found *Sanctuary* by accident. After eating and cleaning up a bit, his plan was to set off and try to find the KKK headquarters.

Martin glanced at Patrick. "Can you please explain what happened?"

That shade of green, Patrick thought. What are the odds?

"Well, it's a long story, but I know this man and I came because he needed some, ah, help."

"Yes, he said he would take me back to my plantation," Jacob sighed.

"Plantation?" Martin said.

Patrick nodded, hoping Martin didn't think he was rude for staring so much. "Is there somewhere quiet and private where the three of us can go?"

Martin seemed to spring to life. "Sure. My office."

Jacob stiffened. Now what could these two black buggers possibly want of me, he wondered. Then he sighed. Well, if it means I'll be returned to my plantation, it might be worth the risk.

He heaved himself up out of his chair and followed the two men.

Closing his door Martin pointed at the two chairs in front of his desk and then slid into his seat. Resting his chin on his hands he looked at Patrick expectantly.

"Well, I'm not exactly sure where or how to start," began Patrick. "So, I guess I'll just dive in."

Martin nodded. "Please do."

"The reason I came here today was to find Jacob and return him to his plantation, which is where he feels he belongs."

"Are you a worker there, Mr. Williams?"

"Of all the—. Of course not!" Jacob sputtered.

Martin shot a look at him and thought, man, this guy is a first rate asshole.

"But I was planning to take him on a bit of a tour first."

Looking at Patrick sideways, Jacob grunted, "Tour? I don't want a tour. All I desire is to return home!"

"Mr. Williams, why do I feel I know you?" ventured Martin, hoping the guy wouldn't blow a gasket.

Jacob sneered, "I am certain I have no idea."

"I think I may know," Patrick offered.

The two men looked at him. "You do?" said Martin.

"Well, it's because—" Patrick started, and then pressed his lips together, wondering how in the hell to say what he knew would sound incredible. "Ok, what I mean is, I think it's because you two might somehow be, uh, related."

There was a silence as the pair stared at him and then at each other before Jacob erupted. "Of all the preposterous suggestions!" He stood up so quickly, his chair fell over.

"Calm down, Jacob, and listen!" said Patrick.

"I don't have to listen to you," snarled Jacob.

"Look, Jacob. Your last name is practically the same as Martin's. Yours is 'Williams', his is 'Willems'. And your eyes—you've got the same green eyes, Jacob."

Jacob glanced again at Martin, who was looking at him intently. He averted his gaze.

"And Jacob," continued Patrick, "I strongly suspect you've had your way with your field hands or house girls. Whenever you so desired."

"Of all the impertinence!" snapped Jacob.

"Look. I just don't get what you're saying, Patrick," said Martin, his green eyes flashing. "Just how does all this make me related to this man?"

Patrick looked at down at his hands, which were so dark they almost blended into the black fabric of his pants. Suddenly he remembered that dream where he'd been about to strike a cowering Jacob with a whip. With renewed conviction Patrick looked back up at Martin and said, "This man used to be, or should I say, *is* a slave owner with a cotton plantation, Martin. Just outside of town. And it's possible he may have had sex with an ancestor of yours."

Martin's mouth fell open. "What? Now you're really talking crazy!"

Patrick held up a hand. "Here me out. And that ancestor could have been, let's see... your great, great, great, great, great grandmother."

"C'mon," said Martin and then burst out laughing. "You're kidding, right? Wait. I get it. There's a hidden camera in here somewhere." He got up from his chair and looked around his office. "I'm being punked, right?"

"No, I'm not kidding, Martin," said Patrick. "There's no camera. It's all true."

Martin shook his head as he sat back down. "True? But, but that's impossible, man! What is this guy?" He gave a little snort. "A ghost?"

"No, Martin. He's not a ghost. He's a—." Patrick hesitated.

"What? What is he?"

"Jacob's a time traveler, Martin."

Martin burst out laughing.

"It's true, Martin," said Patrick. "Jacob Williams is from the past.

He's a cotton plantation owner who lived 175 years ago."

"A time traveler?" said Martin. "C'mon, man. This is a joke, right? There's no way. It's goddamn impossible!"

"It is possible," murmured Jacob, his eyes fixed on the family photo on Martin's desk. "He speaks the truth."

"What?" Martin looked back at Patrick, who raised his eyebrows and gave a slow nod.

"As he says," Jacob continued, jerking his thumb at Patrick, "I am a plantation owner."

Now Martin was hanging onto Jacob's every word.

"My cotton plantation is approximately ten miles outside of Memphis," said Jacob. "Just over a week ago, I woke up in my own bed, but, instead of it being the year 1837, it had somehow become the year 2012."

"1837? I... No, I don't believe it," said Martin, shaking his head.

"What this—what this man is saying is correct," Jacob continued, "although I confess, I reject the implication you are related to me."

And then a vision filled Jacob's head: all that sweet black and brown flesh. A vixen named Sadie had been his most recent conquest. He pressed his lips together and said nothing more.

Martin's long slender fingers kneaded his forehead as he attempted to compose himself. "Ok, let me get this straight." He looked hard at Jacob. "What you're saying is this man has—" He stopped and stared at the ceiling for a moment, took a deep breath and let out it out in a low whistle. "What you're saying is this man has somehow traveled through time. And not only that, you think I'm related to him." Gripping the edge of his desk, he looked up at the ceiling. "Goddam."

There was a knock on the door. Martin gave a start, and looked warily at the door. "Yes?"

Brenda, his *Sanctuary* manager, poked her head in. "Excuse me, Martin, but there's someone from the newspaper here."

"What? Now?" He glanced at Patrick. The man looked alarmed and gave his head a quick shake. "Brenda, uh look, I'm busy. Can you deal with it?"

"Well, he's looking for someone." Her eyes flicked to Jacob.

Martin thought fast. "Brenda, tell him he left. That you're not sure where he went."

She arched her eyebrows. "Oh?"

"Yes! Please!"

Her head vanished.

"Are you going to take me back to my plantation now?" mumbled Jacob who was staring at the floor.

"Yes, all right," sighed Patrick. "I'll take you back now, Jacob. It seems we best get out of here now that the press might be on your trail. Martin, would you like to come?"

Martin gave a quick nod: "Sure. What the hell? Let's roll."

48

July 1850

Wherein Sadie and her kin decide to take another risk, for very excellent reasons.

WATER TRICKLED DOWN HER CHEEK AS SADIE shaded her eyes from the brilliant afternoon sun. There went Henry racing with his cousins and some other boys across the square. She grinned in satisfaction. It did her heart good to see him make friends so quick. Humming a tune she'd heard played on a fiddle the day before, she plunged her hands back into the laundry tub. Rain had been falling steady since the day after she and her kin crossed the river, but had finally let up. Putting on clean clothes would be a blessed event.

How different she felt from that night she and her family had crawled up the riverbank into Canada. She'd collapsed onto a narrow cot, her body shaking so hard she feared she might never sleep again.

It was a few days before they allowed themselves to truly believe the words of the folks who had welcomed them: it was against the law for the men that had shot at them to come across the river to Canada.

Sadie stiffened. A strange man was approaching her. She lowered her head and studied him through her eyelashes. His dark brown face was handsome, but there was a black patch covering one of his eyes. As he drew close, his white teeth flashed as he gave her a quick smile before tipping his hat. She allowed him a shy smile back, but then frowned and looked down at her washing. He passed her by without speaking.

Her parents appeared at the end of the barracks as she wrung out Henry's spare shirt. They'd been visiting some Harmony friends living over in the next row. As they came closer Sadie noted their long faces. She let Henry's shirt splash back into the water.

"What's wrong?" she said, dreading to hear what they would say.

Her Pa looked at the ground and his mouth worked, but it was as if he didn't want it to make any words. "Sadie," he said finally, a catch in his throat, "We're gonna have to move on … now! We're not safe here!"

"What, Pa?" She felt like she'd been kneed in the stomach. "Not safe? How … why?"

"Friends told us Slavery Law just took hold! And now bounty hunters gonna come on over to this side!

Sadie looked around the square, half expecting she would see one of those evil buggers lurking behind a tree waiting to snatch Henry.

"We're too close here," said her mother, her face tight. "We need to run again!" Then she hugged herself and started rocking back and forth. Sadie was shocked to see how old she looked. The hard journey had taken its toll. And then her mother whispered, "They can even snatch up freed slaves and burn their papers."

Jeremiah put his arm around her. "Hush now, Ellen."

She laid her head on his chest and began to sob.

He raised his eyes to Sadie and sighed. "Them greedy bastards figure they're gonna get rich quick 'cause if they bring an escaped slave over to Detroit, they get a whole lot of money."

"No …" said Sadie shaking her head vehemently. "I can hardly believe what you're sayin'."

"They lock 'em up in Detroit before they try 'em," he continued patting Ellen's back. "Then they ship 'em back on down to hell in chains. And if any folks helping fugitives get caught, they get fined 1,000 dollars!"

"Oh, dear Lord in heaven!" Sadie cried, feeling as though she might faint. Then a movement caught the corner of her eye. Looking across the green, she saw Henry racing toward them, a big smile lighting up his face. How she wished he could keep it there forever.

Before crossing into Canada the family hadn't given much thought to their next move. Running had been on their minds forever it seemed, and they didn't have much room to squeeze into their heads what they should do next when they finally crossed over.

Windsor was so far south it was one of the best points for U.S. slaves taking the Underground Railroad to cross into freedom. In fact, there were so many runaways streaming in, the people in charge of the village of Windsor didn't know where to put 'em all. Then somebody remembered the barracks. Situated a little ways from the Detroit River and no longer used by the army, they'd been turned into a haven for the fugitives.

Now the refugees had a rough but fairly comfortable place to rest and decide what to do next. And this setup meant they were kept from spilling over into the community. Sure there were good white folk who helped and supported the runaways, but there were many others who were none too happy that hundreds of coloreds were living in their midst.

No matter what kind of thinking was behind the use of the barracks, Sadie and her kin were grateful for the shelter. And they were sure thankful for the donated food and cooking supplies, too.

After a few days rest the family considered settling in Windsor. It seemed a nice enough place; there could be jobs, but most of all they didn't wanna run any more. The thought of tramping another 40 miles inland to Buxton, a town founded by escaped slaves, was too much to bear.

But now, it seemed they had little choice but to pack up and carry on. Even spending one more night in Windsor was a frightening idea.

As Ellen and Sadie began quickly folding their things to pack into their bags, their friend Sam poked his head through the door. He and his wife had left Harmony back in Ohio a few days before them. With a broad grin he announced, "Y'all don't have to worry none."

"What are you talking about, Sam?" Jeremiah growled. "We gotta get outta here! And you should too, if ya know what's good for you."

"But, you don' understand," insisted Sam. "Some people are comin'. They got a plan … a good plan … for everyone!"

Sadie's mother stopped folding the clothes and straightened up to give him a long look. In spite of being so upset, Sadie smiled to herself. She knew her mother thought Sam was a bit of a prankster.

Rubbing her lower back, Ellen said, "And just who might these people with a plan be?"

"Henry and Mary Bibb," Sam replied, almost hopping up and down on one foot.

"Who they?" said Sadie's Pa. "And why should we risk our lives to stay here and listen to whatever it is these two gots ta say?"

"'Cause they're famous, important folks," Sam explained, and smiled so big his wide face looked like it would crack in two.

"That right?" said Sadie, looking down at her cot to put some folded things into her sack. "Well, they so famous and important, why they got time for people the likes of us?"

"Because Mr. Bibb used to be a slave," Sam said.

Sadie looked back up at him skeptically.

"True!" he assured her. "Then, he turned into an abolitionist. His wife's an abolitionist too, 'cept she was born free."

Sam put his hand on Jeremiah's shoulder and peered up into the big man's dark brown eyes. "Stay 'n listen, Jeremiah. You won't be sorry. Ah promise."

Jeremiah gave a little grunt and then both parents looked at Sadie. "What you think?"

She closed her eyes and sighed. The she turned to Sam and said, "When they comin'?"

"After noon." He pointed at a big tree in the square. "Meeting under that big pear tree yonder."

She gazed across the square at the tree. After a few moments of thought, she looked up into her father's face.

"I think we should stay, Pa. Hear him out. We can leave right after, if need be."

"Hm. I don' know..." he said and then looked down at his wife. She sighed and said softly, "Maybe listen for a spell, Jeremiah. And then decide."

"All right," Pa said slowly. "But we leave before sunset if we don' like what we hear."

After a quick midday meal Sadie and her kin joined a cluster of folks sitting in the shade of the giant tree. Rumor had it the pear tree had been there since the Indian days. Sam had set up two chairs for the two special guests who had already arrived. They were smiling and nodding at people as they settled in on blankets spread on the grass. Sadie's heart skipped a beat when she noticed the man who'd tipped his hat at her was sitting a little ways over. As if he could feel her looking at him, he turned his handsome face around and winked his one eye at her.

He's got some nerve, she thought, but, my, oh my, he's sure one handsome devil. Before she could help it, she smiled back.

"Hello good folk! Thank you for meeting us. My name is Henry Bibb and this is my wife, Mary."

Relieved to turn her attention elsewhere, Sadie looked at Mr. Bibb and saw him gesturing in her family's direction.

"Welcome newest refugees! I understand you had an eventful river crossing."

"Uh, yessir, you could say that," replied Jeremiah slowly.

"I do hope your little one is all right," continued Mr. Bibb, looking at Sadie's mother. She nodded her head, and then tilted her face down toward Adeline, who was dozing in her lap. "Praise the Lord, it weren't her eye. I doctored her up," she said with a smile tinged with pride and relief. Little Jenny, who was tucked in beside her, gave her a kiss on the cheek. Ellen smiled and squeezed her daughter's hand.

Sadie studied Mr. Bibb. She saw a medium-dark man with wavy brown hair slicked down and parted on one side. He had a high smooth forehead over deep-set eyes that seemed to bore right through you. She would bet a dollar he had a lot of white in him. She thought back to the time another famous abolitionist, Frederick Douglass, had interviewed her in Harmony about her escape from the Williams Plantation. She'd been so nervous … she dreaded talking about those days, but the man put her at ease right away with his kind words about her home and her son, Henry.

She looked over and saw her son sitting with his new pals. She could tell he liked the fact that he shared the same first name with the famous Mr. Bibb.

"I am certainly relieved to hear that," Mr. Bibb said to her mother, his full lips curving into a gentle smile. "How unfortunate you had to go through such a terrible ordeal so close to the Promised Land."

"Well, it weren't pleasant, but we're here now," said Jeremiah. "I think we have to get a move on, though."

"That won't be necessary," replied Mr. Bibb. "And I'll tell you why, but first, I wish to share my story with you, if I may?"

"Yessir, please!" cried several children, scooting up closer to his feet.

"All right with me, I guess. If it don't take too long," said Jeremiah. Ellen elbowed him in the side. "Uh, beggin' your pardon," he said sheepishly.

Mr. Bibb smiled and nodded his head, then stretched his arms wide as if to embrace the expectant group before him. He turned to his lovely wife who was beaming down at the little ones sitting at their feet. She looked up at him and said, "Go ahead, Henry. These folks don't have all day."

He laughed, cleared his throat and in a strong voice began.

"I too am an escaped slave. I was born Henry Bibb in Kentucky in 1815. They say my father was Patrick Bibb, a white Kentucky state senator. I never met the man, and if I had, I'm certain it would have made no difference in my life."

Many heads nodded. If your mother was a slave then every sibling was a slave too. And if your father was white, most likely he was a 'step aside'—he'd have nothing to do with you, especially if he was someone important. Your white half brothers and sisters would live lives of luxury while you were forced to serve them. And you'd be beaten for no real reason.

Mr. Bibb regarded the children sitting quietly in front of him. "Myself and all six of my younger brothers were sold to different owners. And I was sold again and again after that. The year I was 10 was the first time I ran away. I didn't make it far. But I tried and then tried again. I kept on trying for another 17 years until finally I broke my bonds.

"Praise the Lord!" cried several people in the crowd.

Mr. Bibb nodded and looked at his wife. "Now, Mary here was born a free woman in Rhode Island."

"All black folk born free there?" asked a young man sitting a little ways in front of Sadie.

"No, not all, I'm afraid," she replied with a sad smile. "Even though slavery was supposedly abolished there in 1774. I was one of the lucky ones."

"She was indeed," said her husband, squeezing her hand. "And she received a good education, too. She's a teacher, a writer and an abolitionist."

She smiled back at him with clear affection.

Sadie felt a twinge of envy. Would she ever allow herself to love a man like that?

As Mr. Bibb turned back to the crowd his smile faltered. "Now, when I was young I fell in love with someone else—a woman who toiled on another farm not far from the plantation I worked on." He looked down at his left hand, still entwined with his wife's. "I hope Mary doesn't mind if I tell this part of my story again."

"It's all right, Henry. It was a long time ago. At any rate, I should get back to my school."

Her beautiful eyes swept the group of folks in front of her. "I have begun a small school here. If anyone … young or old … would care to attend, please do. Henry can explain where it is." She smiled. "I would be honored to have you."

And then she trained her gaze on Sadie's family.

Looking into the woman's eyes Sadie felt a little jolt. Mary Bibb had been born free, but now she too could be thrown into chains because some white man's law demanded it.

"I do hope everyone chooses to stay on in Windsor, at least for a little while," Mrs. Bibb said. "Now, if you will please excuse me."

Mr. Bibb watched his wife gather up her skirts and step into the bright heat of the afternoon sun. "Now, where was I?" he said, turning back to the crowd. "Ah, yes. Malinda's owner gave us permission to marry, but only if he could continue to have uh, certain relations with her." He frowned. "As you can imagine this was an extremely upsetting proposition. I vowed we would try to escape."

Sadie's shifted her legs to get more comfortable, her face burning at Mr. Bibb's words. She looked down at her lap and willed herself to keep bad memories from resurfacing.

"My first chance was in 1837. I decided to attempt it on my own as I thought I would have an easier go of it. Then, I would return, with help I hoped, to rescue my wife and our little daughter. Mary Frances."

His face fell. "Unfortunately, I didn't get far. Even though on my second attempt I had the assistance of the Underground Railroad and succeeded in reaching Ohio. I was recaptured after returning to Kentucky for my wife and daughter."

There was a collective groan from his listeners.

Mr. Bibb seemed not to notice for his attention had been drawn to a delicate yellow butterfly, which had alighted on a blade of grass at his feet. "So beautiful," he murmured. Then, as if coming out of trance, his brows knit and he continued his speech. "We were sent off to a Louisville slave auction, and bought by a deacon from Louisiana—a cotton planter. Deacon Whitfield was by far more of a devil than a man of the cloth. And he had one of the cruelest overseers in that part of the country."

Sadie shook her head. She didn't know how much more of the man's story she could bear.

"When I learned the Deacon ordered me to feel the lash 500 times for attending a prayer meeting without his permission, my wife, daughter and I fled into the Louisiana swamps."

"500 lashes!" a woman cried. "You surely would have died!"

Mr. Bibb nodded gravely. "Very likely, madam. Which is why we risked our lives to flee. But we found ourselves trapped on a small island where we encountered a pack of wolves."

"Wolves?" piped up Sadie's Henry. "Did you fight them off?"

"Yes, son," Mr. Bibb replied with a quick smile. "We did. My wife held a club in one hand and our baby in the other and I had a two-foot bowie knife. When I thought all was lost I yelled at the top of my lungs and rushed toward the pack. The wolves scattered and we were spared. But then, not two days later, we were captured."

"What happened next, sir?" said Henry with that keen expression Sadie knew all too well.

Mr. Bibb looked out at some children playing in the sun-baked square. When he turned his attention back to the assembly, his eyes seemed to have lost their shimmer. "I was tortured and whipped nearly to the point of death," he said. "Afterwards, my master had an iron slave collar riveted around my neck. It's prongs extended above my head, with a bell on each end. I wore this device for six weeks and forced to sleep with my feet in stocks or chained to a log."

"That man was the Devil, for sure!" exclaimed Sam, his broad face serious for once.

"Even worse," Mr. Bibb continued, "I was separated from Malinda and Mary Frances. The Deacon was determined to sell me."

"How could you bear it?" Sadie asked in a small voice, wondering how the man could even speak of it. Pushing her memories into the darkness was the only way she could manage.

"What's that miss? Oh, I don't rightly know," he replied, lifting his shoulders. "I just kept hoping and praying that the Lord would step in and help me."

"Yes, sometimes hope and prayer are the only things left," Sadie acknowledged, looking back up at him with a small smile.

"One day, when the Deacon had me working at the cotton gin house near the road," he continued, "a group of Southern sportsmen rode up. They saw the load of iron around my neck and asked the Deacon about it. He told them the bells were to keep me from running away. They asked to purchase me. After they struck a bargain, I went off with them. The men cut off the iron and dressed me in finer clothes as they wished to sell me. How relieved I was to be freed of my burden, but distressed at being forced to leave Malinda and Mary Frances behind."

A raggedy ball rolled over from the square, stopping at Mr. Bibb's feet. He glanced down at it as a little girl ran over from the square.

"'Scuse me! May I have my ball, mister?" she asked shyly.

Mr. Bibb picked up the ball. "Of course, honey chile." Tossing it gently to her he said, "What's your name, sweetheart?"

"Frannie, suh."

He stiffened, and then his eyes searched the tiny girl's face.

Sadie gave a little start as she realized he was thinking it might be his own child.

After a few moments, Mr. Bibb smiled at the little girl and said, "Well, that's a lovely name, Frannie."

"Thank ya, suh." She gave him a quick curtsy and ran back to her friends.

Mr. Bibb watched the little girl scamper off with a far away look in his eyes. Sadie assumed he'd decided the little girl was a stranger to him.

"Now where was I," he said, after clearing this throat. "Ah, yes. I asked the men if we could please go back to the plantation. Even though they were gamblers with wicked ways they treated me far better than the Deacon ever had. I hoped they might buy my wife and child. I promised I would help find someone to purchase all three of us."

He took a sip of water and continued in a halting voice, "When we arrived, the Deacon was furious to see me out of my irons and wearing fine clothes. He refused to sell my family. Malinda rushed up with Mary Frances. The Deacon ordered her back to work. She and Mary Frances clung to me. The Deacon began to lash Malinda with all his might. 'Shame!' the gamblers shouted. 'We will give you $1000 for the wife and child!'"

Sadie buried her head in her hands. How he suffered!

Mr. Bibb took a deep breath. "The Deacon refused and we had to leave them. We could still hear the lashings as we rode off. Some of the sportsmen were weeping from what they had seen. They promised when they sold me they would give me some of the proceeds and tell me how to escape to Canada."

"Praise the Lord!" shouted young Henry and several others in the crowd.

Mr. Bibb smiled. "Yes, even though they were sinners, they were decent men, deep down. They said I should act very ignorant once we arrived at our destination to improve my chances for sale. I agreed to the plan.

"The deacon was by far the greater sinner," said the stranger who'd winked at Sadie.

Mr. Bibb nodded. "Yes. I was a very lucky man the day the men came along."

Sadie smiled to herself. Maybe the one-eyed man was a decent fellow, she thought.

"We rode on into Cherokee Territory," continued Mr. Bibb, "so the men could wager on horse races. A wealthy half-Cherokee wanted to purchase me. I liked the idea because he wished me to be his manservant—I wouldn't be required to work in the fields. Best of all, the sportsmen told me his place would be easy to escape from. When the men received their money from my sale, true to their word, they gave me my share, and then explained how to get to Canada.

"My new owner treated me well so I stayed with him, but he died not very long after purchasing me. I made my escape the morning after his death. I fled northward, and after a long, difficult journey, the details of which I will spare you, I reached Ohio and freedom in 1841. I made my way north to Detroit the following year. I received some education and, beginning with a speech I made in 1844, I found audiences ready to hear my story."

A miracle, Sadie thought. Not only had this man managed to escape when all seemed lost, Henry Bibb had gotten himself educated and could speak so beautifully.

"As I became better known, people helped me try to find my family," he continued, but then his face clouded once more. "I was devastated to learn that in order to survive, Malinda had made herself the concubine of a white Kentuckian. As far as I could tell our child was taken along with her into that household. They have become lost to me … forever."

A silence fell over the crowd. Then Sadie's mother spoke up. "Truly sorry for your loss, Mr. Bibb." Her father reached an arm around her. Sadie knew her mother would like nothing better than to give Mr. Bibb a big ole hug.

"Thank you, ma'am," Mr. Bibb said, lost in thought. "I can only hope their life is better than it had been with the Deacon." He took a long drink of water. "I was alone for eight years. And then I met Mary." He visibly brightened at the memory. "It was at an abolitionist gathering in New York. I was captivated by her devotion to the anti-slavery cause and, well, as you saw …" Mr. Bibb paused for a moment and winked, "she is quite pleasing to the eye."

Sadie noticed the handsome stranger gazing at her again. He nodded before turning back to Mr. Bibb.

She felt her face flush.

"And, a year later, we were married," continued Mr. Bibb. "I had been blessed with another miracle: I was alone no longer."

"The Lord favored you, Mr. Bibb," commented the handsome stranger and then glanced at Sadie again.

She quickly looked down at her hands. Part of her mind not confused by the man's attention, was noticing how smooth her skin was despite all the laundering she'd done, thanks to the special cream she'd concocted a few years ago. It was good for bartering, too.

"Yes, it does seem that way, good sir," said Mr. Bibb. Then he spread his arms wide. "And please, I'd be honored if you all called me Henry."

"Yessir, Mr. Bibb," said a little girl. "Ah mean, Henry!" and she collapsed into a fit of giggles.

Mr. Bibb's body shook with laughter and soon everyone in the crowd was laughing and slapping their thighs.

My, it is such a relief to laugh after listening to such a sad story, thought Sadie.

"Why did you come over here, Henry? To Windsor?" asked her son when things had calmed down.

"The same reason you and your family are here, my boy," smiled Mr. Bibb. "I could have been forced back into slavery. And even though Mary was born free she was in danger, as well."

"Very good reasons," said young Henry.

One of Sadie's son's new friends playfully pushed him over. He pulled himself up, a wide grin on his face, and gave the fellow a couple of mock punches.

"Now, with so many fugitives coming across because of that horrid law, which as you no doubt have heard means bounty hunters will be crossing over to this side of the river with impunity, Mary and I saw a need," continued Mr. Bibb. Noting some puzzled faces, he quickly added, "impunity means without breaking the law."

He grew quiet and then said, "I assume most of you arrived with little to your name."

Many people nodded. Sadie's father frowned and looked down at his hands, thick with calluses from years of hard labor. He had refused Sadie's cream, saying he needed his hands to be tough.

"Please, I do not wish to offend," said Mr. Bibb sincerely. "I too had very little when I escaped."

Sadie's father explained, "My family, well, we started out with a whole lot more, but had to keep leavin' things behind along the way. Easier to keep goin' with less of a load."

"I understand perfectly well, sir. That's why Mary and I came today. We are part of an organization called the 'Refugee Home Society'."

Jeremiah raised his eyebrows.

"We want to offer slavery refugees 25-acre farms in the countryside."

There were cries of excitement.

"Oh, my goodness!" said Sadie's mother, clutching her father's arm. "You hear that Jeremiah?"

When the commotion died down, Jeremiah piped up once again. "Well then, what's the catch?"

"All right, we do have some rules," said Mr. Bibb. "Five acres will be granted for free, but 20 acres will be sold at cost. One tenth of the purchase price must be paid before possession of the land, and the balance is to be paid in eight annual installments. And settlers cannot buy, sell or use alcohol."

"Hunh. Sounds fair to me," Jeremiah nodded.

"Settlers are obliged to clear the first five acres within two years," Mr. Bibb added. "Houses must be at least two rooms and purchased lands can only be transferred to spouses or children. Otherwise lands will fall back to the Society. We still have some fundraising to provide sufficient moneys to buy our first acreages—"

Jeremiah's face fell.

Mr. Bibb hastened to add, "But we're very, very close! Just one more week! I beseech you all to wait."

"A week? How can we wait that long when bounty hunters can snatch us up now!" demanded Jeremiah.

"Yeah!" cried others in the crowd. "We don' wanna get taken again!"

"Have faith," said Mr. Bibb, his hands reaching out to them. "Please have faith, all of you. If you watch out for each other, you will all be safe."

There were a few moments of quiet and then a voice broke the silence.

It was Sadie's.

"Sign us up!"

49

August 15, 2012
Wherein two doctors do some investigating and get a lucky break.

"AFTER DINNER, ARE YOU UP FOR CHECKING OUT a couple of shelters?" asked Roger as he and Abby drove to Neely's, one of his favorite restaurants. He'd been craving their famous BBQ spaghetti for months. "We probably should be looking for Jacob before too much more time goes by," he added.

"Um, yeah. You're probably right, Roger."

He studied her delicate profile.

God, she's a beauty, he thought. Do I even have a chance?

"But I don't have much time tonight," she sighed. "Don't forget, I've got an early surgery tomorrow."

Her schedule had unexpectedly changed that day so Roger had picked her up earlier than planned. In fact they were going to enjoy more of a late lunch than dinner.

"Well, there's a place not far from Neely's. It's a day shelter actually called Sanctuary. If you're not starving, why don't we try there first?"

"Sure. And what will happen if we find him, Roger? What do we do with him?"

"Good question. Have him join us at Neely's, maybe?"

"You're kidding, right?"

"Oh, yeah, right. Not your favorite guy."

"Not only that Roger, but think about the kind of place we're going to. I'm sure our charming bigot would be thrilled with the clientele, not to mention the staff."

"Right again. Although he would probably love the food," he chuckled.

"Yeah, maybe he'd mellow right out as soon as he tasted one of their pulled pork sandwiches."

"Yup. I'm sure he'd be purring like a great, big pussycat."

She laughed for a second. "Huh. I'd like to see that. Wait, what am I saying?

A few minutes later, he turned onto Beale. They quickly scanned the street. "Ok, I see it just up the block," said Roger. "Now if I can just find parking."

Abby sighed again.

"What?"

"Sorry. I've never been to a shelter. I hope it's not too disturbing. Ok, now I'm sounding like a wuss. Or a prissy pants, or a—"

Roger chuckled. "Don't worry about it, Abby. I've never been inside one either. I'm sure it won't be all that bad. And besides, I don't think we'll be there long, especially if he's not around."

"Ok, but if he is inside, maybe I shouldn't go in. I don't think he'd be exactly thrilled to see me," she grimaced. "And I think you'd have better luck convincing him to leave with you if you're alone."

Roger considered this and said, "You know what? You might be right. You don't mind waiting in the car then?"

"Not at all."

Roger tucked his Prius into a spot near an alley, not too far from the shelter's entrance. "Ok, wish me luck."

"Luck."

Flashing a smile, Roger extricated his lanky frame from the car and loped toward the shelter. Abby leaned back against the headrest and settled in to wait.

God, I'm always so tired, she thought. Maybe I'll catch a few ZZZs while I've got the chance.

Locking the doors she looked up and down the block and across the street. A few people strolled the sidewalks. While not the best part of Beale it didn't seem all that terrible.

As she was about to doze off, she glimpsed a man with a camera climbing into the car parked just ahead of theirs.

50

August 15, 2012
Wherein a reporter gets an inkling.

BRIAN DRUMMED HIS HANDS ON HIS STEERING WHEEL while he collected his thoughts. He'd downloaded the jpeg of Jacob off of Facebook and when he'd shown it to the Sanctuary's manager, she'd momentarily pursed her lips. Then she'd said, "Just a moment, please" and walked off to ask if anyone had seen him.

Something's up, he thought.

While he'd waited for her to come back, he'd scoped out the shelter in case he could spot Jacob himself. He'd been surprised by how absolutely packed it was. For a Friday afternoon the number of young people and kids in evidence was remarkable. A few faces eyed him with curiosity—or maybe it was suspicion, and if they spotted his camera, most looked away.

When the manager had returned, Brian thought she seemed slightly flustered. She'd told him, "yes, a man that looked like the one in the photo had been there, but he'd left. We don't know where he's gone".

His reporter's sixth sense had barked: what's she hiding? She'd seemed just a little too earnest. Maybe the man was still there and she knew his true identity, but she'd been told to keep it to herself? Or, maybe Jacob had been taken somewhere and hidden? But, if Jacob departed on his own accord, where would he be going next?

And then Brian got an idea. He smiled and turned the key in the ignition.

51

August 15, 2012
Wherein two men and a time traveler walk into a bar.

JACOB WATCHED PATRICK CAREFULLY AS he slid into the seat behind what looked like a small wagon wheel. He noted the small black device in Patrick's hand, which he put into a little slot next to the wheel. There was a slight rumbling sound and then they began to move. Jacob gasped slightly and clutched the seat in front of him. He'd seen how fast these four-wheeled contraptions they called 'cars' could go. He caught Patrick's eye in a small looking glass that appeared to be floating near his head. He quickly averted his gaze.

How Jacob wished he'd fashioned some sort of weapon. He did not like the thought of being enclosed inside such a small space with two big niggers without protection. Nevertheless, he was heartened by the prospect of finally returning to his plantation.

He studied the top of the other man's head, poking up above the chair in front of him. The color was black but not overly nappy—more like loose curls. Of course he'd fathered some half-breeds, but he'd never acknowledged any. Sheila had been furious each time she discovered one of the little bastards.

He frowned. Thoughts of his wife reminded him of the argument the night before his life changed so dramatically. He knew that in addition to her anger at him, she was frustrated that Sadie was gone. She'd run off shortly after he'd taken her. His wife had missed her chance to take out her anger and vengeance on her.

When his overseer told him that not only was Sadie missing, she was eluding capture, he'd been angry and surprised that she hadn't been found right away. That other wench—that Suzanne—certainly hadn't made it far. And she'd paid for her transgression with a new web of lashes on her back.

He hoped Sadie hadn't been found yet. He could still taste her. He hoped her capture happened after his return—if he did return—so he could provide a personal punishment. But not with the lash. No, he intended to mount her again straight away; if she were to receive a whipping, it would delay his pleasure. He'd waited over a month before he'd could take Suzanne again; it had been excruciating to wait that long.

The memory of his house girls had aroused him. He forced himself to study the scene flashing by his window. An enormous portrait of a mulatto woman on the side of a building loomed into view. He sat up a little to see better. What a beauty! Her perfect face with its luscious full lips was framed by a halo of golden hair cascading in soft curls to caress the tops of her divine breasts. They nearly spilled out of her skintight, low cut red frock. Golden letters shimmered above her head: Beyoncé. Who was this vixen, he wondered?

Lord, not only did he want Sadie at that instant, he desired Suzanne as well! He forced himself to think of his wife once more. The urge disappeared.

Patrick glanced at Jacob's face in the rear view mirror. When their eyes met, Jacob immediately looked away. Patrick was a bit surprised by what he'd seen in them. Despite his bravado, Jacob actually appeared frightened.

Patrick glanced at Martin. He was staring straight ahead, arms folded across his chest, one knee bobbing up and down like crazy. No doubt the guy was in shock.

Hell, he was too. He certainly hadn't expected this twist of fate: not only had he tracked down a time traveler, but also one of his progeny. It was almost too much.

His plan to teach Jacob a lesson needed to be altered. Having Martin in tow made things a bit more complicated. So what should he do now?

No matter how hard Martin tried, he just couldn't keep his leg still. It was as if it was wired up to an electric current flowing non-stop from his spinning brain.

It still felt like some kind of elaborate, practical joke, but, somehow, it was real. He could practically feel Jacob's eyes boring into the back of his head. Green irises did pop up in the family bloodline from time to time. None of his folks knew exactly why, although it was a given there must've been white blood mixed in, back in the day. He was the only one in his immediate family who had them.

His parents and grandparents had shared a few tales passed down from slavery days, but they couldn't provide many details. They understood some of their slave ancestors had escaped, but there were no last names. After the Civil War, some of his ancestors had stayed on at their slave plantation to work as sharecroppers. But nobody knew exactly which plantation that was. There had been so many in Tennessee. He did know for certain that one set of his great, great grandparents had moved north, in search of work. Years later, their descendants—his grandparents—moved back down to Tennessee, which was when they took up farming.

He had scoured ancestory.com for further information about his past, but then work got in the way. And now, here he was, sitting in a car with a nasty white man with the same eyes as his, who claimed to have been born over 200 years ago.

Suddenly, Patrick realized what he should do. In fact it was almost too obvious.

"Anyone feel like a drink?"

"Hell, yeah," replied Martin.

There was a moment of silence, and then Jacob's voice: "Yes."

There was a small sports bar not too far away. A few minutes later Patrick pulled into its parking lot. After exiting the car, he looked around to make sure they hadn't been followed. He led the way to the bar and as he pushed the door open, he had to chuckle to himself. A time traveler walks into a bar—.

Martin almost hadn't wanted to get out of the car. As soon as he'd realized where they were, a night of heavy drinking flashed through his mind. It had not ended well. He'd had way too much to drink, but that wasn't too surprising given the fact he'd gone out with some friends to drown his sorrows a few days after his brother Solomon died in a car accident. He'd been underage. His father found him and dragged his sorry ass out of there. Hadn't been back since.

Shit. Of all places.

He gave a rueful laugh and followed Patrick to the door. For a moment, he thought he could hear his brother laughing with him.

"You here, Solomon?" he whispered. "If you are, can you believe this, bro?"

52

August 15, 2012
Wherein Abby and Roger give chase.

ABBY AWOKE WITH A START TO HEAR A CAR DOOR OPENING.

Oh, God. Hope I wasn't snoring, she thought.

"Hello, Sleeping Beauty. Sorry to wake you," Roger said, thinking, adorable even while sleeping with her mouth open.

She smiled at him, stifling a yawn. "That's okay. So, no luck, I take it?"

"Nope. Well, not really. But, when I described who I was looking for, I got a funny look."

"Yeah? What kind of look?"

"Well, now that I think about it, that kind of look someone gets when they know something, but are pretending they don't. I should go back."

"Was there a reporter in there?"

"Not sure, but I did notice a guy with a camera. He left just after I went in."

"And I saw him get into the car ahead of us."

They looked at the empty spot where the car had been.

"I'll bet you ten bucks he was from the paper, Roger. Maybe Jacob is still in there."

He drummed his fingers on the steering wheel and then stared at her with admiration. "I think you're right Dr. Shields. You're obviously the brains of this operation."

She gave a little laugh. "Obviously."

"Too bad we hadn't shown up sooner." he asked.

"Well, did you tell them he'd been your 'patient'"?

"Uh, no. I just described him and asked if he'd been there."

"Well, I think you should definitively go back in, tell them you're from the hospital, that Jacob was your patient, and he checked himself out. Tell them it's vitally important you find him!"

"Brilliant. Be right back."

As she watched him run over to the shelter Abby shook her head.

Men. Well, at least, he's amusing. Now, if we do find Jacob what are we going to do with him? Damn. I wish I had given this more thought. She frowned. The media seem to be on the chase, too. We're going to have to be extra diligent.

A side door a little ways down the alley popped open. A head poked out, looked around and then a man quickly stepped outside. Two more men followed him and the trio walked off. They were in a hurry.

"Oh, wow," said Abby, sitting up.

One of them looked very, very familiar.

She jumped out of the car and dashed toward the shelter. She found Roger pushing back out through the door.

"C'mon on! I saw him!"

"Jacob?"

"Yes! He slipped out a side door with two men."

"Really? Did you see which way they went?"

"I did! We can catch up to them if we hurry. Run!"

They raced back to Roger's car and clambered in.

"The car went through the alley. Red Mazda. Four-door. Managed to get most of the license plate."

"Good!"

He raced the car down the alley and darted onto the street one block down. They craned their necks searching up and down the street.

"There it is!" she yelled, pointing to her right. "A few blocks down. Step on it!"

53

August 15, 2012
Wherein Jacob, Patrick and Martin engage in tentative male bonding.

THE BRANDY IS INFERIOR, Jacob thought, but it'll do. He took another sip and smacked his lips. Lord in heaven, it seems a lifetime ago since I've felt that soothing fire in my chest.

From the corner of his eye, he considered the two niggers. The light skinned one—supposedly his progeny—was lapping up his second scotch. And the other—dark as Hades—was polishing off his first bottle of beer. He shuddered as he recalled that morning he'd seen the man's ugly black face hovering only a few inches above his own. Then there was that horrid dream. And now here he was—in the flesh.

He sighed. Hopefully they wouldn't get drunk and forget to take him back to his plantation. He'd seen more than once, especially during Christmas holy days, how their kind simply could not hold their liquor.

One of those infernal boxes droned on the wall opposite the bar. Trapped inside was a horde of long limbed darkies chasing each other up and down a wooden floor. They seemed to be fighting over an orange ball as white men dressed in black and white striped shirts periodically intervened. Were they trying to keep them from killing each other?

He turned on his stool and surveyed his surroundings. Then he grimaced. A nasty place. Dark, foreboding, the only other customers a sprinkling of motley looking niggers staring at him like he was the man on the moon. More than likely they were pondering what a man like him was doing with two of their own kind.

"So, Jacob..."

What now? He kept his eyes on the box and stayed silent. Waiting. From the corner of his eye, he watched Patrick put down his beer and wipe his fat lips with the back of his hand then turn away from the box to look at him.

"You sure you want to go back?" he said.

Jacob gave a snort. "Of course I want to go back!" Shooting the man an annoyed look he swallowed the remnants of his drink and banged the glass down on the bar. "When do we depart?"

Patrick smiled at him. "I have to admit I'm surprised to hear that, Jacob. I thought with all our modern inventions and conveniences you might like it here."

Jacob grunted and pressed his lips together. He certainly would not admit how he enjoyed the coolness inside every building, which was indeed a welcome relief from the heat of the streets. And then there was the marvelous luxury of indoor running water and piss pots. Light whenever one wanted it was also splendid.

Patrick signaled to the man behind the bar. "Bartender, another Coors and a brandy for my friend, please." He looked at Martin. "Another whisky?"

He gave a little start, and then checked his glass. "Sure. Might as well."

Would they ever leave this infernal place? Jacob fretted. But, then again, another brandy couldn't hurt, could it?

Martin stared at the TV. A game was on but if anyone asked who was playing he wouldn't be able to tell them. He was more than a little freaked out. It would probably take a whole bottle of whisky before he even felt a buzz. Never did he expect to be back in this dive. And never, ever in a million years would he have imagined when he'd woken up that morning that his day would take this bizarre twist.

He thought of his mother. What would she think of all this? Could he even tell her? And what would Dad say if he were still alive? No doubt he'd have a few choice words for Mr. Jacob Williams.

He shook the ice cubes melting into his scotch. Yeah. Why not ask the bartender for the whole bottle? He gave Jacob a sidelong look. He seemed to be enjoying his brandy, but looked a little bewildered by the TV not to mention everything else. Trying to take in modern life, let alone the notion blacks were free, would definitely be a shock for him.

Even though his parents were fairly dark, he was lighter skinned, Martin had felt hostility and hatred from white people countless times. And because of his 'paper bag' skin, darker blacks occasionally gave him grief because he was so fair. Some days it felt like he just couldn't win. But the reaction from Jacob was unlike any form of racism he'd ever experienced. The guy was practically spitting venom. Hell, it seemed like Martin wasn't even a person to Jacob.

Even though that was wrong on so many levels, he could actually understand it. Jacob had been conditioned to think of blacks that way, even if his blood was coursing through some of their veins.

And now here Jacob was, a slave-owning plantation owner, sitting with two black guys, in a black bar, with blacks playing basketball on TV. And the topper—a brother was running the country. Man, it would be hard enough trying to cope with traveling forward in time, but to have to deal with your worst nightmare too?

Patrick studied Jacob as he sipped his second brandy. He seemed to be enjoying it, but who could tell for sure with that frown on his stony face? Goddamn, he was one ornery, stubborn bugger. Probably willing himself to stay sober. Maybe my plan to loosen him up a bit is a dud. What the hell can I do to break down his armor... make him realize we're all human?

He turned his attention back to the game while a part of his brain ruminated about the best way to crack Jacob. A commercial came on for Disneyland.

Hm. Wonder if he has any kids? Besides the illegitimate ones, that is. And if so, maybe there's a chance he's missing them.

Keeping an eye on the TV, he asked casually, "Do you have any children, Jacob?"

Silence. But it seemed Jacob's body relaxed a little before he took another sip of brandy. And then finally he answered.

"Three."

"Boys? Girls?"

Jacob hesitated and then, "A son. Two daughters." He added in a low voice, "One daughter is a little one… a baby."

"Hunh. I guess you miss them. And, they must miss you."

Jacob sat up straighter and turned to face Patrick. "Which is why I must return to my plantation as quickly as possible."

"Well, hopefully you will, Jacob. And I will try to make that happen."

"What do you mean, 'try'? You said you were taking me there."

Patrick chose to ignore him.

"Me, I really want kids. At least a couple, but when the economy tanked, we decided to wait a while."

Jacob stared at him blankly.

"Martin, you got kids?"

"Uh, no man. Not married yet. But my mom's holding up a stop watch."

Patrick laughed. "That right? Guess she's looking forward to spoiling some grandkids, huh?"

"Oh yeah. I swear she's already got outfits picked out for them."

"Ha, ha!"

Patrick liked this guy. Somehow he felt a little sorry for him. He'd watched how he kept nervously shifting his gaze from the TV, to the scratched-in initials on the bar in front of him, to Jacob.

"Well, I don't blame her," Martin continued. "She's kind of lonely and anxious I guess. My dad passed a few years back. My brother died too. Before. Almost 10 years ago now. It's taken her a long time to get over his death. In fact, I don't think she ever will."

Patrick frowned. "Oh, man. That's tough, that's real tough. Sorry to hear that."

"Yeah. Thanks." Martin shrugged his shoulders. "So, the pressure's on to keep the blood line going, you know." He gave Jacob another quick sideways look before glancing down at the bar again.

Patrick guessed Martin was regretting his choice of words, but Jacob didn't even seem to notice. He kept toying with his glass and staring at the TV. He looked completely mesmerized by it but Patrick wondered if he might be thinking of home. Or, maybe he was simply choosing to ignore Patrick and Martin once again. Then again, perhaps he was thinking about someone else entirely. Someone other than his wife, like maybe one of those poor slave girls he'd had his way with. Must be pretty annoying to have to deal with the consequences like this.

A slab of light pierced the gloom of the bar as the outside door opened. Every head in the joint turned to look.

A tall man and a petite woman stood silhouetted in the doorway.

54

August 15, 2012

Wherein Brian listens to his gut.

Almost bumping into the car behind him, Brian quickly maneuvered away from the curb. If he wanted to see for himself just where Jacob had supposedly jumped into the 21st century from he needed to get to the Williams' Plantation before it closed. Hopefully, the plantation staff would provide some clues to help him find the guy.

At first, Brian's editor had been skeptical when he'd pitched his story idea about a possible time traveler roaming the streets of Memphis. In fact, he'd been dead set against it, but Brian had pushed hard. In fact, he'd just gotten the green light that morning. Next he'd convinced his editor to promise he wouldn't tell anyone at the paper. His rationale was he didn't want his colleagues to scoff, but the fact of the matter was he didn't want to share the glory. If he could prove that Jacob Williams had traveled through time, and his story broke about a real, live time traveler, he'd be famous.

The concept of time travel had fascinated Brian since he was a kid. Along with UFOs. And the paranormal. In fact his parents used to worry about him. But then they figured it was a passing fad. Brian did tone it down as he got older, but his interest continued to percolate; he was still a "geek seeker" at heart.

Over the years he'd studied some of the theories on time travel: Einstein's, Feynman's, Hawking's. There was no doubt in his mind that the typical concept of time, where everything followed a linear path forward, was too simplistic. The law of causality—or cause and effect—sometimes called the Butterfly effect, where one event happens in the universe and leads to another in an endless one-way string of milestones, particularly intrigued him. But to imagine a different reality, say where a murder victim could die of his or her gunshot wound before they had been shot, violated what people considered "reality". As a result, many scientists believed time travel into the past was impossible.

But going into the future? Maybe that was more likely? And if his hunch about the re-enactor was right, maybe he was about to prove that.

The conspiracy theories about time travel intrigued him, but were pretty far out. The claim that President Obama had taken part in a Mars visitation-training program thirty years ago was downright laughable. Then there was some guy who'd invented a 'hyper dimensional' device that he said could transport people through time. Christ. The thing was a metal box about the size of a toaster oven with a few knobs and switches. Total malarkey, but people actually bought devices from the guy. Brian dug up an old interview with him where he described a trip some scientists took using his device. Said they went into the future to the year 2013 and discovered all life on Earth had been wiped out thus proving the world would end on Dec. 21, 2012, as based on the Mayan calendar. Brian was definitely not in the camp of believers who fell for that particular prophecy. It just didn't make sense.

Then he'd discovered a story that had riveted him. Two men were driving on a secondary highway in Louisiana. The road was quiet—they almost had it to themselves. The pair spotted an old car up ahead that was traveling well below the speed limit. As they caught up to it they saw it had a large bright orange license plate with the year 1940 printed on it. As they started to pass the car, they noticed a woman at the wheel wearing a fur coat and a hat with a long colored feather even though it was a warm day. A child was standing on the passenger's seat.

They were struck by the look of fear and panic on the woman's face; her head was swiveling back and forth like she was lost. It seemed as if she were about to cry. One of the guys called out to her and asked if she needed help. She nodded "yes"but was giving their vehicle a very puzzled look. They motioned for her to pull over.

The men passed her then pulled over onto the shoulder. She coasted in behind them, but then—poof! Her car vanished. Another car stopped, a man got out and ran toward them shouting, "What happened? Where did it go?" The trio stared at the spot where her car had been in disbelief. They checked the environs in case she had somehow driven into a ditch, but nothing. Since the three of them had witnessed what happened they surmised the woman, her child and her car had done the impossible: slipped through a crack in time.

The tale had yet to be disproven.

Man. He just had to find Jacob Williams. When he'd questioned Leisha, the girl who had posted a picture of him on Facebook, she'd said he'd behaved like he owned the house. After he collapsed, the staff told her class he had taken his role as a re-enactor too seriously. When Leisha explained to Brian how the man had charged down the stairs yelling and waving a fireplace poker around, he suspected this was more than just a case of an actor overacting. And the clincher: Leisha described how the man came into focus out of nowhere.

55

August 15, 2012
Wherein Jacob makes a painful confession.

ONCE HER EYES ADJUSTED TO THE BAR'S GLOOM, Abby spotted three men sitting at the bar. She nudged Roger.

"There they are."

Abby tried not to look as nervous as she felt as they crossed the room. A dozen pairs of eyes followed them with interest.

Roger smiled. "Hello, Jacob."

Jacob was visibly flustered. "Hello," he murmured, avoiding eye contact with Abby.

Roger extended a hand to Patrick and Martin. "Hi, I'm Dr. Roger Eaton from Memphis Memorial Hospital. This is my colleague Dr. Abby Shields. Jacob was recently a patient of ours, but released himself."

"I see," said Patrick, his interest piqued. "I'm Patrick Monroe, and this is Martin Willems."

"Nice to meet you," said Martin.

Even in the low light, Roger and Abby noticed Martin's eyes.

Roger turned back to Jacob. "How have you been feeling?"

Jacob looked down. "I ... well, I have been as well as can be expected."

"Well, good. I'm glad to hear that."

Patrick looked at the doctors and raised his eyebrows. "I expect you know who Jacob is?"

"Yes, we figured it out," Abby said glancing at Jacob who turned his gaze back to the TV. "He was quite an interesting patient, I must say."

Jacob squirmed slightly.

She regarded Patrick and Martin. "Excuse me, but can I ask why you two are with Jacob? How do you know him?"

Patrick took a quick sip of his beer. "It's like this, I was at Jacob's plantation the morning he had his heart attack. I performed CPR on him."

"Oh! Well then, my goodness," Abby replied touching his arm. "You saved his life."

Jacob looked up at Patrick as if he had never seen him before. Patrick gave him a slight nod.

"And apparently, I'm related. To Jacob, that is," said Martin. There was a pause as the doctors took this in. "Yeah. I know. Kind of a stretch, huh?" he added.

"Well, this just gets more intriguing by the second," remarked Roger.

"We were about to take Jacob back to his plantation," explained Patrick. "But then I thought we should try to get to know each other a little better first. And here we are."

"Take him back to his plantation?" said Abby with alarm. "Already?"

"Madam, I told you at the hospital that I must go back," said Jacob looking at her with disdain. "But you didn't believe me."

"I know you did, Jacob," she replied trying her best not to sound irritated. "But you were in very bad shape at the time. Anyway, why go back? There's nothing for you there, Jacob."

"I hope you're wrong, madam."

"We think you should come with us, Jacob," said Roger quietly.

Patrick intervened. "Look, I mean no disrespect, but we promised to take Jacob to his plantation and I don't break my promises."

"If it weren't for this delay, we would be there by now," grumbled Jacob.

Patrick frowned. "Look, Jacob. I've had just about enough. You should be god damn grateful we're even taking you."

"How dare you speak to me in that manner, you bloody big— " growled Jacob before he caught himself and looked around the bar. His outburst had garnered extra attention; all eyes were on him.

"'Bloody big what, Jacob?" said Patrick. He stood up, put his hands on his hips, and leaned over him. "Just what were you going to call me, man?"

Jacob shrank away from him. "Nothing," he muttered.

"Maybe I should have just let you die, Jacob. But, noooo. I couldn't do that. No matter what you were or who you are, I had to try to save your life."

Jacob was silent.

"You were very lucky he was there, Jacob. You should be grateful!" said Martin shaking his head.

"Yes, you should!" said Abby sternly. "Without Patrick, you would have died, Jacob." Then she dropped her voice. "I know you find it hard to believe that a black man would have been the least bit inclined to save you, but times have changed."

Jacob stared at the scratched up bar and slowly shook his head.

"And for the record, there are hundreds of thousands of female doctors in this day and age, Jacob. Black, white, brown, yellow, red—you name it," she whispered, an impish smile on her face. "Oh, and women can vote too."

Jacob grew pale. "I don't feel very well," he said with a grimace. "I need to find the washing room."

"It's over there," said the bartender who had been meticulously wiping the bar, trying to eavesdrop on their conversation. He pointed toward a door on the far wall.

With a start, Patrick wondered how much the man had overheard and whether he could make any sense of it. They had been careful to keep their conversation neutral, and the female doc had whispered, but they need to be more diligent.

Jacob slid off his stool and trudged across the room, keeping his head down, as he was obviously the focus of everyone's attention. He furtively glanced behind him when he got to the door, then stepped inside.

"You might as well sit down while we wait for him to return," said Patrick to the doctors. "Why don't we get a table?"

"And how about a drink?" added Martin.

Abby and Roger looked at each other. Abby hesitated for a second, and then nodded.

"A drink is probably a good idea right about now," chuckled Roger. "I'll have a Heineken."

"You wouldn't have some Pinot Grigio?" Abby asked the bartender.

"Um, 'fraid not." He looked at her like she'd asked for a bottle of Dom Perignon.

"Ok, I'll have what he's having."

"That was quite the speech," said Patrick to her as they settled into their seats.

She blushed. "Well, he had it coming. He was an absolute pain in the butt at the hospital."

Roger whispered, "You should have seen him watching TV for the first time. His reaction was priceless. You won't believe this, but he thinks Abby's some kind of a witch and that it was her doing!"

Patrick and Martin looked at each other and laughed.

"Anyway," continued Roger, "he was homeless, penniless and didn't have ID or family. At first I assumed I was looking at just another case of some poor soul who was living in a dream world." He stared at the Men's Room door as he searched for the right words. "I wanted to keep him at the hospital not only for his own safety, but to study him in case he proved to be a very unusual amnesia patient, or possibly someone having a past-life experience, but he checked himself out. When Abby and I compared notes, it seemed Jacob was much more than I first thought."

Abby concurred. "His behavior certainly made me wonder. But, never in a million years did I suspect that we would have a real live—" she glanced around the room and decided to not finish her sentence.

"Yeah, we know," agreed Patrick. "Who in their right minds would believe it?"

Jacob came out of the Men's Room, paused for a moment as if reluctant to rejoin them before heading to their table. Patrick pulled out a chair for him. "Feeling better?"

"Yes. Somewhat." He sat down with a slight thud.

Martin's phone buzzed. "Excuse me," he said to the group. "I have to take this call."

Jacob's eyes followed him as he stepped outside.

"Jacob, how does it feel to meet one of your, uh, relatives?" asked Roger in a low voice. "I can't even begin to imagine how confusing this all must be for you."

Jacob sighed and said, "Yes, of course it is confusing for me. And I find it difficult to believe that man is my relation."

There was a silence. He added in a near whisper, "And it's not because he's a ni—, uh, colored."

"No?" said Patrick. "Then why is it difficult, Jacob?"

"Because of the way I treated them," he whispered.

Another silence.

"Them?" asked Abby at last.

Jacob looked at her and then closed his eyes.

Damn, she thought. If I didn't know better I'd say he looks ashamed of himself.

"Those slave girls I uh, had relations with. Most of their—" He stared at his hands. "Almost every one of their babies died. Because of me."

Jacob shrunk down in his seat and folded his arms across his chest.

Patrick nearly spit out his words. "How many, Jacob?"

Jacob hesitated before finally whispering, "I don't know for certain.

My wife, well, she—" He scrubbed his face with his hands. "My overseer keeps track. I would have liked to have added them to my—" Jacob paused, considering his words, and then added, "my slave stock, but Sheila would not have it. She wouldn't even let me sell them."

He looked up at the ceiling and then his eyes slid back down to Patrick's face.

"She wanted them all dead."

56

May 1866

Wherein a young man returns to his country of birth: the United States of America.

SADIE GAZED UP INTO HER BELOVED SON'S bewitching green eyes. He's become such a tall, handsome young man, she thought with pride. "Goodbye, Henry," she said. "Be careful and don't forget to send word a soon as you get to New York City."

"Don't worry, Ma. I'll be fine." He gently brushed a tear off her cheek. "Did I ever tell you how pretty you are?"

"Go on with you," she said, dabbing her eyes with her handkerchief. Her face was still wrinkle-free despite years of hard labor in the fields. She credited her special facial cream concoction made from various secret ingredients and the honey she harvested from the bee hives she kept.

"Now promise me you'll be sure to let us know you made it safe and sound."

"I promise, Ma. Cross my heart."

Nathaniel stretched out a broad hand toughened to the consistency of boot leather. "Take care of yourself Henry. Here. This is for you."

Henry looked down at the folded bills nestled in his stepfather's open palm. His eyes widened.

"Pa! You don't have to give me any money. How did you— "

"I know son, but I want to," he said a little gruffly. "Take it, please."

"I don't know what to say, sir."

"Say 'thank you' and take it, Henry."

Henry scrutinized his face. His stepfather's one eye was crinkled at the corner. He guessed Nathaniel was only pretending to sound stern.

Henry smiled at him. "Thank you, Pa. I sure do appreciate it."

Sadie stood on her tiptoes and kissed her husband's cheek. "Nathaniel! You ole softy." The man never ceased to surprise her. From the very first day when he'd tipped his hat at her by the barracks in Windsor, she knew he was different from the other men who had tried to woo her. Soon she began accepting his attentions and slowly got to know him. His story of how he'd lost his eye during a vicious lashing by his former overseer broke her heart. Little by little she felt relaxed enough to share what had happened to her on the Williams' plantation. To her relief, Nathaniel did not shun her or Henry. When Sadie saw how gentle he was with her boy and how her Ma and Pa approved of him, something unexpected happened. It was something she'd longed for, but didn't dare allow herself to feel: love. 'True' love, she believed. They married later that same year. Together they built their homestead on the Home Society land allotted to them in a little community a ways east of Windsor called Puce.

Today Henry was taking the ferry from Windsor to Detroit to catch a train to New York. After receiving news that the long Civil War was finally over and colored folk were free he'd decided it was time to go back and seek his fortune. Once he'd made his mind up, she saw that he couldn't wait to leave their farm in Puce and head south to the United States.

His Ma had insisted on accompanying him to town and Henry didn't relish the thought of a long, drawn out goodbye. But then he realized how hard she was taking his leaving. Besides, he knew she was longing to pick up some pretty cloth in town to make some new clothes. His step dad had offered to drive the wagon, but Henry knew his real reason for coming; it was not just to say goodbye, but also to support Sadie as she watched her son return to a country that had driven them all away.

Henry's little brother and two sisters had remained back at the farm with his Grandma and Grandpa. As he'd said his final goodbyes to everyone, the girls had leaped into his arms for one last hug. His brother Joseph, hands shoved in his pockets, stood nearby, scuffing at the dirt with his toe. Henry put his sisters down and turned to him. Their eyes locked and Joseph stuck out a hand. Henry marveled at how much his brother had grown—nearly past his shoulder already. If they were to meet again, he would likely be as tall as Henry.

It was a long dusty ride into Windsor. The family rarely had time to journey far from the homestead. It all seemed new to them. They craned their necks as they tried to take everything in. The town had boomed after the railroad arrived in '54. Now it was four times bigger than when they had taken that fateful voyage across the river from Detroit in '51.

Had that really been 15 years ago?

They admired the shady tree-lined streets with their tidy homes. His Ma's eyes lit up at the variety of shops and other businesses that had sprung up in the bustling downtown. Henry couldn't resist buying her a penny ice cream cone—her first ever—at one of the souvenir shops catering to American tourists. The smile on her face was enough of a treat for him; he was too nervous and excited to eat.

He'd thought of going down South, but didn't think he'd be able to find work that would pay there. And he was sick and tired of farm chores and getting up before dawn. He hoped today was the last time he would ever have to milk a cow.

His family had kept in touch with Joe (Missus Margaret died several years back). He'd offered a place for Henry in Philadelphia. While that was a tempting offer, Henry balked. He liked the sound of New York City. It seemed to him anything was possible there. And he had a feeling he was the kind of person with enough smarts to make it.

His heart was pounding with excitement as he stepped aboard the ferry. He turned and blew a kiss to his mother. Raising her hand, she pulled her shawl tighter from a sudden gust of wind. Nathaniel wrapped an arm around her and nodded one last time at his son.

Henry walked over to the railing and waved at his parents until they were tiny specks.

Ten minutes later he stepped onto U.S. soil.

It felt right.

57

August 15, 2012

Wherein the past meets the present, again.

Brian whistled under his breath. He'd gotten lost but had finally found the plantation. It felt like he'd arrived at the set of *Gone With the Wind*. He stepped out of his car and stared up at a magnificent white mansion which nearly engulfed a small rise. Massive antebellum columns stretched to the roof, which poked out over a deep balcony stretching across the entire front façade and sides of the house. The only feature interrupting the vast expanse of the white mansion was the front door, which was a rich, dark brown.

"Man, this is some house," Brian murmured.

His gut did a little flip. He gave his stomach a little pat. "I hear ya." He'd trained himself not to ignore what he called his 'second brain'. He'd found this technique invaluable during his career as a reporter. His stomach was telling him that Jacob was inside.

Pocketing his keys, he pressed his cameras against his body to keep them from bouncing as he trotted from the parking lot up to the house. It was difficult to contain his eagerness. If all went well, he was about to capture, for all the world to see, a real time traveler. And not just any old time traveler. This was a southern U.S. slave-owning-time-traveler from the 1830s who had arrived in a future where blacks were free.

He raced up the front steps. The hours of operation were etched on a polished brass plaque beside the front door. He still had time. He took a deep breath and pushed the door open. He found himself in the Great Hall. He was alone. A magnificent curved staircase arched toward a second floor landing that must have been twenty feet up. A stunning crystal chandelier was suspended from the center of an ornate plaster ceiling. A gleaming polished hardwood floor was accented by an intricate red Persian rug. The Williams' Big House was as grand inside as out.

He listened carefully for voices, but all was quiet. Had the tourists already left? Where were the staff?

"Hello?" he called.

Ambling into a room adjacent to the front hall, he gave a low whistle. He was staring straight into the eyes of Jacob Williams. Well, his portrait at any rate. The resemblance to the photo Leisha had posted on Facebook of the man shouting from the landing was uncanny.

Jacob nearly swooned as they rolled up an expansive lane way leading to the front of his home. He was almost beside himself with joy. But his happiness was tinged with fear.

If I cannot go back, what will I do? What will happen to me?

He thought of the KKK men he'd seen. Would he still join them? Or, would he take his own life, according to his earlier plan?

He looked quickly at the two men in the car. His thoughts felt muddled. With a start, he realized that he felt a bond with them. Would they continue to help him if he could not travel back in time?

His hands clenched. I will not think about failure. Whatever barrier opened for me to travel here will allow me to slip through again and I will go back to my time. I must.

It *will* happen.

Patrick glanced into the rear view mirror at Jacob's face. It was clear the man was excited to see his "home" again. As Patrick looked up at the grand white mansion the memories of their first encounter came rushing back. While he no longer felt that Jacob loathed him, if the man remain trapped here in the future, he felt pretty certain they would never become bosom buddies.

Before they'd left the bar, Patrick had watched the two doctors closely as they'd said their goodbyes to Jacob. He couldn't help bur wonder if they harbored some disappointment about Jacob's departure. It was certainly possible that they'd been expecting to gain fame and fortune with their discovery of a real live time traveler. But they didn't strike him as the type; they appeared to have a genuine interest in Jacob's well-being and had decided to do the right thing: allow him to attempt a return to his own time.

As he turned off the engine, a new thought made Patrick catch his breath: So, what was "Plan B" if Jacob was stuck here?

He broke into a sweat as he realized there was no "Plan B".

"Holy shit," said Martin under his breath.

The last time he'd driven by the plantation, it had been a dilapidated mess. Now it glowed like a king's palace.

He swallowed hard as he tried to imagine his ancestors living there—well, not in the Big House, of course. If it weren't for them and the other slaves, there would be no mansion, nor any of Jacob's other possessions, or his incredible wealth.

As they had arrived almost at closing time, there were only a sprinkling of other cars in the parking lot.

It's a good thing we left the bar when we did, he thought.

Then he felt the hair on the back of his neck stand up.

What if this doesn't work, Martin? whispered his brother Solomon into his ear. What are we gonna do with Gramps?

Patrick helped Jacob unbuckle his seat belt.

"Ok, this is it. Are you ready for this, Jacob?"

His eyes trained on the house, Jacob nodded. "Yes. I am ready."

As the three men began walking toward the house, Patrick turned his head to Jacob. "What if this doesn't work out? What do you want to do, then?"

Jacob turned to Patrick, his green eyes glittering.

"It will happen."

The Great Hall was empty when the men pushed through the heavy oak door into the front hall. Without a moment's hesitation, they headed to the stairs. The strip of thick carpet running down the center muffled the sound of their steps as they began to climb. On the landing they paused so Jacob could catch his breath.

A man and a woman slowly entered the great hall from a side room. The man was carrying a camera. The couple spotted the men on the landing.

"Excuse me. May I help you?" said the woman. And then she gasped. "Oh, my god. It's him!"

Patrick grabbed Jacob's arm. "Go! Go!"

Brian raised his camera to his face.

"And that teacher, too!" she cried. "Wait! Please wait! This man wants to talk to you!"

Brian started running up the stairs.

Patrick dragged Jacob down the hall.

"This room," Jacob panted as he pointed to the second closed door on the right

Patrick yanked the door open and pushed him inside.

"I hope this works," Patrick whispered. "If it does, goodbye Jacob!"

Martin gave Jacob a salute. Their green eyes locked.

"It's been a slice," said Martin.

Jacob raised a hand and nodded. "Goodbye, Martin," he rasped, his chest heaving as he tried to catch his breath. "And, thank you. Both of you."

Patrick gave him a quick nod as he pushed the door shut just before the man and woman descended upon them.

"Is he in there?" demanded Brian. "I need to talk to him!"

He grabbed the door knob and gave it a frantic turn.

58

Wherein a family is reunited?

JACOB FELL UPON HIS BED and pressed his hands into eyes. The room began to whirl and then seconds later—nothingness.

He was unsure how long he lay unconscious. One moment all was black and then he was aware of something thick and soft pressing against his cheek.

He opened an eye. He was lying on a carpet. But where?

As he lifted his head to look around, he winced. His fingers found a large bump on his forehead.

"Jacob!"

He stiffened, and then eased over onto his back. He looked up into his wife's face.

"Oh, Jacob!" she cried, reaching down to cradle his head. "Are you all right?"

He stared at her in shock. Not believing it was she. Not believing he was home. That he had returned.

Sheila's eyes were large with fear and worry, and there was something else—something he hadn't seen in such a long time: love.

"Oh, Papa! I don't think I've ever been so frightened!"

He turned his head to see his two eldest children kneeling beside him. They were in their nightclothes. Rosalie was cradling Baby Chloe in her arms.

"I heard a terrible crash," she continued breathlessly. "I ran out to the landing and saw you down here in a heap on the floor!"

"What happened, Father?" asked his son Jonathan. "Did you hear an intruder?"

The baby gurgled and crawled out of Rosalie's arms to give Jacob a slobbery kiss.

Tears sprang to his eyes. He'd done it. He was back. He was home!

Sheila took his hand and gave it a gentle squeeze. It had been his family's custom to gauge Jacob's mood before they spoke freely. Now it seemed they had no fear. Could it be they all loved him now? If so, how extraordinary.

His wife picked up the fireplace poker, which lay beside him.

"Now, what on earth is this doing here, Jacob?"

Jacob's eyes widened as he stared at the poker. Then he slowly shook his head. Had he actually been trying to chase a group of children out of his house with it? How could he?

"Please say something, Jacob!"

He pulled his eyes from the poker to look at his family. His dear, nearly lost family. At last he managed to croak, "Hello, Sheila."

She sighed in relief. "Oh, thank goodness. Can you rise. Jacob?"

He nodded and attempted to stand, but found he only had strength to push himself up onto his elbows.

"Here, let us help you. Jonathan, quick, put your father's arm over your shoulders and help him up. Careful now! And Rosalie, go ask Suzanne to bring your father a cold, wet cloth."

Taking great care not to jostle him, his wife and son got Jacob to his feet and then helped him hobble over to the parlor and onto the settee. Sheila was arranging cushions beneath his head as Rosalie hurried back in with Suzanne.

"My goodness, Mr. Williams. That sure is quite a bump you've got there," Suzanne said, her pretty brown face puckered in concern. She bent and placed a soothing wet cloth on his forehead. "You gave us all such a fright!"

Jacob's heart gave a lurch. Suzanne. She was one of the house girls he'd taken. Why did she not fear him!

He closed his eyes in shame. Not only had he raped her, he'd ordered 70 lashes after she'd been caught attempting to escape the plantation. Suzanne had fled not only because of what he'd done to her, but because she likely feared his wife's retributions. And now she was showing them both such kindness. How was it possible? How had things changed so?

"We need the doctor," declared Sheila. "Jonathan, go fetch Dr. Edwards. Tell him to come as fast as he can. Tell him your father's had a bad fall. And hurry!'

"Yes, Mother," Jonathan yelled over his shoulder as he snatched his hat and ran off, yelling for Samuel to bring 'round a horse.

Jacob smiled. He hadn't noticed before how tall his son was getting.

"Rosalie, stay here with your father. I must go back and help Suzanne in the kitchen. Oh, my land, how are we going to be ready in time for the governor and his wife tomorrow? Perhaps I should cancel the dinner?"

"Don't you fret, Mrs. Williams. We'll manage. We always do," Suzanne reassured her and marched back to the kitchen.

"Oh, I do hope so, Suzanne," Sheila called after her. She stared down again at Jacob, her long fingers pressed to her mouth. Sighing, she bent down to gently flip the cloth over on his forehead so it felt cool again.

"I do wish you could tell me what happened, Jacob. Was there an intruder?" She looked around nervously. "I certainly hope not."

He stared at her. How could he even begin to tell her what he'd been through? What would she even believe?

Sheila turned to Rosalie. "I'll be right back with a bell for your father to ring, just in case."

"Don't worry, Mama. I'll watch him. But perhaps it might be better if Chloe went to the nursery with Nanny."

"Why yes, of course," said Sheila, scooping up the baby who squawked and squirmed, stretching her chubby arms toward Jacob.

"Wait—"

Sheila jostled the baby, trying to calm her. She looked down at Jacob.

"Yes, dearest?"

"Let her stay, Sheila."

The baby gave Jacob a wide gap-toothed smile. He felt his heart skip a beat.

"Are you sure?"

"Please. I miss her."

"Miss her?" Sheila searched Jacob's face in wonderment. He smiled and nodded.

"Very well then, my love." She returned the baby to Rosalie's lap.

With a trembling hand Jacob reached over and stroked Chloe's soft pink cheek. "Hello, honey chile."

"Pa... Papa," the baby chortled.

"I'll be right back," said Sheila, brushing a tear from her eye as she darted out of the room. Bustling back in a few moments later with a small silver bell, she placed it on the end table next to the settee.

"Now Jacob, don't you worry one little bit. The doctor will be here lickety split." She moved toward the kitchen and paused in the doorway. "And I'm close by. Now, Rosalie, just ring that bell for your father if you need to." She looked at Jacob again. "Oh, darling—I am so relieved that you, well, that you seem to be all right."

Jacob smiled. "I think it is a good idea to have the doctor look me over." Then he added a word he hadn't used in a long time: "Darling."

She smiled back, blew him a kiss, and then disappeared.

Jacob blinked and then stared at the empty doorway. He was remembering the last time he'd seen her. She been in a different doorway—the dining room's, and she had been crying and cursing him. Jacob rubbed his eyes as if to banish that image from his mind.

Other than the bump on his head and some weakness, he didn't feel all that bad, considering. Not like... before. He gave a little shudder and closed his eyes again. He lay still and tried to ponder why things had seemingly altered while he was—away. In fact, it appeared a downright miracle had occurred. Now it seemed his family loved him and the house girl Suzanne wasn't afraid of him.

And, what of the others? Perhaps all his slaves no longer feared him? Had he received a second chance? Was that the reason for his journey into the future?

His thoughts turned to that other house girl—Sadie. Had she been found? But, no, of course she hadn't. For then how could he have met Martin—his progeny who lived in the future? If Sadie's baby had been born here, then his wife would have seen to it that it was killed. But... wait a moment....She certainly wouldn't have done that now, would she?

Lord, it was all so confusing. If only he could understand what had really happened to him—everything that had transpired before he'd woken up on the carpet. But now, as he tried to think back it seemed the memories were growing hazy. He could still envision tall buildings, giant dragonflies, speeding horseless vehicles and a small box with people trapped inside, but the images were not sharp. In fact, the harder he tried to recall them the more they seemed to become fantasies of his mind.

Opening his eyes again he realized with a start that he was in his nightclothes.

"My word," he murmured.

Might all that had happened to him been a dream? An incredible, disturbing, yet wondrous dream?

"Papa?"

He gazed up into Rosalie's sparkling green eyes. She gave him a sweet smile.

"Are you feeling better now?"

He thought for a moment, gave her a nod and smiled. "Yes, indeed, darling girl. I am. Much, much better."

He breathed a long sigh of contentment. It was best to think about the here and now, and to not dwell on—before. He was home. And his family loved him. He did have everything he could want now, didn't he? Yes, it did indeed seem that a sort of miracle had occurred.

He closed his eyes again and drifted off to sleep.

What seemed only moments later, Jacob was poked hard in the side. He opened his eyes, but at first could see nothing, only a light... a searing intense light. He realized it was the sun.

"How ... how did I get outside?" he mumbled. The settee was gone and instead, he was lying on the hard ground.

It was so very hot.

A sudden wave of nausea engulfed him as he felt himself start to spin.

"Oh Lord, I'm going to be sick. What did the doctor give me?"

He turned his head and vomited, then wiped his mouth with the sleeve of his nightshirt. Mercifully, the spinning had stopped and the torturous light was extinguished by the shadow of someone stepping between him and the sun.

"Sheila? Is that you, darling?" he called weakly.

He could hear the rasp of someone breathing.

"Sheila...?"

Powerful hands gripped the front of his nightshirt and wrenched him up off the ground. His feet dangled helplessly as a hideous face, smeared with thick, white paint, loomed inches from his own. He jerked his head away, trying not to look at the red-rimmed, black eyes that seemed like they could bore a hole into his own.

He saw a row of tall, shining bodies holding shields and spears.

"Sheila!" he screamed.

There was a sharp blow to his head, and then, all went dark for Jacob Williams.

Acknowledgments

It certainly was a challenge making time travel believable, imagining how my protagonist would react to his strange new world (let alone a black president), let alone how modern day people might react to him. And there was the additional challenge of telling the stories of the characters he'd left behind at his plantation in 1837. Weaving a tale that went back and forth in time was a writing and editing feat as well.

I'm hoping that people haven't grown tired of reading about slavery ("Please, not another whipping scene!") After 2012, it seemed there was a burst of literature and film about the subject. I think incorporating the time travel aspect is a unique twist. I hope it captured your attention (and made you forget about the gruesome bits).

Over three years of my life went into research, writing, revising, submitting to first readers, incorporating their suggestions, and revising again. After, the first limited edition of this novel was released in Dec. 2014, I decided I could make it even better.

Special special thanks to my husband Chris Edwards for his encouragement; his editing help, for the design and layout of the book and cover, (both editions).

Special thanks to my "first look readers" who gave me helpful feedback: Sue Vignola, Renka Gesing, Ira Rosalyn, Pat Jeflyn, Carol Chedour, Dee Dee Hull, Jan Dean, Kimba Elliot, Irene Moore Davis, Lois Larkin, Barb Moluchi, Howard Weeks, Doug Weeks, Patrick Clarke, and Julia Nelson.

Thank you to those who loaned me books that aided my research: Freda Clark, Julia Burgess, Howard Weeks, and Marian Anger.

Special thanks to my daughter Rosalie for listening to me read chapters aloud and giving me her honest opinion. And I'm grateful to my dear friends Adele Steinberg, Gloria Goodman, and Patricia Grom, who offered their undying support and encouragement throughout the whole process.

I could not have completed the first edition of this book without the help of my friend and very talented editor, Mary McNamara, who provided key insights regarding the direction and development of plot, characters and voice. Thank you, Mary!

I'm especially indebted to Patricia Grom for her brilliant idea of using my son Jon's mysterious self-portrait for the book cover. (If you would like to see more of his haunting work – much of it created using old Polaroid cameras – go to: jonestwards.com. Prints of his work are also available through that site.)

For this second edition of Time Trespasser, my friend Patricia was again invaluable. She helped me when I was revising the first and last chapters and also the back cover blurb, (after we devoured a southern-style dinner she cooked to get us in the mood), plus she provided other important feedback.

In addition, my second cousin by marriage, Dee Dee (Diane) Hull, was most helpful regarding corrections and improvements for this new edition.

My sister, Brenda Weeks-Clarke, trained her keen eye on my book and caught the pesky typos that the auto spell-checker can't catch, i.e., words that are spelled correctly, but just aren't the correct word. She also helped me with some grammar issues. Thanks so much, sis!

I'm also grateful and thrilled by the wonderful response from readers to my first edition. I think you will like this one even better.

Endnotes and Sources

MODERN DAY SLAVERY

Everything that is really great and inspiring is created by the individual who can labor in freedom.
Albert Einstein

Unfortunately, slavery is not a thing of the past. Today, millions of men, women and children are enslaved worldwide. A tremendous amount of illegal money is being made buying, selling, and exploiting humans – about $32 billion a year. It happens in greater numbers in developing countries, but it also happens in developed ones. Over $15 billion of that comes from industrialized countries, including the United States. As I wrote this novel, I kept track of on-line slavery estimates. Much to my dismay, they continued to climb with every report I read. I thought 23 million was an outrageous figure, then, when it jumped to an estimated 29.8 million, I was shocked. Currently, (April 2017), the estimate is up to 45 million!

Walk Free Foundation is dedicated to finding and ending modern day slavery. More than 8 million people worldwide are helping Walk Free in their efforts.

www.walkfreefoundation.org

There are many other groups and organizations dedicated to fighting on behalf of the enslaved. Please do your part by signing their on-line petitions and sharing their work to help raise awareness. We must end this modern-day evil!

Re the song: *Great Day!*

The work song Jacob hears his slaves singing in his dream (Chapter 9) is from *Great Day!*, which may or may not be a Negro spiritual, depending on which source you believe. In my research, I was unable to find a work song (rhythmic a Capella song intended to increase productivity while decreasing boredom) for the cotton fields as surprisingly, there were few songs linked to cotton picking. Pick a Bale of Cotton is said to be a work song, but no documentation is available before the 1930s.

Slaves focused their minds upon the concept of freedom, distilled it into music and created the spiritual to protest the injustice of their lot. Their owners believed they were singing the praises of Christianity and enjoyed these songs thinking they represented a conversion and submission to European-based ideology.

I decided to use *Great Day!* at the start of Chapter 9 because I felt the lyrics suggested an uprising or rebellion. The slave threatening to whip Jacob (who he doesn't realize at first is Patrick – the black teacher who saved his life at the plantation) is dressed in modern day clothing not only as a clue to his identity and Jacob's journey forward in time, but to suggest the reality that slavery continues to exist in the modern world

The full lyrics for *Great Day!*:

Great Day! Great Day, the righteous marching.
Great Day! God's going to build up Zion's walls!
Chariot rode on the mountain top,
God's going to build up Zion's walls!
My God spoke and the chariot did stop.
God's going to build up Zion's walls!
This is the day of Jubilee,
God's going to build up Zion's walls!
The Lord has set His people free.
God's going to build up Zion's wall!
We want no cowards in our band,
God's going to build up Zion's walls!
We call for valiant-hearted men.
God's going to build up Zion's walls!
Gonna take my breast-plate, sword and shield,

God's going to build up Zion's walls!
And march out boldly in the field.
God's going to build up Zion's walls!
Great day! Great day, the righteous marching.
Great day! God's going to build up Zion's walls!
No more driver's lash for me, no more, no more. . . .
No more peck of corn for me;
Many thousand go."
"Slavery's chain done broke at last;
gonna praise God till I die."

BLACK HISTORY RESEARCH

Books

This Is Detroit 1701- 2001 An Illustrated History, Arthur M. Woodford, Wayne State University Press, Detroit, Mich. 48201, Copyright 2001

A Stolen Life – Searching for Richard Pierpoint, David Meyler and Peter Meyler, Natural Heritage Books, Toronto, Copyright 1999

Broken Shackles – Old Man Henson from Slavery to Freedom, edited by Peter Meyler, Natural Heritage Books Toronto, Copyright 2001

A Shadow on the Household: One Enslaved Family's Incredible Struggle for Freedom, Bryan Prince, McClelland and Stewart Ltd., Copyright 2009

One More River to Cross, Bryan Prince, Dundurn Toronto, Copyright 2012

I Came as a Stranger, The Underground Railroad, Bryan Prince, Tundra Books, copyright 2004

Harriet Tubman – Freedom Seeker, Freedom Leader, Rosemary Sadlier, Dundurn Toronto, Copyright 2012

Slaves in the Family, Edward Ball, A Ballantine Book New York, Copyright 1998/9

From Midnight to Dawn – The Last Tracks of the Underground Railroad, Jacqueline L. Tobin with Hettie Jones, Doubleday New York, Copyright 2007

The Long Road – A History of the Coloured Canadian in Windsor, Ontario 1867-1967, Charlotte Bronté Perry, Sumner Printing & Publishing Co. Windsor, Copyright 1967

Legacy to Buxton, A.C. Robbins, Ideal Printing, Chatham, Ontario, Copyright 1983

The Book of Negroes, Lawrence Hill, Harper Collins Publishers Ltd. Toronto, Copyright 2007

Web (Partial list)

Slave life in Virginia and Kentucky; Or, Fifty Years of Slavery in the Southern States of America. By Francis Fedric, An Escaped Slave. 1863
http://docsouth.unc.edu/neh/fedric/fedric.html

Beating of female servant for pouring too much molasses: Testimony of the Late Rev. John Graham, American Slavery As It Is: Testimony of a Thousand Witnesses, written by Slaveholders (1837-1839), Assembled by Rev. Theodore Dwight Weld and Angelina and Sarah Grimké (1839) NEW YORK: Published by the American Anti-Slavery Society, Office, No. 143 Nassau Street, 1839
http://medicolegal.tripod.com/weldslaveryasis.htm#p17-hmowlton

Reconstruction after end of Civil War: http://en.wikipedia.org/wiki/

Reconstruction_era
http://www.dailymail.co.uk/news/article-2167996/Why-progeny-slaves-strike-gold-Olympics.html

The Slave Experience of the Holidays, (highlights) Documenting the American South:
http://docsouth.unc.edu/highlights/holidays.html

Narrative of the Life and Adventures of Henry Bibb An American Slave, Written by Himself with an Introduction by Lucius C. Matlack. New York: Published by the author; 5 Spruce Street. 1849
http://docsouth.unc.edu/neh/bibb/bibb.html#bibb39
Fugitive Slave Act:
http://en.wikipedia.org/wiki/Fugitive_Slave_Act_of_1850

Ku Klux Klan to rally in Memphis in protest to park's name change:
http://www.theguardian.com/world/2013/mar/20/ku-klux-klan-memphis-rally

People against slavery reparations:
http://www.saveyourheritage.com/slavery_reparations.htm

Suit Seeks Billions in Slave Reparations:
http://www.blacknewsweekly.com/bin101.html

How the end of the war led to slavery and death for millions of black Americans:
http://www.theguardian.com/world/2012/jun/16/slavery-starvation-civil-war

Descendants of slaves and slave traders meet:
http://www.npr.org/2012/12/25/167977051/descendants-of-slaves-slave-traders-come-together

African American work songs:
http://en.wikipedia.org/wiki/Work_song

Is *Pick a Bale of Cotton* a work song?:
http://pancocojams.blogspot.ca/2013/11/the-real-history-of-song-pick-bale-of.html

Frederick Douglass, African American social reformer, orator, writer, statesman, escaped slave:
http://en.wikipedia.org/wiki/Frederick_Douglass

For too many African Americans, prison is a legacy passed from father to son:
http://www.theguardian.com/commentisfree/2012/jan/15/jail-reflects-collapse-black-communities-us

Paper Bag Test – discrimination within the black community: if your skin were darker than a paper bag, you wouldn't be into clubs, universities, etc.:
http://www.urbandictionary.com/define.php?term=brown%20paper%20bag%20test

The Black Community in the History of Quebec and Canada:
http://www.learnquebec.ca/en/content/curriculum/social_sciences/features/missingpages/

House Slaves – what it was like:
http://spartacus-educational.com/USASdomestic.htm

Sojourner Truth (1797-1883): Ain't I A Woman?:
http://www.upworthy.com/163-years-ago-a-former-slave-rocked-the-world-with-these-words?c=upw1

Post Traumatic Slave Syndrome:
http://joydegruy.com/resources-2/post-traumatic-slave-syndrome/

The Price of a Black President:
http://www.nytimes.com/2012/10/28/opinion/sunday/the-price-of-a-black-president.html?pagewanted=all&_r=1&

What is Voodoo? Understanding a misunderstood religion.
http://www.huffingtonpost.com/saumya-arya-haas/what-is-vodou_b_827947.html

TIME TRAVEL RESEARCH

Web

Urban Legend Time Traveler and Focal Character of "I'm Scared":
http://en.wikipedia.org/wiki/Rudolph_Fentz

Stephen Gibbs' description of scientists who travel forward in time, but cannot pass through barrier into 2013:
http://www.klimaco.net/timetravel_pages/time.htm

Beam me up, Obama: Conspiracy Theory Claims President Teleported to Mars:
http://www.universetoday.com/92359/beam-me-up-obama-conspiracy-theory-claims-president-teleported-to-mars/

My Very Own Hyper Dimensional Resonator:
http://mysteriousuniverse.org/2013/04/my-very-own-hyper-dimensional-resonator/

Did this man find a wormhole under his kitchen sink?:
http://www.strangerdimensions.com/2012/03/06/did-this-man-find-a-wormhole-under-his-kitchen-sink/

Mother and child time motorists from the past disappear after other drivers attempt to help:
http://www.strangemag.com/highstrangenesstimetrav.html

A Brief History of Scientists Hunting for Time Travelers:
http://gizmodo.com/a-brief-history-of-scientists-hunting-for-time-traveler-1641272404?utm_campaign=socialflow_gizmodo_facebook&utm_source=gizmodo_facebook&utm_medium=socialflow

All the Evidence that Time Travel is Happening All Around Us:
http://io9.com/all-the-evidence-that-time-travel-is-happening-all-arou-1446262029

Three Old Time Traveler Cases – These People Say They Saw the Future and the Past:
http://www.messagetoeagle.com/threeoldtimetravelcases.php#ixzz3KHswIMA2

Time Travel is 100% Real - Facebook group:
https://www.facebook.com/pages/Time-Travel-is-100-Real/134050586658505

Notes

About the Author

Elaine Weeks was born and raised in Windsor, Ontario, a primarily blue-collar, Canadian city one mile south of Detroit, Michigan.

Married to her business partner, Chris Edwards, they have two grown children – both artists. (Son Jon's mysterious self-portrait graces the cover of this book.)

Elaine has a B.A. in English and 35+ years experience in marketing, advertising, public relations, publishing, writing, editing and photography. She and Chris co-authored six non-fiction books, which they published through their company, Walkerville Publishing Inc. Two titles: Best of The Times Magazine, *&* 500 Ways You Know You're From Windsor *are Canadian Best Sellers.*

A community activist, Elaine's mantra is: one person CAN make a difference. She has led or been involved in various worthy causes for much of her adult life.

In her younger days, Elaine was a serious track and field athlete, qualifying for the 1984 Olympic Trials. She's always loved "time" traveling to far flung places. Portions of this book were written in Bali, Gili Air, Thailand, Malaysia, Cambodia and Hong Kong.

Time Trespasser *is Elaine's initial foray into fiction. A sequel is in the works.*

64044068R00140

Made in the USA
Lexington, KY
26 May 2017